PRAISE FOR ROUGH WAY TO THE HIGH WAY

Kelly Mack McCoy spins a riveting yarn of a long-haul truck driver, Mack, who must overcome challenging road blocks on the highway as well as in his personal life. He struggles with grief, regrets over perceived failure as a minister, and questions his spiritual wellbeing. If all this was not enough, he is confronted with hijackers, smugglers, and a mysterious hitchhiker. This fast-paced novel puts the reader into the thick of the action.

HENRY SPEARS, AUTHOR OF THE APOCALYPTIC ELEPHANT

It's not every day you have the opportunity to read an engaging novel about a truck driver, written by one. Kelly Mack McCoy is the real deal as an emerging author.

PHILLIP TELFER, PASTOR AND AUTHOR,
FOUNDER AND PRESIDENT OF MEDIA TALK 101.

Kelly Mack McCoy's first novel is sure to be a hit. The long hours of driving a tractor-trailer can give a trucker many hours to consider life, and perhaps, to even get insight from a mysterious hitchhiker. Mack's delightful Texas wit and trucker lingo gives humor throughout as he tries to determine how he will bring a killer to justice. Ride along with Mack, the preacher-turned-trucker, and experience the twists and turns he takes to get the answers he seeks.

JUDY SHEER WATTERS, AUTHOR OF THE ROAD HOME:
THE LEGACY THAT WAS, IS, AND IS TO COME AND
PANNING FOR GOLD IN OUR GOLDEN YEARS:
A JOURNAL FOR POSITIVE AGING.

Kelly Mack McCoy's exceptional writing style will leave you laughing and crying along with the characters in his novels.

Kelly Mack McCoy has a unique writer's voice, and it comes through in his pages with an easy style to keep you captivated until the very end. He uses dialogue to charm, intrigue and guide the readers to many conclusions--some truthful and others, well...he'll keep you guessing. Excellent writing, colorful characters, and a plot with plenty of twists and turns to shadow the highways of life Mack and the hitchhiker have traveled.

A Novel

Rough Way
to the
High Way

A Novel

Rough Way to the High Way

by
Kelly Mack McCoy

ELM HILL

A Division of
HarperCollins Christian Publishing

www.elmhillbooks.com

Rough Way to the High Way

Published in Nashville, Tennessee, by Elm Hill, an imprint of Thomas Nelson. Elm Hill and Thomas Nelson are registered trademarks of HarperCollins Christian Publishing, Inc.

Elm Hill titles may be purchased in bulk for educational, business, fund-raising, or sales promotional use. For information, please e-mail SpecialMarkets@ ThomasNelson.com.

Publisher's Note: This novel is a work of fiction. Names, characters, places, and incidents are either products of the author's imagination or used fictitiously. All characters are fictional, and any similarity to people living or dead is purely coincidental.

Library of Congress Cataloging-in-Publication Data

Library Congress Control Number: 2018965300

ISBN 978-0-310103721 (Paperback)
ISBN 978-0-310103738 (Hardbound)
ISBN 978-0-310103745 (eBook)

To Patrick, who would have been a far better writer than me;
we'll have eternity to create stories together.

ACKNOWLEDGEMENTS

Rough Way to the High Way would never have seen the light of day had I not had help from many people along the way. Space does not permit me to list them all by name. Here are just a few of the many who helped make this dream a reality.

To my wife Emily, a hardworking, wood-chopping kind of gal who is fully capable of doing all the manly-man kind of things around the house while her husband stares stupidly at a computer screen for hours until he finally gets some serious writing done, only to delete it in disgust the next day: thank you, Babe. In answer to your question as to where my head has been, please keep reading to the end.

To my friend, author and publisher John Floyd Mills, who has gone on to be with the Lord. John was as much of a sentimental softie on the inside as he was tough on the outside of his well-honed gruff exterior. It was he who approached me with the concept of the two of us partnering together to write a series of novels about the adventures of a long-haul trucker.

We never wrote together, but I don't know that I would have written this novel or perhaps even other books I've had rolling around in my head had John not suggested we partner as writers. His passing was the motivation for me to pick up this on-again-off-again project once more and see it through to completion.

To my good friend Dr. John W. Lovitt, who often told anyone who would listen what a good writer I was, in spite of the sparse material I had to show in my early days as a writer: your encouragement helped keep my writing alive when I was ready to just throw in the towel and forget about the notion that I could write a novel anyone would want to read.

Thanks to Al Mendenhall for giving new life to this novel with his great cover design. Al offered to design the cover for *Rough Way to the High Way* when he first learned I was writing it. I made no suggestions about what I wanted in a cover but just sent him a brief synopsis along with the first few chapters.

The design was one hundred percent his, yet when I saw it my reaction was, "Wow! That's it!" I knew Al as one of the pastors at Living Water Fellowship in Bulverde, Texas. But I had no idea what a multitalented man he was until I saw his work.

To Ninfa Castañeda, PhD, my editor, who provided me with an education that will last a lifetime with the copious supply of notes she provided along with her edits. She took on this project as she was enjoying the last days on earth she would spend with her mother. Ninfa's mom—once a barefooted, two-dress owning, dirt-poor woman—left an invaluable treasure that lives on long after her passing. Perhaps a book will be written to tell her incredible story.

Ninfa explained in her notes the reason behind every jot or tittle and why I may want to consider changes here and there in the text. Yet she understood when my rather loose use and abuse of the language was intentional, so she left those parts as they were and suggested changes where needed. *Rough Way to the High Way* is so much better than it would be because of the contribution of her considerable talent. Any errors in the text of this novel are due to changes I snuck in after her edits were completed.

Thanks, Ninfa (sorry, I had to sneak that in).

Special appreciation goes out to Brenda Blanchard, president of the Christian Writers Group (CWG) of the Greater San Antonio area. She helped to draw out the writer in me from the time of my first visit to

CWG, even when I wasn't sure I had anything to share. Thanks to Brenda and all the members of the CWG for welcoming a greenhorn like myself into their company. Your critiques and encouragements helped motivate me to take this project from beginning to end.

I would also like to thank Judy Waters and all my fellow members of the Hill Country Christian Writers Group. When I found this group near my home in the Texas Hill Country, I was so impressed with the level of talent in the group I sometimes felt I was a little out of my league. The writers there helped give birth to this novel.

Both of my writers groups include some talented, published authors, as well as talented writers who don't aspire to publish anything to share with the general public. The one thing all these people have in common is that these busy, accomplished professionals and dear Christian friends freely gave of themselves, filling my heart with gratitude in the process.

CONTENTS

CHAPTER ONE

THE HITCHHIKER

Friday, 9:00 A.M.

Mack's eyes locked onto the sight in his mirror as his rig's eighteen wheels rolled away from his boyhood home of Pampa, Texas. The DO NOT PICK UP HITCHHIKERS sign above where a man once stood now topped a bare metal post. The man was gone but the memories his image evoked seared into his soul like a branding iron.

He indulged in the perverse pleasure of wallowing in the memories until his stomach twisted into the same old knots he could never seem to untangle. The memories brought comfort to him in a strange kind of way—as in the way a man hangs onto a grudge because it feels familiar and is easier to hang onto than let go.

When the sign faded from sight Mack eased back onto his seat. He shook the memories off with humor, like he always did, driving them back into a forgotten graveyard in his mind.

Maybe that was the ghost of dear old Dad leaning against that post, he thought, though dear old Dad died long ago in the Huntsville state prison. He chuckled to himself and glanced at his watch before turning his thoughts to Chicago, where he would unload his first load in decades. *Almost three full days to make it there. Guess I can take the scenic route.*

But his peace of mind vanished like a vapor as he eyed the solitary figure of a man walking toward a midmorning Texas sun that brought the promise of another blistering day to the Panhandle Plains. Even with the man's back to him, Mack recognized the hitchhiker as the same one he passed on the way to the slaughterhouse.

He steered his new Peterbilt onto the shoulder and watched in his mirror as the man jogged to his truck. The hitchhiker flung the passenger door open and tossed his bag onto the floor before plopping himself onto the seat and turning to face Mack.

"Where're you headed, son?" Mack asked.

"Away from this God-forsaken place," replied the hitchhiker.

Mack turned his eyes to the highway and floated through ten gears before casting those eyes toward his new passenger. "Good luck with that. Unless you have somewhere to go your mind will stay locked up in that prison back there as long as you live."

The hitchhiker fixed his eyes on Mack and smiled. It was a one sided, tough guy kind of smile. "How'd you know I just got outta prison?"

"You may as well have it stamped on your forehead." Mack glanced left and then right at his West Coast mirrors. He shrugged and attempted to suppress a grin but failed. "Besides, I saw you on my way to the slaughterhouse to load. You were leaning on a signpost beneath a 'Do Not Pick Up Hitchhikers' sign just down the road from the Jordan Unit."

The hitchhiker laughed. "I just set my bag down to rest. I never read the sign. A cop came along an' told me if I didn't wanna go back to the joint I better hightail it out of his territory." He snatched up his bag and rested it on his lap for a long moment before tossing it onto the floor by the sleeper. "So why'd you pick me up?"

"You wouldn't believe me if I told you." Mack studied the hitchhiker's eyes before focusing once again on the painted lines darting past his Pete. "Let's just say you remind me of someone I once knew."

He watched his speedometer needle rise until it reached the speed limit, set the cruise control, and placed an arm on the armrest. "I'm taking a load of swinging meat to Chicago. So buckle up. I haven't driven a big rig in a month of Sundays. Should be an interesting ride."

The hitchhiker settled onto his seat and folded his arms before cocking his head in Mack's direction. "Swingin' meat?"

"Yeah. Swinging meat." Mack thrust a thumb over his shoulder. "Picture a bunch of cows hanging from their tails back there in the trailer. That's about how unstable the load is. Actually it's sides of beef hanging from hooks. Anytime I make a sudden move, you'll feel those babies get to swinging around. And if I jerk the wheel too hard, we could end up with the truck shiny side down."

"Shiny side down?"

"Yeah. You know, upside down, dirty side up. Whatever you want to call it. This rig could easily end up that way." Mack scanned his mirrors before facing his passenger once more. "Like I said, it's been awhile since I've driven one of these things, and I've forgotten some of the lingo." He inclined his head toward the hitchhiker and grinned. "You may be dead when that happens, so I don't think the terminology will really matter at that point."

"It can't be that dangerous." The man turned to face the highway and laughed. "Listen, I just spent the last four years of my life thinkin' I might get the shiny side of a shank to my jugular vein any day—just 'cause maybe I hung around with the wrong people or somethin'." He flopped his head around to face Mack and smiled his one-sided smile. "I ain't scared of no swingin' meat."

"Whoa!" Mack yanked his steering wheel hard left, dodging a slow-moving combine before jerking the wheel back to the right and returning to his lane. The shifting carcasses in the trailer sent it reeling left before tilting back to the right as the rig swerved across both lanes.

After slamming on his brakes, he watched as his trailer skidded across the highway and slid around toward his Pete. Mack spun the wheel right and back to the left, but his trailer just loomed ever larger in his mirror.

Attempting to reign in the out-of-control rig Mack wrested his wheel back hard to the right, sending his truck careening off the highway. He veered off to the edge of the shoulder as his rig hit a soft spot. A chill shot up his spine upon hearing a *whump* when the carcasses shifted as the trailer leaned toward the embankment.

"Hang on!" Mack hit the brakes once more, easy this time. His truck continued rolling along the shoulder until the big rig's wheels wound down and rolled to a stop. He gripped his steering wheel with arms locked forward and listened to his rig creak like an old rusted door as his trailer tilted inch by inch farther to the right.

"Whewww…" Easing air from his lungs as if too much at once might unbalance the rig and send it crashing over the side of the highway, Mack considered his options. His best option at this point seemed to be to abandon ship by hopping out of his truck. But after glancing at his passenger, he decided against it.

"Hey! You crazy, man?" the hitchhiker shouted as he fumbled around for the door handle. "I'm gettin' outa here!"

His door flew open, sending him sliding out of the cab. He grasped for the grab handle and peeked over his shoulder at the jagged concrete and steel left by a highway construction crew. Clutching the handle with both hands now, he tightened his grip and glared at Mack.

"Okay." Mack eased his hands away from the wheel before holding them up "Look, Ma" style. "Hopefully the truck won't fall over on you when you get out."

The hitchhiker punched a foot hard against the side panel and pushed himself onto his seat before releasing a hand from his grab handle. He leaned in toward Mack. "Okay. So what're you gonna do?"

"Well, if we just sit here the truck will turn over for sure. And if we drive off, the rig *still* may flip over. But there's a chance it won't." Mack positioned his hands onto the top of his steering wheel before sliding his moist palms into place and facing his passenger. "So I say we drive forward and pray."

The hitchhiker clicked his seatbelt into place with his free hand. "I'm with you man," he said before digging his fingers into his armrests. The man stared lock-jawed at the highway ahead. "Let's do it."

CHAPTER TWO

DIVINE OCCURRENCE—
TURNING BACK

Friday, 10:00 A.M.

Mack guided his Pete along the shoulder, leaning left in unison with the hitchhiker as the truck leaned right. The rig groaned in protest as he attempted to pull his truck back onto the roadway. Third gear, fourth gear, fifth gear...

He popped it into high range and eased back onto the highway. The rig righted itself as the cargo shifted. Mack eased his viselike grip from the wheel upon reaching highway speed once more. There was blessed silence in the cab now, save for the *click-click*, *click-click* sound of the eighty-thousand-pound tractor trailer rolling over highway expansion joints.

The hitchhiker slammed his door shut, crossed his arms, and stared dead ahead at the highway.

Mack settled onto his seat, and emptied lungs filled from the deep breath he took before pulling the truck forward. "Thank God."

"Did you do that on purpose?" The hitchhiker cast ice-cold eyes Mack's way.

5

After turning to stare into the young man's eyes for a moment, Mack returned his attention to the highway. "What?"

"Jerk the wheel around like that." The hitchhiker thrust his fists forward and mimicked his motions with the steering wheel. 'Make the truck rock back and forth.'

"I'm not that crazy." Mack plopped an arm on his armrest and inclined toward his passenger. "Didn't you see that combine?"

Still glaring at Mack, the passenger blinked. "That what?"

"That farm machinery. The farm machinery we almost ran over back there."

"I didn't see no farm machinery. I was lookin' back at you. Last thing I remember you was tellin' me how scary it was to haul swingin' meat." The man jabbed an accusing finger in Mack's direction. "Then you started drivin' crazy to prove it."

"Oh yeah. Now I remember." Mack lifted an index finger and motioned it toward his passenger. "You were saying, 'I ain't scared of no swingin' meat.'"

"Then you tried to *make* me scared." Still pointing his finger, the hitchhiker gave it a firm shake. "That wasn't no coincidence."

Mack looked at the young man's finger and then back up at his spitting-mad face. He shrugged and turned his gaze back to the highway. "No, you're right. I don't believe in coincidences." He glanced at his passenger and smiled. "I call things like that divine occurrences."

"Huh?" The hitchhiker lowered his finger-pointing hand and gripped his armrest. "What?"

"Divine occurrences. You know, things people call coincidences. Happenstance. Strokes of luck…or bad luck. Fate maybe." He turned and looked the hitchhiker dead in the eye. "But those things happen by design."

As his Pete lumbered along down the highway now, he enjoyed the rocking rhythm of the road for that moment in time. Facing the highway in silence, Mack smiled once more, this time to himself. He turned his gaze toward his mirror and watched his hometown fade away in the distance. He glanced at his passenger and nodded. "It's a God thing."

The hitchhiker turned to his window and watched the monotonous landscape pass by like a passenger on a train bound for nowhere. After sitting in silence for some time, he rolled his head to face Mack. "You *are* crazy."

"Maybe. But like they say, 'Just because I'm paranoid doesn't mean they're not out to get me.'"

"An' what's *that* suppose' to mean?"

"I may be crazy," Mack said matter-of-factly, "but that doesn't change the fact that God often uses events in our lives to get our attention. He just did that to you."

"Oh yeah?" The hitchhiker scoffed. "An' just how did He do that?"

Mack placed a hand atop his steering wheel and spread his fingers to make sure all the little red needles on the truck's gauges were pointed in the right direction. *All systems go*, he thought, using a phrase Uncle Jake used when Mack stood barefooted behind him, feeling the rumbling floor beneath his feet. Mack would lean over his uncle's shoulder, point to the gauges, and confirm the assessment. "All systems go."

"What's your name, son?" Mack turned to face his passenger and smiled.

"Ricky. My name is Ricky. People call me Rocky."

"Rocky? You don't look like a Rocky to me. Where did you get that nickname?"

The hitchhiker tapped a finger to his head. "Some dude in the joint said I had rocks for brains. So I got stuck with that name ever since. You know…Ricky…Rocky? I tried to just go by Rick after that. But they called me Rock then, so I gave up."

"Uh-huh. Well, I'll think I'll call you Ricky if you don't mind." Mack extended a hand across the space separating the two men. "I'm Robert. Robert McClain. People call me Mack."

The hitchhiker wiped his palm on his jeans before shaking Mack's hand, but remained silent.

"Pleased to meet you." Still grasping the young man's hand, Mack inquired, "How much time did you spend in prison, Ricky? Four years?"

"Yeah." The man withdrew his hand and shrugged. "Somethin' like that. I was suppose' to anyways. They let me out early for good behavior."

"Ever been locked up before?"

The hitchhiker turned to his window and laughed. "Ever'body back there has at leas' been in county jail before."

"So you ignored the people and signs that told you what would happen when you violated the rules." Mack focused his eyes on his unresponsive passenger. "Violating those rules got you into trouble before, but you didn't stop doing things you *knew* would get you in trouble."

The hitchhiker shook his head. "What's all this got to do with you drivin' crazy?"

"I told you how unstable the load we're hauling is. But you were so cocky about the danger involved…" Mack stretched out his shoulder strap and snapped it to his chest. "You didn't even buckle your seatbelt until the truck almost flipped over."

"Well, now I know, man. You didn't have to almost kill us both to prove your point."

"Maybe. But sometimes it takes a dramatic event like that for God to get our attention. Things happen for a reason, Ricky. He may have used that little adventure we had to get the attention of both of us. Thank God for combines." He lifted an index finger from the wheel and pointed to an old, closed down weigh station.

"I'm going to pull off here to get turned around and head back into town. I wasn't going to stop anywhere else in Pampa, but there's a truck stop I'd like to visit that I haven't been to in years. I don't plan on coming back here anytime soon if I don't have to, so it may be the last chance I get for a very long time."

Mack paused for a long moment before continuing. "I think I might change my route anyway and go the way my uncle did when he was dodging scales back in the day. We'll have a cup at that old truck stop if it's still there and check things out before we hit the road again. I need to make sure we didn't lose anything back there other than a year or two off our lives."

CHAPTER THREE

PAST EPISODE

Friday, 10:45 A.M.

After parking his rig at the antiquated truck stop Mack stepped down from his Pete. As he viewed the scene around him, he took in a deep breath and savored the smell of diesel from some of the old rigs parked nearby. Grinning like a kid with his first car he popped open his side compartment and grabbed his hammer. Still smiling, he raised it to bump his tires.

The hitchhiker eyed an object which glistened in the light flooding the cab when Mack opened the door. After slipping it into his pocket, he hopped down from the truck, bag in hand, and hurried around from the passenger side. But the man skidded to a dead stop upon eying Mack as he turned toward him, raised hammer in hand.

"Hey, man! I was just kiddin' 'bout that crazy stuff." The hitchhiker's bag slid across the truck stop parking lot as he thrust out his hands and shook them side to side. "I don't want no trouble. Just let me grab my bag and get outta here."

Mack eased back against his trailer, dropped the hammer to his side, and chuckled.

"What's so funny, man?"

"I was just about to bump my tires, Ricky." Mack raised his hammer and waved it about like a finger-wagging schoolmarm. "This is my tire thumper."

"Tire thumper?"

"See these big ol' tires?" Mack smacked one of the driver tandems with the palm of his hand. "There are eighteen of them." One by one he whacked the tractor tires with the hammer—*thump-thump, thump-thump*. He used the hammer as a pointer and poked its head to the side of a tire. "One of them can go flat without you ever knowing about it. If you don't check them periodically, a lot of bad things can happen."

He counted them off with his free hand, thrusting his fingers out as he spoke. "You can ruin a tire, it could come apart, get caught on something and catch fire, or it can just overheat and cause another tire to blow.

"If that happens with the load we've got..." Mack aimed his hammer toward the highway, "we could be back out there doing the bump-bounce boogie all over the highway again."

"I'll remind you to whump them tires ever' now and then."

"Thanks. I appreciate that." Mack spoke over his shoulder as he strolled back to bump the trailer tires. "Let me finish here and we'll go have that coffee before we hit the road again. Hopefully, the rest of the trip will be less eventful."

He lifted the trailer's sight door and shielded his eyes from the sun to get a better look at the load inside. "Looks like these babies are behaving. Far as I can tell they're all still hanging in place," he said before tugging on the seal.

Uncle Jake had entrusted Mack with doing the walk-around as soon as he was tall enough to reach the seal. And he drilled it into him to make it a matter of routine to check the seal while performing his inspection.

The hitchhiker picked up his bag, followed Mack around to the rear of the trailer, and stopped to listen as he spoke. Mack turned to see him dancing around, attempting to get a peek at the hanging sides of beef. The man stopped mid-step, stuck out a thumb, and motioned it toward the coffee shop.

"I'll meet you inside," he said, lifting his bag. "I need to clean up a bit before we have that coffee."

"Okay." Mack turned to bump the rest of the tires and gave the man a backhanded wave. "See you inside."

After completing his inspection, he tossed his hammer back into the side compartment and walked away. But he snapped his fingers and returned to grab his logbook from the dash before strolling off to the coffee shop.

The *ding, ding* of an old-fashioned bell sounded as Mack entered the café. He found an empty window booth and eased himself onto the torn vinyl seat before slapping his logbook onto the table. A full-figured, red-headed waitress sashayed his way, menu in hand.

"What'll you have, cowboy? We have coffee and sweet tea." After handing off the menu to Mack the server placed a hand on her hip and smiled. "Nobody ever orders anything else here, so I just quit spoutin' out the rest of it. But if you like, I'll give you the whole spiel."

Mack guesstimated the woman's age to be a bit north of fifty in spite of the dye covering every last strand of grey hair. Deep laugh lines on the outer corners of her tired eyes and on the sides of her full lips told a story Clairol couldn't hide. He forked over the menu, returned her smile, and, after eyeing her nameplate, answered, "I'll have the former, Barb. Thanks."

"You got it." Barb glanced about the café before fixing her eyes on Mack once more. "You by yourself, honey?"

"I'm waiting on my new friend I just picked up down the road." Mack punched a fist onto his seat, lifting himself a bit to get a better view of the café. He turned one way and then the other before easing back and returning her gaze. "He'll be along in a minute."

"You just picked him up?" Menu in hand, Barb rested a hand on her hip. "You mean a hitchhiker?"

"I know. I don't look that dumb, do I?" After receiving no confirmation from the waitress, Mack shrugged. "I felt compelled to pick him up. If I told you why, you'd think I was dumb *and* crazy."

The waitress strolled off shaking her head.

Mack pulled a folded piece of paper from his shirt pocket. He read the note on it for the hundredth time since he received it in the mail less than a week after selling everything he had to buy his new Pete.

A call is heard now as it was then;
It was not for the life of one
But this call is to all men:
His will must be done
Now as it was then
Who is freed from sin? No one.

He shoved the note back into his pocket and stared out the window. *Only the doctor would send a note like that. But why?*

Barb returned with his cup of coffee and slid it in front of Mack's folded arms. "So where was he?"

Mack turned his gaze from the window, faced Barb, and blinked. "Who?"

"The hitchhiker. Where did you pick him up?"

"Just down the road a bit." Mack leaned back and threw an arm onto the back of his booth before pointing an index finger at the window in the direction of the highway. "Not far outside Pampa. I first saw him when I was headed into town to pick up my load."

He pulled the cup to himself and lowered his voice. "You're not going to believe this. He was sitting under a 'Do Not Pick Up Hitchhikers' sign just down the road from the Jordan Prison. After I loaded, I saw him walking along the highway and stopped to pick him up."

Mack peered at the furrowed brow of the waitress. He sipped his coffee, returned the cup to the table, and then rolled the warm cup between his hands in silence for a moment. "He...um...he was just released from prison."

The waitress placed an open hand on her hip and sighed. "Honey, are you *driving* a truck, or did you just *fall off* a *turnip* truck?"

"Guess I just fell off the turnip truck, dusted myself off, and then got right up into the big rig." Mack dropped his eyes and smiled. "I know it all sounds crazy."

"That's a crazy story all right. Look, I don't know who you just picked up, honey…" Barb leaned in, slapped a hand onto the back of Mack's seat, and lowered her own voice, "…but I can guarantee you he wasn't just released from the Jordan Unit."

Mack glanced first at her arm, and then eyed the waitress in silence.

Barb stepped back and raised her eyebrows.

"How do you know?"

"Every prisoner in the Texas prison system is sent to Huntsville for a few weeks before being released. From there, they're given fifty bucks and a bus voucher to anywhere in the great State of Texas. And then they're told they'd better get the heck out of Dodge in three hours or less."

She smacked the vinyl backside of Mack's seat for emphasis and inclined toward him once more. "Or else. And, honey, let me tell you, you don't have to explain what *or else* means to an ex-con."

Barb's tossed back red hair and ever-present smile brought back that déjà vu feeling he experienced a number of times since he stepped into his new Pete and hit the road. Mack stared at the waitress as if seeing her for the first time. For that one moment, she became Georgia, and the two of them, Mack and Georgia, were together again at their kitchen table back in Kerrville.

But then, as always, Georgia faded away. Like a kick to the gut, Mack was hit once again by the realization that she was gone. For good. Memories flooded in like the raging Guadalupe River after a storm rolled in from the Gulf.

"You all right, honey?"

Mack dropped his eyes for a moment before lifting them once more to stare into Barb's. "Yeah…sure. I'm okay. If he wasn't just released from the Jordan Unit, where did he come from?"

"I don't know. I haven't even seen him." Barb raised her brows and leaned over to check the level of Mack's coffee. "But I know he wasn't just released from there. And you can bet your bottom dollar no escaped convict would be sitting under a 'Do Not Pick Up Hitchhikers' sign, thumbing a ride within spitting distance of a prison gate."

Barb stepped back, eyed Mack, and winked. "Maybe you just picked up a ghost, honey." She swiveled around on her heels and waddled off to retrieve the pot to refill Mack's coffee, singing a theme song as she left. "Doo-doo, doo-doo. Doo-doo, doo-doo."

CHAPTER FOUR

GOING BACK TO THE FUTURE

Friday, 11:15 A.M.

After glancing down at his watch for the third time in the last minute, Mack gulped down the last drop of his fourth cup of coffee. "Hey, Barb," he said to the passing waitress, "I think I'll have something to eat after all."

"Know what you want, honey? I can recite the menu chapter and verse if you'd like." Barb placed a hand on the side of her hip and winked. "That's the most entertainment you're going to get in this town."

"I'll have a double grease burger with fries." After watching the waitress cross her arms and stare in silence, he grinned and added, "Comfort food."

"You got it. House specialty." The waitress tipped over Mack's cup before tapping it back down onto his table. "Elsie's tied up back there by the barn. We've been saving her for a special occasion, but I'll have Henry grind her up and put her on a bun for you. Be right up."

"Thanks, Barb."

Upon returning with his burger and fries, Barb slid his plate in front of Mack. "So where's your imaginary friend?"

Mack lifted the toasted bun and generously sprinkled hot sauce atop the upper blackened layer of ground beef. Wondering if he would ever eat another burger without thinking of Elsie, he smiled and returned the gaze of the waitress. "Barb, have you ever felt sure you were supposed to do something, but you were at a loss as to knowing why?"

"Hmm..." The server refilled Mack's coffee before resting the pot against her apron. "Sure have. I fell head over heels in love with a cowboy one time. Everybody told me he was no good. But I was sure he was the one for me." She pointed to her well-worn walking shoe and gave it a firm shake before continuing. "He swept me right off these size nines. He was a lot older than me, and believe it or not, I was as shy as a mail-order bride at the time. We were supposed to be married, and I knew we would live happily ever after." Barb placed the coffeepot back onto the table and returned Mack's stare. She ended her story with all the emotion she felt when rattling off an oft-repeated menu item. "So I married him."

Mack glanced at Barb's ring finger. *How long has it been since I've noticed if a woman was wearing a ring or not?* "What happened?"

"Well, the first thing that happened is I found out living happily ever after in this life goes by faster than gossip in a small Panhandle town. Turns out everybody was right. There were a lot of nooses in that cowboy's family tree. If I hadn't been so dumbstruck with love, I would have seen how worthless he was. By all rights he should have been hung himself." Hand on hip, she continued. "Would've saved me a lot of trouble. Anyway, once he cleaned me out he ran off with some barmaid from Amarillo."

The waitress brought the coffeepot back to her apron, raised her eyebrows, and tucked in her chin. "You haven't done something stupid like that, have you, honey?"

"Maybe worse than that. I don't know the end of the story yet."

Barb scanned the coffee shop before locking her eyes with Mack's. "The hitchhiker?"

Mack nodded in agreement. He fought a smile but lost.

"See? Now there you go. I would have pegged you as being a lot smarter than that. Guess I haven't learned anything after all." Barb glanced about the café, inclined toward Mack, and spoke in a hushed tone. "Honey, if I were you, I'd get right back out there in that truck of yours and put my foot to the floor and keep it there until I got to wherever it is I was going. This ex-con, this ghost, whatever he is, he isn't your responsibility."

The black liquid swirled about his cup as Mack turned it between his hands before pushing the cup aside. "I guess not. But I sure felt like he was." He looked at the server's raised eyebrows, noticing for the first time they were painted on. "Do you believe in God, Barb?"

Barb placed the coffeepot onto the table, straightened her posture, and wiped her hands down her apron to smooth out the wrinkles. She nodded toward the glass to Mack's side. "Take a gander out that window."

The bleak landscape looked the same to Mack as it had those many years ago before he left the Panhandle for good.

"How do you think I've survived living in a place like this with all the things I've been through?" Barb said before offering a wink to Mack. "You don't know the half of it, honey." She picked up her coffeepot once more and placed a hand on her hip. "Of course, I believe in God!"

"Maybe you will understand then. The reason I picked up the hitchhiker is that I felt strongly that is what God wanted me to do." Mack shrugged, and fell silent for a moment. "I heard His voice as clearly as I ever have when I passed the hitchhiker the first time when I headed back to town to load. The only reason I was on that road in the first place was because I took a little detour to visit a place I spent the last thirty-three years or so running away from."

"What have you been running from? It can't be the Jordan Unit. It hasn't even been there that long."

"No. But sometimes I felt it was a worse place than that. I went by to visit my old homestead outside of town."

"Wait. You're from Pampa?"

Mack nodded. "I never planned to come here again. But since I was here I thought I would drive out to see if my old home was still there.

Don't know what made me go out that way now. Not like I have a lot of fond memories of the place."

"Then what made you decide to come back to Pampa?"

"I didn't want to. My new boss lady, Ginger, who owns the trucking company I leased out to, she sweet-talked me into it. One of her drivers quit on her so she needed someone to take his load. Seems I was the only one available.

"But it's not like all my memories from here are bad. My Uncle Jake used to come up here when I was a kid and take me out on the road with him when I wasn't in school. We would stop by this truck stop after he loaded."

"So that's why you drove back out this way? I was wondering how you ended up back here. You seem like a greenhorn, but I would think you would be able to find your way out of town."

"I'm beginning to wonder. It was weird, Barb. When I passed the hitchhiker, he was thumbing a ride on the opposite side of the highway when I was headed back into town to load. But I could see him watching my truck pass. It was then I heard a voice telling me to pick him up."

"You're scaring me now, honey."

Mack grinned. "It wasn't an audible voice. But it came from deep inside of me. From a place words could never reach. I've only heard from God that clearly a handful of times in my life."

"Why didn't you pick him up then?"

"Guess I was more afraid of Ginger than God at the time. Ginger would have had my hide if I had been late—which is exactly what would have happened had I turned around to pick up the hitchhiker.

"As I stewed about it while waiting for my truck to be loaded, I made a vow to God that I would pick up the hitchhiker if he were still there when I went back that way. I knew there wasn't a snowball's chance on the Fourth of July he'd still be there, so it's not like I was making much of a promise anyway.

"Sure enough, when I passed the sign again, much to my relief, he was gone. But unfortunately for me, I saw him hitchhiking down the road from there, so I stopped to pick him up. I almost flipped my truck after I took off with him. It scared the heck out of us. That's another reason I came all the way back to town.

"You know the old 'God works in mysterious ways' saying?" Mack leaned in toward the waitress. "Well, I can tell you, that's an understatement if there ever was one. Evidently the hitchhiker has found another ride, so I guess I'll never know why any of this happened."

CHAPTER FIVE

KILLING TIME

Friday, 11:45 A.M.

After finishing off his burger, Mack glanced at his watch, and then watched his plate slide across the table. He looked up to see Barb's now familiar smile.

"More coffee, honey?"

"No thanks, Barb. Got to hit the road. There's some swinging meat out there in my trailer that I have to get to Chicago eventually. I'm not making much progress."

"You may be making more than you think." The waitress winked once more before resting the plate on her apron. "Where'd you say you're headed? Chicago?"

"I am. If I can ever get out of this truck stop, that is."

Barb placed a hand on the booth behind Mack and leaned in toward him. "Well, I'll just get your check for you since you don't like my company anymore."

After snatching Mack's check from the rack at the cook's counter, Barb grabbed her purse and rummaged through it for a moment before returning to Mack's booth. She placed a photograph on the table and slid it in front of him. "This is the one good thing that no-count cowboy left me."

A young man in full-dress military uniform could be seen when the picture came into view. Mack cocked his head in order to get a better angle with which to see the photo. He listened as Barb spoke.

The waitress tapped an index finger on the photo. "My son Billy. The reason I stay here is to look after my grandbaby while he's gone."

"Gone? Gone where? Where is he stationed?"

Barb guided the picture back across the table with her finger and sighed. She slipped the photo into her apron pocket and patted it into place. "Oh, he's halfway around the world now. But he was stationed at the Great Lakes naval base outside Chicago after he joined the Navy. That's where my grandbaby was born—Chicago."

She leaned back in and spoke in a whisper. "But don't tell anybody. I don't want anybody to know my grandbaby is a Yankee." Barb shook her head. "My son was still wet behind his ears himself when he had his own son. His wife was a grown woman and pretty as a speckled pup. But she looked like she was about fourteen. She hit the bottle when Billy left to go overseas and took off with another man.

"That's why I have my grandbaby now—he was with her parents when she took off. She called her parents and Billy and told them that she was leaving. Said she was tired of living a lie and had found another man. It's like she vanished off the face of the earth or something after she left. Nobody heard from her after that. But Billy is still close to his wife's family.

"He's a Navy SEAL now. And he's about to come home on leave." The waitress beamed and then eyed Mack in silence for a moment. "How about you, honey? Do you have family?"

After pulling out his wallet, Mack withdrew a picture of his own and placed it on the table. He pointed to the women in the photo. "Two grown daughters. Faith and Hope. They live in San Antonio. But, you know, they're married and have lives of their own…"

Barb admired the photo for a moment. "Beautiful girls. You must be proud of them." She raised her eyes to face Mack once more. "Got a wife?"

Mack took out another photo and placed it next to the picture of his daughters. "This is Georgia."

"Wow. She's a doll, honey." Barb tilted her head to better view the red-haired, blue-eyed beauty in the photo. She turned to Mack and winked. "Sure it's safe to leave her at home while you're out here gallivanting about the country?"

"She's gone, Barb. If she were still here, she would be in the truck with me. I think...I think I should have just taken her with me on the road instead of chasing vain dreams and trying to prove I'm something I'm not."

"Listen, honey..." Barb punched a fist to her hip, "...a woman would have to be a couple sandwiches short of a picnic to want to leave you. There are plenty of women out there who would give their eyeteeth to have a man like you to come home to."

"Thanks for the compliment, but I'm not sure I deserve it." Mack tapped the photos together and slid them back into his wallet. His eyes fell as he stared into his almost empty cup. "When I said my wife was gone, I meant to say she died. The authorities ruled her death a suicide. But I know now for sure she was murdered."

Barb cupped her hand over her mouth before lowering her arm to her side. She shook her head in silence for some time. "Oh, I'm so sorry. Me and my big mouth. Are they opening the investigation back up then?"

Mack leaned to his side and slid his wallet into his jeans, shaking his own head. "No." He resumed staring into his cup for a long moment, undisturbed by the waitress. With the edge of the cup resting on the table, he tipped it back and watched the last bit of coffee swirl around the bottom. After dropping the cup back down, he glided it along the space separating him from the server. "Okay, Barb. You talked me into it. One last cup and then I absolutely *have* to get out of here."

"Honey, you're going to tell me the rest of your story before you leave." Barb inclined toward Mack. "Or I'm going to go out there and throw the biggest monkey wrench you ever saw into your truck to make you stay."

Ding, ding.

22

The two glanced toward the door as a man pushed it open with a shove. Barb rolled her eyes.

"There's my manager poking his nose through the door. He hates it when I stop to chat with customers. Says my yakking interferes with the sweet sound of the cash register ringing. But people tell me they go out of their way to stop by here." Barb winked. "And you know it's not for the food.

"And besides that, the only time the till is short is when he's on duty. Oh, by the way, honey, please don't pay with cash if my manager is at the register—at least not with exact change. He may decide to comp you and then take your money in his hot little hand and slip it into his pocket. How does a lowdown dirty snake like that get away with it?" Barb strolled off to get Mack's coffee. "Drives me crazy."

The manager scanned the coffee shop before asking in a loud voice, "Is there a TGN Trucking driver here?"

Mack shot his hand upward, extending an index finger. "I drive for TGN." He pushed himself away from his booth and stepped toward the manager. "Why?"

"The police are looking for you outside."

23

CHAPTER SIX

CRIME AND BUNGLEMENT

Friday, 12:15 P.M.

Striding out the door past the manager, Mack asked, "Where are they?"
"Out by your truck."

As he rushed across the lot, Mack heard the manager bark in a shrill voice. "You can pay your check when you come back, driver."

The police officers and truckers clustered about the rear of Mack's trailer turned toward him as he approached his rig.

"What's going on?" Mack demanded.

A tall, scrawny officer whose uniform hung on his bones as if draped over a broomstick looked Mack up and down as he waited for him to catch his breath. To Mack, the officer resembled a long, blue pipe cleaner with a cowboy hat and sidearm.

"This your rig, driver?" Officer Pipe Cleaner asked with a raspy, singsong kind of twang.

"Yes, sir, this is my truck. What's going on?"

The second officer, a round-faced man, sported a neatly trimmed mustache above his plump lips. He stuck his thumbs under his belt before extending his elbows to either side of his substantial frame. "These boys here said they saw someone messing around at the back of your trailer.

They called us out, but the bad guys took off before we got here." Officer Round Face turned to a bull hauler standing at his side. "What did you say they were driving?"

Mr. Bull Hauler glanced at Officer Round Face and then turned to face Mack. He pulled up his britches, which were fashionably tucked inside his boots. The Texas flag design on the boots reached mid-shin to his bowed legs. The man cleared his throat and spoke as one with authority.

"A Ford, I think. Could've been a Mercury. It was kinda old. And blue. No. Yeah. It was definitely blue."

"And you said there was a man *and* a woman back there?" Officer Pipe Cleaner offered helpfully.

"Yes, sir," Mr. Bull Hauler affirmed. "When I got near the truck they hopped in the car and burned rubber."

"I saw 'em, too," chimed in a twenty-something driver dressed in a neatly pressed shirt with his company's logo displayed above the pocket. Heavily starched, thick creased jeans covered his spit-shined, pointy-toed black boots. Stylishly tousled blond hair with just a tad too much grease for effect topped his head.

Officers Pipe Cleaner and Round Face turned to the young driver. Mr. Bull Hauler scowled at Blondie. Mack's eyes darted back and forth between the two drivers.

"They were back there for a long time," Blondie continued. "I thought they were a husband and wife team checking on their load."

"And they just happened to have their car with them?" Mr. Bull Hauler interrupted. He glowered at Blondie before pulling up one side of his britches and then the other. "I knew they were up to no good as soon as I saw those clowns."

"I didn't notice the car." Blondie glared back at Mr. Bull Hauler before returning his attention to the officers. "Not at first. But I knew something was wrong, though. That lady back there kept poking her head around the corner of the trailer like she was on the lookout or something."

"So why didn't you call the cops if you knew they were bad guys?" Mr. Bull Hauler scoffed. "I called in as soon as I saw them. And those skunks hauled tail out of here as soon as I started heading their way." He crossed his arms and turned to face Officers Pipe Cleaner and Round Face.

"Why didn't you tell them about the crack in the window if you know so much?" Blondie demanded.

Mr. Bull Hauler spun around to face Blondie once more. "What crack?"

"I saw it as soon as I noticed their car back there." Blondie leaned in toward Mr. Bull Hauler and pointed to where the car had been. "There it was, right in front of you, bigger 'n Dallas. A big ol' crack in the window."

"Hey, are y'all looking for those guys in the Chevy that hit the highway out there on two wheels?"

All eyes turned and focused on another driver strolling up to the bunch beside Mack's trailer. The approaching driver dug into his back pocket and retrieved a pouch. He pinched some tobacco and tapped it onto the side of the pouch as he waited for an answer.

"It was a Ford," Mr. Bull Hauler said.

Mr. Tobacco dropped a clump into his mouth and worked the leaves over to one side. The man seemed to be savoring the fresh tobacco as if it were fine wine before he responded. He turned, spat on the ground, and then dabbed the side of his lip with his wrist.

"Nope. It was a Chevy. Chevy Malibu. Eighty-two. I know my cars. I had one of those at one time. Worst piece of junk I ever owned."

"Didn't those kind of look like Fords?" Mr. Bull Hauler asked.

"Not really," Mr. Tobacco replied.

Mr. Bull Hauler dropped his hands to his side and slid them into his pockets before lowering his head to stare at the ground in silence.

"This is important, driver," Officer Pipe Cleaner interrupted. "This could be what we in the business call a clue. Are you sure it was a Chevy Malibu?"

Mr. Tobacco chewed with a deliberate, staccato-type rhythm as he appeared to ponder the question. He stopped mid-chew and turned to

Mr. Bull Hauler. "You know, I guess if you saw it from a distance, maybe from the rear, it could be mistaken for a Mercury Marquis. At least the taillights were similar."

Mr. Bull Hauler crossed his arms, nodded, and turned back to face Officers Pipe Cleaner and Round Face.

"Anyway," Mr. Tobacco continued, turning to the officers as well, "if you want to go and check out the car, it's in a ditch by a little side road across the highway. I saw it turn down there on my way into the truck stop. After getting it stuck, a guy and a gal bailed out and took off like a pair of scalded cats."

CHAPTER SEVEN

RETURNING TO THE SCENE
OF THE CRIME

Friday, 12:45 P.M.

Officers Pipe Cleaner and Round Face eyed one another for a moment before hopping into their patrol car and speeding across the truck stop parking lot with lights flashing. Mr. Bull Hauler and Blondie stared bug-eyed at each other before hightailing it in the direction of the police car. Mack and Mr. Tobacco stood beside Mack's trailer as the car sped out of the lot with the other drivers following behind.

"Well, those fellers are on the chase like a duck after a June bug." Mr. Tobacco chewed his wad as if keeping to the beat of a slow love song. He watched the pair of drivers scamper out to the highway before turning to face Mack. "Guess we can all sleep well tonight. Everything all right, driver?"

Mack nodded as he turned to walk around to the rear of his trailer. Mr. Tobacco resumed his slow-motion chew, slid his hands into his pockets, and strolled along with Mack. The man watched as Mack tugged on the seal, lifted the sight door, and peeked inside.

"Yeah, I guess so," Mack answered with a shrug. The door closed with a thud when he dropped it before he whacked it shut with the ball of his fist. "What were those guys thinking? Were they going to throw a couple of sides of beef in their trunk? Seems to me they could have picked a better trailer to break into."

Reaching around to retrieve the pouch from his back pocket, Mr. Tobacco offered some of the fragrant leaves to Mack. The sweet aroma brought back memories of trips to a tobacco shop in Amarillo where Mack's father would often take him on payday before hitting the bars. Although he never picked up his father's tobacco habit, mainly because of his determination to excel at football, he loved the smell of fresh tobacco. Mack shook his head.

"No. Thank you."

"Luckily for you and me, criminals aren't necessarily the brightest bulbs in the box." After extracting a clump of leaves from the pouch, Mr. Tobacco tilted his head back and dropped the fresh tobacco into his mouth. He rolled the pouch back up before shoving it into his pocket. "Keep your shiny side up, driver," he said, before giving Mack a backhanded wave as he walked away toward the café.

"Thanks." Mack watched the man leave before turning to rest his head on the trailer door and shake his head. He chuckled to himself before heading off to the coffee shop to pay his bill.

Barb stood filling Mr. Tobacco's coffee cup when Mack walked through the door. She smiled and nodded in the direction of a freshly poured cup at the booth he left earlier. Upon seeing the just-slapped-housedog's look on Mack's face, she placed her coffeepot onto the table and pointed an upturned hand toward Mr. Tobacco.

"When this gentleman came in, I asked him what all the excitement was about. We all saw the cop car speeding out of here with its lights flashing. He said some TGN driver almost got robbed and the driver was checking out his trailer when he left." Barb lifted her pot from the table and wiped it down with her apron. "You're having quite a day, aren't you, honey?"

Mr. Tobacco cast his eyes back and forth between Mack and Barb. "You two know each other?"

"Yeah, we go way back." Mack placed a hand on Mr. Tobacco's shoulder and gave it a quick squeeze before easing into his booth. He turned back to face Barb. "My friend's coffee and whatever else he's having is on me."

Mr. Tobacco cast a quick nod in Mack's direction. "Thanks, driver."

"You're welcome. Thank *you*. If you hadn't come along, I'd probably be out there for the next couple of hours filling out a report or something."

"Glad to be of assistance."

Mack flipped open the logbook he left on the table. He plucked a pen from his pocket before turning to stare out the window. From the corner of his eye, he watched a piece of pecan pie topped with vanilla ice cream glide across his table and come to a stop next to his coffee cup.

"Dessert's on me, honey." Barb pulled back her hand before sliding it into her apron pocket, along with the other. She rolled back on her heels, and smiled.

"Thanks, Barb." Mack closed his logbook, eyed the waitress, and smiled. "You're a good woman. Someone's going to come along one day and take you away from all this."

"Is that an offer?"

Mack looked at his pie and shook his head. He took his fork and picked a pecan from the top of the pie before resting it back on the table. "I can't even seem to get my rig out of this truck stop. We wouldn't make it very far."

After picking up his pen from the table he tapped it on his logbook for a moment and then returned the gaze of the waitress. "What were we talking about before we were so rudely interrupted?"

"You were telling me about your wife."

"Ah, yes, Georgia. You've heard of the Proverbs 31 woman?"

"Of course, I have. Your wife must have been a wonderful gal." She placed her coffeepot onto the table. "And pretty to boot. She could have made any cowboy in the Panhandle plow right through a stump. Guess you were lucky to snatch her up, as well. Looks like y'all made a great couple."

Mr. Tobacco leaned over his booth. "Where do you find one of them Proverbs 31 gals?" He turned to Barb. "What the heck is a Proverbs 31 woman anyway? Are you one of 'em?"

"Not hardly. I think I'm more of the Lee Ann Womack type."

"Huh? What's the Lee Ann Womack type?"

"A Proverbs 31 woman is what most of us gals wish we could be." Barb winked at Mack. "If we had a man worth a bucket of spit."

"You haven't been talking to my ex-wife, have you?" Mr. Tobacco asked.

"I don't have to, cowboy." Barb reached over and gave the man a firm pinch on his cheek. "I was married to your twin brother."

Mr. Tobacco grinned like a mule eating cockleburs, showing his Red Man teeth.

Barb continued with her explanation. "A Proverbs woman is like the most perfect woman you've ever known."

"You *have* been talkin' to my ex. She's that way. At least to hear her tell it."

"This woman is from the Bible." Barb poked a fist to her hip. "Look it up. She's definitely a much better woman than I could ever hope to be."

"Why did you say that you're more the Lee Ann Womack type?"

"Have you ever heard the country song 'I'll think of a reason later'?"

Mr. Tobacco nodded.

"The song is about a pert-near perfect woman who is hated for no other reason other than she is about perfect as a woman can be. She can be as bright as a new penny and pretty as a pie-supper to boot. That's all a gal like that may be guilty of but she can just walk into a room and bring out the green-eyed monster in me."

Barb snapped her fingers and sang the first lines of the song before raising the coffeepot to her apron and winking at Mr. Tobacco. She caught a glimpse of her manager's scowling face out of the corner of her eye and rolled her eyes like a slow-moving roulette wheel to close her act.

Mack cheered, "Bravo. Encore!"

"Uh-uh. That's all y'all get for the price of the admission you paid." Barb rubbed the bottom of the pot with her apron. "Listen, I know the Proverbs 31 woman is the ideal woman and all of us females should be like her, but I think the bar is set way too high for me."

The waitress fixed her eyes on Mack and smiled. "Honey, I don't want to give away any secrets that would demystify the feminine mystique, but that's just the way us gals think. Most of us feel we can't live up to that standard, and we don't particularly like women who do."

Mack chuckled. "Your secret is safe with me." He continued in a more serious tone. "But really, Barb, we all tend to think like that when we compare ourselves to others. The good news is that God didn't set impossibly high standards for us so we can beat ourselves up when we can't live up to them. Listen, are you familiar with the genealogy of Jesus?"

"Well, yeah, kinda. I'm a little fuzzy about parts of the Bible. I haven't been to church since…uh…" Barb lifted the photo from her apron pocket and fingered its slick cover. She stared at the picture, and then eyed Mack. "Since the last time Billy came home on leave."

She placed the photo back on the table and slid it in Mack's direction with her index finger. "Before that, I can't remember when. He wants my grandbaby to go, so I guess I'll go back. But I'm not exactly thrilled about it."

"Well, when you go home tonight read that genealogy—in Matthew. It includes some women who didn't necessarily exhibit the virtues of the Proverbs 31 woman. Yet, in the end, they are remembered forever as women who bore sons in the Kingly line of Jesus."

Ding, ding.

The bell alerted them to the entrance of Mr. Bull Hauler. He headed toward their booths, easing one bowed leg forward and then the other. The slow *tap-tap-tapping* of cowboy boots on the checkerboard tiles held their attention until he arrived at Mr. Tobacco's table.

Mr. Tobacco stretched an upturned hand across the table. "Have a seat, driver. You just missed the show. Betcha didn't know they offered live entertainment here."

Mr. Bull Hauler wrapped his hand around the back of the booth, looking like a goat that just wandered onto Astroturf. "Thanks," he said, before sliding down onto his seat and turning wide-eyed in the direction of the waitress.

Barb smiled at the new arrival, lifted the coffeepot, and tapped its side with her fingernail. "And all for the price of coffee. Can I interest you in a cup?"

"Uh, yeah...sure."

Mr. Bull Hauler leaned around to eyeball Barb when she left to get his cup and then turned back to face Mr. Tobacco.

"You were right about those taillights. That's why I mistaked the Malibu for a Ford."

Mr. Tobacco nodded.

"Once we got across the street the cops were slip-sliding their way out of the ditch. Then they hopped in their car and took off. I guess they went looking for the bad guys. That smart aleck young fella ran around the corner after them, but I think he must've lost 'em."

After returning with Mr. Bull Hauler's cup, Barb filled it, along with Mr. Tobacco's before stepping over to Mack's booth.

Mack slid his hand over the cup and shook his head. Upon hearing the *ding, ding* of the bell as the coffee shop's door swung open, he looked up to see a police officer entering. Barb followed Mack's gaze and turned her own eyes toward the door.

Officer Pipe Cleaner removed his hat upon entering the coffee shop and scanned the booths. After eyeing Mr. Bull Hauler, he strode toward where the drivers were seated. Mr. Bull Hauler scooted out from his booth and stood to greet the officer.

"Driver, would you mind stepping outside with me for a moment?" Officer Pipe Cleaner asked.

Mr. Bull Hauler cast a glance toward Mack and Barb before looking in Mr. Tobacco's direction. After tugging up one side of his britches and then the other he cleared his throat. He returned his attention to the officer and offered one brief nod before clearing his throat. "Yes, sir. Be happy to."

Officer Pipe Cleaner turned to face Mr. Tobacco. "Sir, would you come out to our car, too? We need y'all to identify the woman we picked up."

Mr. Tobacco nodded and then gulped down a swig of his coffee before standing to join the men as they prepared to leave.

The officer focused his attention on Mack. "Don't go anywhere, driver. We'll need to get some information from you, too."

Mack looked at the waitress, smiled, pulled back his hand, and pointed to his empty cup. Barb placed her hand at the back of his booth and returned the smile before pouring his coffee.

"Yes, sir," Mack said.

Barb watched out the window as Officer Pipe Cleaner and the drivers approached the patrol car. After catching sight of the woman in the back of the car, she slapped her coffeepot down in front of Mack.

"Well, I'll be...that's Maria!"

CHAPTER EIGHT

CHANGING HER TUNE

Friday, 1:45 P.M.

Mack picked up a napkin and wiped away coffee spilled from his cup. He followed Barb's eyes and surveyed the scene by the police car. Officer Pipe Cleaner lifted a hand and pointed to the back seat as Mr. Bull Hauler and Mr. Tobacco gawked at the passenger seated there.

Moving his head from one side to the other, Mack attempted to view the woman but couldn't see around the drivers. He caught a glimpse of a ponytail bouncing side to side as she shook her head. Mack turned to Barb, who continued to stare out the window.

"You know her?"

Barb focused once more on Mack and then looked at the table. "Oh, I'm sorry, honey." After yanking a rag out from her apron pocket, she shook it open with a pop before lifting Mack's cup. She leaned across his table and cleaned up the mess with a wide circular motion as she explained her relationship to the woman in the back of the police car. "Yeah, I guess you could say that. She spends quite a bit of time around here. We have to run her off all the time."

She placed his cup back on the table before stuffing the rag into her pocket and wiping her hands down the sides of her apron. "She's a lot lizard."

Mack cut his eyes toward the window and observed Mr. Bull Hauler and Mr. Tobacco nodding to one another before both men turned to face Officer Pipe Cleaner. The men nodded in unison to the officer.

Turning to face Barb once more, Mack stared long and hard at the waitress. "A lot lizard?"

Barb grinned. "Honey, you weren't kidding. You *did* just fall off a turnip truck, didn't you? Haven't you ever seen a lot lizard before?"

"I know what a lot lizard is," Mack said, returning Barb's grin. He glanced out the window before shifting his focus back to the waitress. "But aren't they usually banging on the door of your truck trying to get in? Why was she trying to break into my trailer?"

"Hmm… Good question. We've never had problems like that with her before." Barb stared out the window for a moment, shrugged, and then snatched up the coffeepot. "Maybe she just got tired of all the strain of trying to make an honest living." Sashaying off to wait on another table and wagging her head, she continued. "Lord knows it's hard to make an honest living around here."

Ding, ding.

Officer Pipe Cleaner strode into the coffee shop, carrying a storage clipboard that swung on his arm like a pendulum of a grandfather clock. Mack looked up to face the approaching officer. Upon arriving at Mack's table, he cleared his throat, but still sounded like a cross between a bullfrog and a barn owl when he spoke.

"Okay, driver. I think we've nabbed the bad guys. At least one of them." He motioned a thumb toward the scene outside. "Bonnie Parker out there is singing like a canary. We should be able to chase down Clyde now and haul him in, too."

Officer Pipe Cleaner popped open his clipboard and shrugged. "Not much we can charge them with, though. Stupidity's not against the law in Texas." He paused, slipped out a form and a notebook, and eyed Mack in silence for a long moment. The officer snapped the clipboard shut. "Are you sure there was nothing missing from your trailer?"

"Not unless you caught Bonnie out there running down the road with a side of beef on her back." Mack placed his hands onto the table and folded them together. He returned Officer Pipe Cleaner's gaze.

The officer laid the form in front of Mack and used an index finger to slide it toward him. He cocked his head, lifted an eyebrow, and stared down Mack. "Is there something else you might want to mention, driver?"

After letting out a deep sigh, Mack nodded and motioned a hand to the seat across from him. "I think I might be able to give you a good description of Clyde."

CHAPTER NINE

GETTING THEIR MAN

Friday, 2:00 P.M.

Officer Pipe Cleaner sat on the seat Mack offered before picking up his notebook and whacking it down onto the table in front of him. He clicked his pen and waited in silence.

"Before I say anything else," Mack said, "I need to know if I should take the fifth. Is picking up a hitchhiker against the law?"

"Like I said, driver," Officer Pipe Cleaner deadpanned, "stupidity is not against the law in the State of Texas."

"Good thing. I'd be facing ninety-nine to life if it was. The man who was with that lot lizard out there..."

The officer leaned in toward Mack. One of his eyebrows popped up and his voice climbed an octave higher when he spoke. "How did you know she's a lot lizard, driver?"

Mack's face turned redder than a cherry pepper. He drummed his fingers on the table and gave the officer a half smile. "The waitress told me." Pointing to the police car outside, he continued. "Seems she does a good bit of business around here."

"She does, indeed. We get calls from out here pretty regularly and have to haul her in every now and then, but never for something like this. Looks like she's diversifying her business."

The officer paused before giving Mack the best gotcha-dead-to-rights look he could muster. "Back to Clyde, driver…"

"Clyde's name is really Ricky is all I know." Mack shrugged. "Says he goes by Rocky, if that helps. Supposedly he was just released from the Jordan Unit. But I understand that can't be true because he would have been sent to Huntsville first and released from there."

"How do you know so much about how the prison system works in Texas?"

Mack motioned to the front counter and grinned. "The waitress."

The officer tilted his head to better view the server.

Barb gave the men a wriggle-handed wave as she paused from taking orders at the counter.

"Barb? The Gray County Gabber?" Officer Pipe Cleaner returned her wave before easing back onto his seat and shaking his head. "That woman could talk the ears off a mule. We don't have need for a newspaper in these parts. Everybody just comes to see Barb for all the news around here." The officer fell silent for a moment and then morphed back into interrogating-officer mode. "You were saying…?"

"That's all I know about him." Mack leaned in toward the officer, smacked his hands down on the table, and sighed. "His name is Ricky. Goes by Rocky. Claims to have just been released from prison. Average height. Medium build. Kind of a scraggly, rough-looking sort of guy." He plopped back against his seat and shrugged. "Young guy. Hard to tell how young, though. Looks like he's had a pretty rough life."

"Well, that really narrows it down, driver. You just described ninety percent of the population of the Gray County jail. And the Jordan Unit for that matter. Except the name. And that's probably made up. Look, these guys go by all kinds of aliases and nicknames. They'll have one for the jailhouse and another for the street. Whatever is useful at the time. Same for their stories. They're all a bunch of con artists. But they're usually not all that good at it or they wouldn't be locked up in the first place."

The officer let out a long sigh, sounding something more like a whistle when he did. "Since you say nothing was missing, we'll wrap up the paperwork and you can be on your way." He scribbled in his notebook, paused, and then jabbed his pen toward the window.

"Miss Parker out there seems awfully nervous. She's about as jumpy as spit on a hot skillet. Looking to pin the rap on anybody she can. And all she's guilty of is being the lookout for Clyde in about the dumbest crime caper we've seen this side of Amarillo."

The officer glanced at the police car outside and shrugged. "But as soon as those drivers showed up she ran off like a spooked buck in hunting season. And then she hightailed it on down the road on foot when she ran her old Malibu off into a ditch. Don't know what she was so scared of. There was nothing in the car, and she didn't have anything of interest on her when we caught up with her."

"The wicked flee when no one pursues." Mack turned to watch Officer Round Face taking notes as he talked to Mr. Bull Hauler and Mr. Tobacco beside the police car. He leaned toward the window, attempting to get a look at the passenger in the back seat.

Officer Pipe Cleaner followed Mack's eyes to the scene outside before turning to face him once more. "What did you say, driver?"

"Proverbs 28:1." Mack eased back onto his seat. "The wicked flee when no one pursues."

The officer tapped his pen onto his notebook, raised an eyebrow, and pursed his lips.

"Ancient wisdom from the book of Proverbs, one of the books of Wisdom from the Bible." Mack rested an arm onto the back of his seat and pointed a finger to the police car outside. "Judging from the way those characters acted, you know that Bonnie and Clyde were afraid of getting caught for something other than shopping for meat for their next cookout."

Mack pulled his coffee cup toward himself and leaned across the table. "Human nature does not change. The book of Proverbs was written well over twenty-five hundred years ago and is as relevant now as it was then."

Officer Pipe Cleaner eased back onto his seat and sighed. "Are you a driver or a preacher?"

"Yes, I am. Or was. A preacher, I mean. *And* a driver." Mack shook his head in silence for a moment. "Look, I don't know what I am anymore. I'm just trying to get out of here and get that load of swinging meat out there to Chicago. Can we please just wrap this up so I can hit the road? That gal out there is obviously up to no good. And as for the hitchhiker... who knows what he was up to?"

"Okay, driver. Just let me be sure I understand what happened." The officer thrust his pen in Mack's direction. "You picked up this hitchhiker outside the Jordan Unit. And he told you he just escaped or something?"

"Not exactly just outside the Jordan Unit. I was driving into Pampa to load and saw him hitchhiking. And, no, he didn't say he escaped. He said, or sort of implied, I think, that he was just released from prison. Anyway, I saw him sitting under a 'Do Not Pick Up Hitchhikers' sign trying to thumb a ride."

"Okay. So you were headed into Pampa to load." Officer Pipe Cleaner scribbled on his notepad. "You stopped and picked up this hitchhiker who was sitting under a 'Do Not Pick Up Hitchhikers' sign. Once you were loaded, you brought him back to where he came from?" The officer jabbed his pen in the direction of the patrol car outside. "And then he ran off after meeting up with Miss Parker out there?"

"Yes. I mean, no. I didn't pick him up then." Mack rested his elbows on the table, laid his head onto his hands, and massaged his forehead. He whacked the backside of his open hands down and angled himself back in toward the officer. "After I loaded, I went back to where I had seen him. I saw him walking a little ways down the road from there, so I stopped and picked him up."

Mack eased back onto his seat. "By the way, you were almost called out to the highway to do a lot more interesting report than this one—a fatality report. I came up on a slow-moving combine after I picked him up and almost flipped my rig. We were having a conversation and I guess I wasn't paying attention to the road.

"Needless to say, we were both pretty shook up. I decided to turn around and come back into town to visit this old truck stop that I haven't been to since I was a kid. He went inside before me. Said he needed to clean up. That was the last I saw of him."

Officer Pipe Cleaner nodded in silence for some time. "What did you call that book you just quoted from, driver? A book of Wisdom?"

Mack bowed his head and shook it to and fro before looking up to face the officer. "Touché. Look, I know it all sounds crazy. But I picked up the hitchhiker because I felt like that was what God wanted me to do."

"Uh-huh," Officer Pipe Cleaner chirped. "Look, driver. The psych wards are full of people who say they're doing God's will." He lifted a card from his clipboard before snapping it shut once more. "I hope you're getting instructions from the right person." The officer guided his card across the table and tapped it with an index finger. "Here's the case number, my badge number, and phone number. If you think of anything else, just give us a call." He plopped a hand down onto the table and pushed himself from the booth. "Be safe out there, driver."

Mack stared at the card for a moment before turning to the window as Officer Pipe Cleaner walked over to the patrol car outside. Officer Round Face closed his own clipboard and thanked Mr. Bull Hauler and Mr. Tobacco. He nodded to his partner, indicating he was wrapping things up, walked around the patrol car, and eased himself down onto the seat. Officer Pipe Cleaner folded his bony frame like a carpenter's ruler and eased into the car, as well. Their car sped off, leaving the drivers in the dust.

Mack slid Officer Pipe Cleaner's card into his wallet, took out another card, and ambled on up front to pay. Barb placed her coffeepot onto the counter and rushed up to the register to greet him.

"Not leaving us already, are you, cowboy?"

"Already? I should be halfway to Chicago by now." Mack retrieved money from his wallet, slipped it across the counter, and motioned to the still chattering Mr. Tobacco and Mr. Bull Hauler outside. "Treat those drivers out there to the house special, as well."

"Sure thing, honey." Barb tapped the bills together on the counter and leaned in toward Mack. "But I'm curious. Just what did those drivers do to you to deserve that?"

"The burger was actually pretty good."

Ding.

Mack followed Barb's gaze to the cook's counter as a fry cook placed an order there and tapped a bell.

"My compliments to the chef." Mack pointed to the smiling fry cook before glancing toward the drivers outside. "Those guys went out of their way to help me. They could have just ignored what was going on and went their own way. That's what most people do these days. Guess there's still something left of the code of honor that drivers once had when I was a kid out on the road with my uncle Jake. It's the least I can do for them in return."

"Listen, honey, you've given us enough gossip to last until the next time you come around here to get a load." Barb placed the bills into the till before sliding the register drawer shut with a clang. "But you haven't told me the rest of your story, yet."

"Still working on it." Mack guided his card across the counter with a forefinger as he spoke. "If you and your son need help with anything, just let me know. I still have some connections around here. Don't hesitate to call."

"Oh, you can count on it, honey." Barb raised the card and held it at arm's length. "You can count on it, Mack." She shook her head before lowering the card onto the counter. "That's it? Just Mack? And TGN trucking? Honey, you're about as mysterious as that hitchhiking ghost you picked up."

"That's all anyone needs to know about me right now." Mack chuckled as he tapped his finger onto the card. "If you call that number, you'll get ahold of my boss lady, Ginger, and she'll relay the message."

Barb ripped out a blank ticket, scribbled her number on it, eyed Mack once more, and winked. "If you call this number, you'll get a poor, red-headed, overaged Cinderella still looking for her prince."

Ding, ding.

Mack stuffed the ticket into his pocket and turned to face Mr. Bull Hauler and Mr. Tobacco as they entered the café. He nodded to the drivers and motioned his head in Barb's direction. "Listen, boys. This lady is about to treat y'all to some of the best burgers in the Panhandle. I'd love to stay and chat, but I've got some swinging meat out there that's got to get to Chicago one of these days."

"Thanks, driver," Mr. Tobacco said. "Be careful out there. You know how those things like to get to dancing around back there."

"Talk about dancin' around? You should haul 'em while they're still mooin' some time," Mr. Bull Hauler said. "You've got to be part cowboy and part rodeo clown, whoopin', and a'hollerin' and a'carryin' on just to get 'em in the trailer."

Mr. Bull Hauler yanked up one side of his britches and then the other. "Try to convince a heifer who's bigger and meaner than my ex-wife and who ain't never seen nothin' but grass and other heifers to get into a little chute and up into a trailer."

"Must be a challenge," Mack said.

"Yes, sir. And once you get 'em in there and hit the road they've got a mind of their own—they think they know better 'n you how to keep the trailer balanced." Mr. Bull Hauler inclined his bowed legs right and then left. "They lean this way and that when you maneuver around curves 'n all."

Mack placed a hand on Mr. Bull Hauler's shoulder. "You've definitely got the toughest job out there, driver. I'll wait until they're stripped down and hung up inside my trailer before I haul them."

Mr. Bull Hauler crossed his arms and nodded, looking first at Barb and then at Mr. Tobacco.

Mack turned to the counter and waved. "See you when I get back this way, Barb."

Barb smiled, giving Mack her wriggle-handed wave. As Mack turned to leave, she winked. "Don't pick up any hitchhikers."

Mack glanced at Barb and returned her smile. "Guess that's not going to happen now." He said to the drivers, "Catch you on the flip side, boys." He paused, wondering if he said that right. "Y'all be careful out there, too."

"Hey. Good news, driver," Mr. Bull Hauler said. "Guess those bears out there are going to nab that ol' boy who was foolin' around at the back of your trailer, too. We heard on their squawk box that they had his '20 before they took off like the donut shop was about to close."

CHAPTER TEN

ON THE ROAD AGAIN

Friday, 2:45 P.M.

Mack strolled out to his Pete, hopped into his rig, and cranked it up. He plopped his head onto the headrest and listened to his powerful Cummins engine purr as if he were enjoying the sound of fine music.

His uncle Jake would often talk to him about fuel injectors, pistons, and compression as Mack sat behind the wheel, straining to reach his leg down to the accelerator. But Mack just enjoyed the *vroom, vroom* sound he heard when he stretched out the tip of his toes and revved up the engine.

Mack pressed the accelerator, watched the rpms rise and fall, and then pressed it harder once more for good measure. *Vroom. Vro-o-o-om.* He smiled, slipped the rig into gear, and drove out of the truck stop, happy that the bright Texas sun dangled in the blue sky on the westbound side now.

Ring...ring. Mack picked up his cell phone. It could only be Ginger, who owned the trucking outfit Mack leased on with, or one of his daughters. He purchased a new phone when he decided to sell everything he had to buy his Peterbilt, and he only gave his number to them. No point in starting a new life if he had to load up all the baggage from his old one and haul it with him. After eyeing the caller ID, he let out a long sigh before answering the phone.

"Hello, Ginger."

"Hey, big guy. Just checking to see that everything's going okay out there. Did you get loaded on time and all?"

"Yep. I made it just under the gun. But I got there on time and loaded without a hitch."

"Great. Good job. You must be almost to Chicago then. Huh?"

"Well…not quite. But I *am* headed in that direction…sort of."

"Just kidding, Mack. I know you're probably still in Oklahoma somewhere. Are you close to Joplin, Missouri, yet?"

"Uh, no. I…uh…I've still got a little ways to go before I get there. If I go that way. I may take the scenic route."

"That's okay. No worries. Your load was actually supposed to be delivered today. But after my other driver quit on me, the loading time had to be changed to Friday, which means you can't deliver it until Monday anyway now. So you have plenty of time. Lord knows you don't need any more stress on you right now. But it's imperative that this load be delivered on time Monday."

"Oh, don't worry, Ginger. I'll get it there on time. And don't worry about me, either. You've got enough on your plate. How's your son?"

"Nicky's going to pull through. He's a tough little guy. Just like his father was. It's going to be a long, hard road, but he's got just one more operation and then he should be done for a while. Thank God I still have him. If I'd lost both Tom *and* Nicky, I don't think I could have survived it."

"As you know, Tom and I built TGN up from the one truck we had when we were out running the roads together years ago. And the company was in pretty good shape when Tom died. The drunk who hit them didn't have insurance, though, so I've already run through most of the money he left me. But if we can just keep it in the green while we're building the company back up, we should be okay. We have some big contracts we're working on."

"*We're* working on?"

"I say we. Just me and Nicky right now. Unless you want a part of the company when you decide you want off the road. I'll help you find another driver for your truck."

"No, thanks, Ginger. I'm happy where I am. I plan to stay out on the road for the foreseeable future."

"Suit yourself, Mack. Just remember, the offer is on the table. In any case, I'm so glad you signed on with me. The last driver I sent up there got himself into some trouble, so I had to send another driver to get his load and deliver it. Then that driver up and quit on me. I had no one to go up there to cover the load you're under right now.

"If I didn't have you to take the load, I could have lost the whole contract for all the business going up from the Panhandle to the Midwest. And that contract is our bread and butter now and the hope for our future as a company. If we lose that, we're in serious trouble. But I know I can depend on you to get that load up to Chicago without any problems."

"Oh, I'll get it there, Lord willing."

"I know you will. By the way, where exactly are you in Oklahoma? You haven't been out on the road for years. I can figure out how far you are from Joplin by knowing where you're at now."

Mack smacked a hand at straight up twelve o'clock onto the steering wheel, plopped an elbow on his armrest, and massaged his temple. "Well…uh…actually…I…um…I haven't quite made it to the Oklahoma line yet. I've barely made it outside of Pampa."

There was a long silence on the line.

"I've had a few issues since I got loaded," Mack explained. "I stopped at a little truck stop just outside Pampa to check things out and then went inside to have a cup before I got back on the road." Mack paused, and drummed his fingers across his steering wheel. "While I was in there someone tried to break into my trailer for some strange reason."

"What? Someone tried to break into your trailer? Mack, you're hauling a load of swinging meat," Ginger reminded him. "All they had to do was look into your sight door to see what you were hauling. Why would anyone break into a trailer loaded with swinging meat? Did they have a refrigerated unit to load the meat into? Was it a butcher shop or restaurant owner or what? That's crazy, Mack. I've never heard of anything like that happening."

"It's a new one on me too, Ginger." Mack turned his hand upward on the wheel. *All systems go,* he thought. He settled back onto his seat and grinned. "A couple of drivers saw a man and a woman in a beat-up old Chevy at the back of my trailer. Evidently they were trying to break into it. But the drivers chased them off and called the cops. I've spent half the day waiting around and filling out reports. The cops caught the gal who was back there and when I left they were headed out to pick up the guy. I managed to get out of there before anything else happened."

"Just be careful out there, Mack. There are a lot of whack jobs out there on the road."

"Tell me about it," Mack chuckled. "I've already met more than a couple since I've been out here."

"And you always have to be on the lookout for thieves. I just never thought you had to worry about anyone trying to steal anything from your trailer with the load you've got. But one of my guys had his trailer broken into when he got stuck in traffic up in New York. The thieves cut the lock on his trailer and stole half his load before he got moving again. Turns out another one of the gang members pretended his car broke down in front of my driver. As soon as the guys behind him got as much as they could handle from his trailer, the car cranked right up and took off."

"Remind me to never take a load to New York."

"Oh, it's just as bad in some places in Chicago. Another one of my guys tells me he sometimes stays in a hotel up there where the neighborhood is so bad that he clears out all the stuff from his truck and keeps his windows down all night. Just so the thieves don't bust his windows out to get into his truck to go shopping around in there to see if there's anything worth stealing. It's kind of a low-end smash-and-grab crime that the cops up there don't even bother investigating. Except in this case, there's no smash when they swing their crowbar because the windows are rolled down and no grab because the truck has been cleaned out already."

"Thanks for the warning. Can't wait to see the Windy City again. Are things really that bad up there?"

"The crime rate would be through the roof if people up there reported most the crimes that happen. But unless the victims expect an insurance payout they don't bother. The police don't do anything in most cases. And truck drivers are considered low-priority victims."

"That could be a blessing. If someone had tried to break into my truck in Chicago, the cops probably wouldn't have bothered checking it out, and I'd be a lot farther down the road."

"You're kidding, Mack, but that's really how it is. One of my guys was waiting to unload somewhere in the South Side and left his truck to see if they were ready for him. When he came back, a couple of characters were hanging on the doors on either side of his truck. He chased off after them but they were young guys, so it didn't take them long to lose him.

"My driver jogged back to his truck a'huffin' and a'puffin and hopped up into his cab. He was frantically searching about his truck to see if anything was missing. About that time a cop car came cruising by, so he started hollering and waving at the cops..."

Mack heard laughter on the other end of the line.

"You should've seen my driver when he told the story. He bulged his eyes out like—like—Don Knotts—you know, Barney Fife? Then he started flailing his arms all around, hollering, 'Hey! Help! H-E-L-P!' But the cops just stared at him and passed on by. No way were they going to get out and go running off into a neighborhood like that for some lowlife truck driver."

"Why didn't you tell me all this *before* you talked me into taking this load? I would have rather taken a beating than go up to load in Pampa of all places to start with. Now it sounds like I have to take this load into a den of thieves to unload it."

"I knew you could handle it, big guy. Besides, after I lost those drivers, I didn't have anyone to cover the load." Ginger paused and sighed. "Mack, it is imperative that you get this load delivered on time. There are some things I haven't told you about the load you're taking up there...."

She continued speaking, but with a strained, patient tone—like a parent with an errant child. "Look, I know it's been a long time since you've driven…"

Mack rolled his eyes, made a hand puppet, and mimicked her tone under his breath, "Wook, I know it's been a wong time since you've biven…"

"And like I said, there's plenty of time to make it. But you can't fool around too much. There's a lot riding on this load for us. After what happened with my other drivers, I'm depending on you to right this ship and make our shippers happy with us again."

"I'll try not to fool around so much the rest of the way, Ginger."

"Good. It's okay to enjoy yourself out there. But if we don't keep our customers happy we're not going to have any freight to haul. And then we'll both be in trouble. You know, I enjoyed it myself when I was out there with Tom. I stayed out there with him until Nicky was born and then ran the business from home. We bought more trucks, so after a while he was able to stay home, too, and we built our business together. But I always felt like Tom was torn between being home with us and wanting to be on the road. I'm sure you can relate to that, can't you?"

"I could until today."

"What? C'mon, Mack. Put on your big-boy britches and deal with it. You're tougher than that. I'm not going to listen to that kind of talk out of you. You're ready to quit just because someone tried to break into your trailer?"

"Don't get your tail up, Ginger. I was only kidding."

"Well, you've got to keep going, big guy. Do it for Georgia. You said you and Georgia talked about going out on the road together after you retired from the ministry. Have you ever considered that God may have another ministry for you out there on the road?"

"Right now I'm just out here to get some peace and quiet. And a little windshield therapy. But the only windshield therapy I've had thus far is when I drove up here from Kerrville. And that didn't last long. I should have left earlier so I wouldn't have been so worn out when I got here."

"Maybe you should think about getting some other kind of therapy, Mack. You've spent almost all of your adult life ministering to others. Don't you think it's time to let someone minister to you? Maybe it would help if you would talk to someone about losing Georgia instead of just going out there on the road and working it out yourself. Talking about my loss sure helped me when Tom died. But you just up and left your church, your ministry, and everything else when she died."

"Ginger, I studied psychology in college. I graduated from cemetery—I mean, seminary. Remember? I was even working on my dissertation to finally obtain my doctorate when I lost Georgia. I know every trick in the book. It's tough for me to go to someone else. I have to get away from everything for a while. I'll work through this. I'm just fine."

"You're just stubborn, is what you are, Mack. I know, because Tom was the same way. I think it's just a man thing. Look, we all need help dealing with things sometimes. Your whole world has been turned upside down. You lost Georgia. You lost your ministry. Your kids are grown and off on their own. You just up and left everything. You're basically alone now."

"Alone is where I need to be right now, Ginger."

"Stop it, Mack!"

Mack turned his phone upward, stretched out his arm to view Ginger's face, and then whacked the phone back down.

"You're acting like you're some kind of cowboy riding off into the sunset," Ginger scolded. "This is not the movies, Mack. You're heartbroken over the loss of Georgia. I get that. But what about your church? What about your ministry?"

"My church is in good hands. I trained my associate pastor. He took over and was doing a great job when I left. He's younger, has more energy, and doesn't have the baggage that I have." Mack paused for a long moment before continuing. "Unless I get a clear message from God telling me otherwise, my ministry is over. I once thought I was called to the ministry—if there is such a thing as being called to the ministry. But I just don't know anymore.

"Maybe I was trying to please my uncle Jake. He thought I had something special to offer the world—that I was gifted or something. So much so that he paid for my seminary education. In fact, he provided just about everything I needed to get my degree. I'm just now really beginning to understand what he went through to do all that for me.

"Uncle Jake drove a truck nearly all his life. It was his ticket out of the Panhandle. He was as hard drinking as my dad. And meaner, too, if that were possible. He moved to Dallas and stumbled into some truck stop ministry service and found the Lord." Mack chuckled. "You should have seen my daddy's eyes when Uncle Jake came back to the Panhandle talking about Jesus."

"Oh, Mack," Ginger interjected. "I remember what I called you for. Someone came by here looking for you. Do you know a Ahmad Hashim?"

"Ahmad Hashim?" Mack lifted his hand from the wheel and glanced at his speedometer after realizing he just punched the accelerator with his foot. "Yeah, I know him. He's a doctor. Works at the medical center there in Kerrville. Georgia went to see him. He's actually the one who diagnosed her. She invited him to our church, and he came a couple of times. Why?"

"He came by here. That man gives me the creeps, Mack. This Hashim character—this Dr. Hashim—said he heard you bought a truck and were going to drive for TGN. I told a little white lie just to get rid of him. Told him you were already on the road. Then he asked for your phone number. He was rather insistent. I told him you had an unlisted, private number and I was not authorized to give it to anyone."

"You didn't give it to him, did you?"

"Ha! Are you kidding? You swore me to secrecy, remember? Told me you'd change your number and go lease on with another company if I gave it out to anyone."

"Good. That man is one brick shy of a load if you ask me. The first time he came to our church, I gave a lengthy sermon about the Jewish origins of our Christian faith and how Jesus was the promised messiah. I looked out toward the back of the church while I was preaching and caught the eyes of Dr. Hashim. You should have seen him, Ginger. He was staring a hole right through me. I thought he was going to blow a fuse.

"That sermon was actually part of a series, and to my surprise he came back. I guess out of curiosity. We had the most powerful move of God I've seen in all my time of ministry. A number of people came to the Lord that day and even some long-term members were crying and repenting of their sins."

Mack scanned his mirrors and shook his head. "But not Dr. Hashim. I was ministering to others then, but I was told he was still at the back of the church with a death grip on his seat. He left before that service was over and never came back.

"Anytime I saw him after that, he always wanted to engage me in some kind of debate about religion. But I would never take the bait. I learned a long time ago to just preach Jesus and leave the results to Him. Talk about being insistent—Dr. Hashim would not give up trying to make me debate him. I tried to reason with him in a calm manner, but he became angry every time we talked about the Lord."

"That's what made me remember why I called you, Mack—when you mentioned Jesus. Dr. Hashim tried to draw *me* into a long, drawn-out debate about religion when he asked if you were still preaching. When I told him about my own faith in Jesus, his face dropped like I had just told him about a death in the family."

Ginger paused for a long moment. "Mack, I didn't mean to, but I... um...I let it slip that you were going to pick up a load in Pampa."

"What? Why didn't you call me before? I would have liked to have known."

"Sorry, Mack," Ginger snarled. "I'm a busy lady. I didn't want the job of being your answering service in the first place."

Mack heard a long sigh on the other end.

"What made me call you, Mack." Ginger spoke in a measured tone now. "Is that Dr. Hashim called later and asked if you were in Pampa. Said he would find someone there to deliver his message."

Ka-pow! Mack's truck swerved into the other lane, causing him to almost crash into a passing car. He gripped his wheel and watched in his mirror as rubber peeled off from one of his tractor tires. Mack hit the brakes and pulled his truck off the highway. He felt his rig sway to the right as his load shifted and then felt a slap from the rear, *whump*, as the sides of beef swung forward, giving him an extra nudge after his Pete rolled to a stop.

"Mack! What happened?"

"Gotta go, Ginger. Looks like I just had a blowout."

CHAPTER ELEVEN

THE CALL

Friday, 3:15 P.M.

After hopping down from his rig, Mack planted a large boot print on the side of the blown tire. He inspected the rest of his tires for damage, stepped back into his cab, and snatched up his phone before punching in the number of the first truck tire shop he found in Pampa.

A man answered after several rings.

"Howdy. Panhandle Tire. How may we help you?"

Mack shook his head. *This guy sounds like he's from so far out in the country, a possum and a six-pack would be seen as a seven-course meal.* "I...um...I'm out here on the side of the road with my Peterbilt. Not too far outside of Pampa. Just had a blowout. Can you send someone out here with a tire?"

"Sorry, driver. We're about as busy as a stump-tailed bull in fly season right now. Our road-service truck is out. Can you nurse your truck on over here?"

"I don't know. Will it hurt anything to drive it over there?"

"If your tire is blown out, you're going to have to replace that tire anyway. If you drive slow, you shouldn't damage any other tires. But I can't guarantee you won't. Hope you brought a good book with you if you plan to wait out there, though. You're not going to be able to get anyone to come out anytime soon."

"Why are y'all so busy?"

"Summer may have officially just started, but it's already hotter 'n Hades out there, driver. When it gets this hot those tires get to poppin' like firecrackers. There's more alligators out there on the highway right now than in a Louisiana swamp."

"Okay. I'll nurse my rig on over. Where are y'all located?"

"Know that little truck stop just outside Pampa?"

"Unfortunately, I know it very well."

"Ha! The food's not that bad there, driver."

"No, it's not. But someone tried to break into my rig when I was parked behind the café. I spent half the day there already."

"That was you? You ain't having no luck at all today are you, driver?"

"You don't know the half of it. Where's your shop?"

"Right next to the truck stop."

"Be there as quick as I can get this thing turned around."

Mack eased his Pete back onto the highway and began looking for a place to do just that. After driving for some time he rocked his head to and fro and mimicked the tire shop man: "You ain't having no luck today are you, driver?" The old song "Give Me Forty Acres" by Red Simpson came to mind. Mack started humming the tune. "Give me forty acres, dah, da, da, da, da, ta…"

The words came to him in a flash as he headed down the road the opposite way he wanted to go. He yawped out the song while looking for a place to turn around so he could head back to the truck stop to replace his tire.

Mack grinned when he spotted a place large enough to get his rig going the other direction. He whipped the Pete back around, faced that blazing Texas sun once more, and made a beeline for the truck stop. Once there, he found the Panhandle tire shop next door, parked his rig in front of the bay door, and hopped down from his truck.

The tire man ambled on out from the shop to greet him. He wore a once white T-shirt now stained grey and black. Mr. Tire Man pulled a rag from his back pocket and wiped his hands together for an even mixture of dirt and grease on both hands. He stopped and offered one of those hands to Mack.

"Howdy, driver. How can we help you?"

"I blew out a tire down the road apiece." Mack shook the hand and pointed to the blown tire. "I called and was told I'd have to drive my rig down here to have a new tire put on anytime soon."

Mr. Tire Man strolled over with Mack to inspect the blown tire. "Yes, sir. That was me you talked to." He stuffed the grease rag back down into his pocket. "I heard they caught those scoundrels who tried to bust into your truck." Mr. Tire Man smacked his hands onto the Pete's front tandems before poking his head under the trailer to get a better look at the tires. He turned to face Mack. "These are brand-new tires, driver."

"They caught both of them? They only had the gal when I left."

"Yes, sir. I went over and picked up lunch at the coffee shop. I heard it straight from the horse's mouth."

"From the horse's mouth? The waitress? Barb?"

"You know Barb?"

"I've known her for a long time, it seems."

"Everybody knows Barb. Anyhow, the cops brought that sorry son of a biscuit eater to the truck stop and had a couple of drivers identify him." Mr. Tire Man grinned and pointed an index finger to Mack's chest. "By the way, driver, you were headed in the wrong direction. Barb said one of the drivers told the cops that you left and were on your way to California."

"They already knew I'm on my way to Chicago," Mack chuckled. "I don't think the cops care about talking to me anymore anyway. They've probably already released those characters. One of the officers said they don't really have much to charge them with anyway."

"Well, I don't think that lot lizard will be knocking on any doors around here for a while." Mr. Tire Man thrust a thumb toward the coffee shop. "The manager didn't mind her plying her trade around here too much. But if it gets out that thieves are breaking into trucks out there, drivers will go on down the road somewhere else to eat."

Mack looked out to the lot behind the coffee shop where his rig had been parked, nodded, and then turned to face Mr. Tire Man. "How long before you get to my truck?"

"Might as well put on your sittin' britches, and visit with us awhile, driver." Mr. Tire Man pointed to several rigs parked beside the tire shop. "See those trucks out there? They're all ahead of you. I've got my partner in there working like a one-armed paperhanger trying to catch up. We'll get to you as soon as we can."

Mack glanced at his watch. "That's okay. I've got to call my boss lady back and let her know what's going on. By the time she's done talking you should be finished with the tire."

Mr. Tire Man pulled his rag from his pocket and strolled off wiping his hands. "Women."

Mack climbed into his truck and parked it next to the other rigs waiting for tire repair. He took a deep breath, flipped out his phone, and entered Ginger's number. He hung up before the phone rang. *Better go in and have another cup and catch up on my logs.* He slipped his phone back into its case. *Once I get out of here, I want to get as far down the road as I can.*

After grabbing his logbook, he hopped down from his rig and walked by the front of the tire shop. He spotted Mr. Tire Man with his demounting tool in hand, working a tire off its rim. Mr. Tire Man's partner slapped a tire onto the rig next to him. The man kicked it into place, gathered lug nuts scattered by the rig, and snatched up his impact wrench.

"I'm going to the coffee shop," Mack said.

BRRRREEEWWWWNNNNTTT! BRRRREEEWWWWNNNNTTT!

Mr. Tire Man turned to face Mack. "What?"

Mack pointed to the coffee shop. "I'm going to..."

BRRRREEEWWWWNNNNTTT! BRRRREEEWWWWNNNNTTT!

"What?" Mr. Tire Man asked again.

Mr. Tire Man's partner lifted a lug nut from the floor, readied his wrench, *brrnt*, and then dropped the lug nut.

"I'M GOING TO THE COFFEE SHOP!"

Mr. Tire Man wedged his demounting tool into place. He stood, pulled his rag from his pocket, and wiped his hands together. "You don't have to yell, driver."

"Sorry." Mack cupped a hand to his mouth and whispered. "I'm headed to the coffee shop. Will you let me know when you're ready for me?"

"I will. If you promise not to yell if it takes too long."

"I make it a policy never to yell at men with large tools in their hand."

"Fine. Then I'll let you know when we're ready to pull your rig in."

"Thanks."

Mack walked over to the coffee shop and found his old booth before slapping his logbook onto the table with a *whap*! After easing onto the booth, he tapped his pen onto the table and turned to gaze out the window. He turned to see Barb guiding a cup over in front of him.

"Well, look what the cat dragged in. Did you come back to pick up that ghost you left behind?"

"One of my tires blew out just down the road, Barb." Mack pointed an index finger toward the highway. "I had to come back here to have it fixed."

Barb rested a fist on her hip and shook her head. "If you didn't have bad luck, you wouldn't have no luck at all, would you, honey?"

"Tell me about it."

"Well, things got pretty exciting after you left." The waitress explained what all the excitement was about as she poured Mack's coffee. "The cops came back with Maria's partner in crime, so your two friends could identify him."

"Let me guess." Mack raised an open hand and held it between himself and Barb. "He was a young, rough-looking character? Looks like he just got out of prison?" He lowered his hand down onto the table and leaned toward the server. "And then took a ride in a tractor-trailer, with a hard-luck truck driver? Only to end up in an old truck stop, from which he vanished, never to be seen again?"

"No, no. That was your imaginary friend you picked up. I just saw this character at a distance in the police car. He actually appeared kind of clean cut. Almost looked like a cop himself." Barb placed her coffeepot onto the table and stared out the window for a moment. She faced Mack once more. "I think I've seen him around here before, but I couldn't get a good-enough look at him to be sure."

"Well, the hitchhiker said he was going to clean up when I last saw him. And he *was* carrying a bag with him. Probably changed clothes before he met up with Bonnie."

"Bonnie?"

"That's what they called her." Mack pulled his coffee to himself and rolled the warm cup in his hands. "The police mocked your lot lizard friend and her partner in crime—called them Bonnie and Clyde. They already had Bonnie in the back of the patrol car and said they should be able to nab Clyde, as well. Evidently they were able to chase him down, too."

"Evidently." Barb brought her painted eyebrows together, and eyed Mack. "What did the hitchhiker say his name was?"

"Ricky. He said his name is Ricky. But the officer I talked to seemed to think that was a made-up name."

"Hmm… If your friend *is* a ghost, he needs to come up with another name. Ricky doesn't sound too scary for a ghost. But Bonnie and Clyde *do* sound a lot better than Maria and Ricky. I think I'd call them Bonnie and Clyde, too—especially if I were telling my buddies about the bad guys I chased down." Barb raised the coffeepot to her apron. "Maria and Ricky sounds like some sort of pop music duo or something."

Mack sipped his coffee and then tapped his cup back onto the table. He shook his head. "If Bonnie and Clyde's brains were both made of leather they couldn't saddle a flea between the two of them. But nobody would be dumb enough to try to break into a trailer loaded with swinging meat. And the hitchhiker *knew* I was hauling swinging meat. What were they going to do with it if they were successful in breaking into my trailer?"

"I don't know. Maybe they got the trucks mixed up. I heard the manager talking to someone on the phone earlier this morning just before you came in. They were looking for some other TGN driver. I couldn't hear him very well." Barb strolled off to wait on another table and shrugged. "But they were trying to hunt down some guy named Robert something."

CHAPTER TWELVE

PARTING SHOT

Friday, 4:15 P.M.

*D**ing, ding.*
Mr. Tire Man poked his head into the coffee shop and looked up and down the booths until he spotted Barb. "I'll have another glass of that sweet tea, gorgeous." He ambled over to Mack's table and thrust a thumb over his shoulder. "We're ready for you out there, driver. Just had to patch a couple tires, and then single one out. We got 'er done quick as we could. Don't want you hollering at us out there."

Mack slid out from his booth, retrieved some bills from his jeans, and tossed them onto the table. "Thanks," he said, before turning to face the waitress. "Gotta go, Barb. I've got to get that load out there to Chicago someday. Hopefully it will be a little longer before I see you next time."

He chuckled as he reached out to touch Barb's arm. "Sorry. I do enjoy your company, though."

"I'll bet you say that to all your women out on the road, honey." Barb crossed her arms and stuck out her lips in her best Marilyn Monroe impersonation. "That's okay. I'll be here pining away for you until you get back."

"I'm sure you will, Barb." Mack patted her arm, and grinned. "I'm sure you will."

He walked back out to the tire shop with Mr. Tire Man. Upon arriving at the shop, Mr. Tire Man pointed to the empty space and said, "Ease 'er on in there, driver, and we'll have you out of here in no time."

Mack scanned left and right to check for clearance as he drove his rig through the old shop doors. He noticed a piece of paper stuck under his windshield wiper, hopped down from his rig, and gave a thumbs up to Mr. Tire Man before walking away toward the front of the shop.

He turned to get the paper but stopped dead in his tracks, snapped his fingers, and yanked out his phone. After raising a finger to call Ginger back he looked at her picture and hesitated a moment before punching it in.

"Mack! What happened to you?"

"I'm at the tire shop now, Ginger." Mack pushed open the shop door and walked back out under the hot Texas sun. "After I hung up with you, I checked out my tires and sure enough, there it was, one of my brand-new tires had blown out on my brand-new truck."

"You have new tires, Mack. How could you have a blowout?"

"Hang on, Ginger. I have to check with the tire man." Mack turned around and walked back into the shop. He spotted Mr. Tire Man, already kneeling by the blown tire, readying his impact wrench. Mack muted his phone and said with a wink, "My boss lady wants to know how I could have a blow out."

Mr. Tire Man raised himself from the floor and massaged his knees. He eyed Mack and grinned. "Does she want physics or philosophy?"

"I don't think she likes philosophy too much."

Mr. Tire Man pulled out his rag, wiped his hands, and pointed to one of Mack's tires. "Good. Because the physics of the situation is pretty cut and dried. There's about a hundred psi of pressure in those tires. That's a lot of pressure, driver. When there's just an iddy biddy opening allowing that compressed air to escape..." He balled his fists, and brought them together before throwing his arms to the side. "Ka-blewee! Stuff goes everywhere. And you better not be anywhere near the tire when that happens."

Mack stepped back and nodded. "That's what I thought."

"But I prefer the philosophical explanation myself." The tire-repair man pointed to a deep scar on his forehead before he tapped Mack's rim with his knuckles. "I was putting air in a new tire, but I didn't know there was a crack in the rim. That thing exploded and went flying by me like greased lightning. I could've been killed, but I was lucky." Mr. Tire Man brushed his fingertips across his scar. "It just grazed me."

"Sounds like the Lord was watching over you." Mack leaned in and inspected the scar. "He must have a purpose for you."

"Maybe He does." Mr. Tire Man nodded in silence for a moment. "Maybe He does. But I always just considered myself lucky—or unlucky, depending on how you look at it." The man paused and shook his head. He wiped his hands together on his rag before summing things up. "That's the way it is, driver. There ain't no justice in this world. A man's either lucky or unlucky."

Mr. Tire Man stuffed his rag down into his britches and smiled. "I think you fall into the latter category. That's about the best explanation I can come up with as to how you could have a blowout." He knelt back down to work on the tire, lifted his wrench, and faced Mack. "Tell that to your boss lady."

"Thanks." Mack chuckled as he grabbed his phone. He turned to walk out the shop door. "I'll tell her that. I just needed to hear an expert's opinion."

BRRRREEEWWWWNNNNTTT!

After glancing back at the paper under his wiper, he made a mental note to take it off before he backed out. As he walked out of the shop, he looked at Ginger's picture on his screen, took a deep breath, and unmuted the phone. "Okay. I talked to the tire guy."

"What happened?"

"Do you know what the original Murphy's Law said, Ginger?"

"Yeah...uh... If anything can go wrong it will." Ginger paused for a long moment. "Or something like that. Don't change the subject."

"That's actually Finagle's Law. The full name is Finagle's Law of Dynamic Negatives." Mack stuck a finger to his chest. "Murphy's Law is more applicable in my case."

"Don't wax philosophical on me. What happened to the dang tire?"

"It's flat. Blown out. I told you that." Mack glanced over toward the coffee shop and grinned. "But you asked me how could I have a blowout."

"Mack, you drive me crazy sometimes."

"When I get back from this trip maybe we can get adjoining rubber rooms. The original Murphy's Law says..." Mack balled his fist and then thrust out two fingers before continuing his explanation, "'...if there are two or more ways to do something, and one of those ways can result in a catastrophe, then someone will do it.'"

"I really shouldn't do this Mack."

Mack heard laughter on the other end of the line.

"But what's the difference?"

"Finagle's Law suggests we live in some kind of perverse, negative universe where things just naturally go wrong. We Christians attribute that rule as applying to a fallen universe." Mack stopped and looked at the line of trucks waiting for repair. "Bad things happen because of sin. The devil was cast out of heaven because of his pride. He got madder than a wet hen and has done nothing but wreak havoc on the earth since that time."

"Yeah...well, that's kind of what I believe. He's wreaked a lot of havoc in my life lately, that's for sure."

"Maybe so, Ginger. But the problem with Finagle's Law is that it's fatalistic—*que sera sera*—what happens, happens. It's not really consistent with the Christian faith."

"Forget about *que sera sera*." Ginger spoke in an almost strident tone. "If we don't get that blasted load you're sitting under to Chicago on time, I *know* what's going to happen. We're going to be in real trouble. That's what's going to happen."

After the line fell silent for some time Mack turned the phone to view Ginger's picture. He listened as she spoke with a tone as level as a hockey field and just as frigid.

"Call me when you're back on the road, Mack."

"Will do." After lifting a finger to hang up, he paused and pointed it forward, giving it a good shake instead. "I'll leave you with this: Murphy's Law is about design. Murphy was an engineer, not a philosopher. God, the Engineer, is still fully in charge. Good-bye, Ginger."

"Hey, driver!" Mr. Tire Man stood at the door of his shop. "We're almost done with you in here. My partner's putting on your new tire as we speak. If you want to come in and settle up, by the time we're done, you should be good to go."

Mack dug out his wallet and walked back to the door. "How much do I owe you?"

"Four hundred, eighty-five dollars, and ninety-nine cents."

"There goes my profit for this run." Mack stepped through the door held open by Mr. Tire Man and walked with him through the shop. "Not sure if my warranty covers stupidity. I must have run over something when I dodged a combine out there. There was some road construction going on around there. Guess I ran over some debris or something."

"Let me show you something." The man stopped at Mack's blown tire, raised it to the side, and pointed to a hole before dropping the tire back down onto the shop's floor. "Your warranty may not cover stupidity. But it may cover sabotage."

Mr. Tire Man pulled his rag from his pocket and wiped his hands. "Someone shot out your tire, driver."

CHAPTER THIRTEEN

ON THE ROAD AGAIN, AGAIN

Friday, 5:15 P.M.

M ack backed out from the shop and pulled his Pete around to a spot by the exit heading back onto to the highway before stopping and popping his parking brakes. He jumped down from his truck and gave the new tire a swift kick before stomping around his rig, looking for more damage.

After looking through the sight door at the rear of his trailer, he dropped it back down and punched it shut with the ball of his fist. He bolted back up into his truck and snatched up the clipboard containing his paperwork before storming back to the rear of his trailer once more and checking the seal number against his bill of lading.

Well, at least something is going right, he thought after confirming the matching numbers. He remembered the time Uncle Jake told him about being scammed by warehouse employees stealing items from his load after putting the wrong number on the bills. *First someone tries to steal a side of beef from my trailer. I'd hate to think I'd been scammed out of one, too.*

He tossed his clipboard back into his truck after walking around to his cab and resuming the inspection of his rig. Satisfied there was no more damage, he grabbed the paper from his windshield and climbed into his Pete.

Thinking the paper was some kind of ad for truck service, he balled it up and aimed for his trash bag, basketball style. After chunking the paper dead center, he fist-pumped the air upon hearing the paper land in the trash as if from a winning free-throw shot.

Mack slipped his truck into gear and steered toward the exit. After glancing back at the trash, his curiosity got the better of him. He sighed, popped the brakes, and leaned across his cab to retrieve the paper. What looked like poetry appeared after he smoothed out the paper on his steering wheel. Easing back onto his seat, he read the poem aloud.

> "A sound is heard once a day times five
> All must stop and heed the call
> In between are four times?—No, but five!
> These things are known to all
> To all but those in darkness, yet alive
> They hear, but ignore the call
> Now they live, but soon must die."

He stared long and hard at the paper and then out the windshield of his Pete. Mack crumpled the paper once more and threw it at his trash bag. The paper bounced off before rolling to a stop on the passenger-side floor. He once again stared at the paper.

After climbing down from his rig, he placed his hands on his hips, took a deep breath, and surveyed the lot. He walked around, opened the passenger-side door, grabbed the paper, and gripped a hand on the door's handle. Mack read the poem once more.

"A-sound-is-heard-once-a-day-times…five!" He slammed the door shut before stomping around and climbing back up into his Pete. Mack snatched up his briefcase, folded the paper once again, and dropped it down onto a pile of paperwork before snapping the case shut.

He propped the briefcase across his steering wheel and crossed his arms on top of the case. After watching traffic pass on the highway for some time, Mack grabbed his phone and punched in Ginger's number.

"Mack!" Ginger shouted as soon as the phone stopped ringing. "Are you back on the road yet?"

"Just left the shop, Ginger. Listen, someone called the truck stop looking for me. You didn't tell anyone where I was, did you?"

"Look, Mack. I told you that Dr. Hashim came by wanting your phone number. I wouldn't give it to him. But I let it slip where you were going, and that's it."

"Well, someone called up here looking for me. Said they were looking for Robert. Robert from TGN. There are only two people I can think of who know me as Robert—Pastor Robert McClain. Dr. Hashim and Ben Garza from the Texas Rangers."

"*I* don't even know where you're at except that you're at some truck stop in Pampa, having a tire changed. How many truck stops can there be in Pampa? Maybe they just called the truck stops to track you down. By the way, who is Ben Garza?"

Mack paused, let out a long sigh, and shook his head. "I guess it's okay to tell you about this since nothing's come of it. Ben Garza is a captain with the Texas Rangers. After the Kerr County authorities ruled Georgia's death a suicide, I sought help from the Rangers. Unfortunately, I didn't get anywhere with them, either. They just kind of brushed me off and said something about how it's often difficult for family members to accept a loved one's suicide."

"Well, I couldn't believe she did that, either, Mack. But she did have cancer. Who knows what she was going through inside?"

"She was just diagnosed with cancer, Ginger. Georgia was a fighter. She was a lot stronger than me. She would have fought that battle, and by the grace of God she would have won it. No way did Georgia kill herself."

"But who would want to hurt Georgia? She was one of the kindest people I've ever known."

Mack popped open his briefcase and read the note once more.

"Mack?"

"I'm going to find that out, Ginger. And they're going to tell me why. It looks like I'm going to have to do this on my own."

"Do *what* on your own? There you go with your stupid Lone Ranger stuff again. Just let the professionals handle it. If you are right about what happened to Georgia, they'll find out."

"They're not even looking, Ginger. Didn't you hear what I said? I raised so much stink that I got the attention of a captain with the Texas Rangers. And I couldn't even get *him* to believe me in spite of the bizarre circumstances of her death."

"Just be careful out there, Mack. If you want to go home and talk to people there again and try to get some answers, I'll get you a load going that way as soon as I can. But you have to get that load to Chicago on time."

"I'm at home *now*, Ginger. And don't worry about your precious load. It will be in Chicago on time."

"Mack..."

"Good-bye, Ginger."

Mack tossed his briefcase onto the passenger seat, dug out his billfold, and pulled out Officer Pipe Cleaner's card. After staring at it for some time he shook his head and slipped the card back into his wallet. He yanked his phone from its case and flipped through his contacts to find Captain Garza's number.

After glancing at his watch, Mack rocked his head back and forth, mimicking Ginger's tone as he repeated her words to himself. "If we don't get that woad to Chicago on time…we're going to be in *weeeaaal* trouble."

I'll never get out of Pampa, if I call someone now. I'll give Captain Garza a call after I unload in Chicago. If I call now, I'll have to deal with those two locals first since shooting at a truck is a crime they would be called out on first.

Mack stuck his phone into its case and tapped it down with the ball of his fist. He put his rig into gear and drove out of the truck stop. Once he reached the speed limit, he settled back onto his seat and focused on the highway ahead.

Whatever else the hitchhiker is, he's definitely not a poet. As he peered into his mirror and watched the truck stop fade from sight, he thought about Officers Pipe Cleaner and Round Face. *Maybe I should have called those cops. They were able to track down Bonnie and Clyde after all.* He chuckled and shook his head.

After grasping his steering wheel tighter with each thought, he scanned his gauges and took a deep breath. *How could I not have seen it? After I saw him at the funeral and shook his clammy little hand, I should have trusted my gut.* He glanced at his watch once more. *Still plenty of time to get there.*

His white-knuckled grip on the wheel reminded him that he was letting this get the better of him. He loosened his grip and ran his fingers across its edge. *I don't know what he's up to. But he can follow me all the way to Chicago, if he wants. The worst he can do to me is send me to be with Georgia sooner than I had planned.*

CHAPTER FOURTEEN

THE TRAVELER AND THE
TROOPER

Friday 5:45 P.M.

Mack scanned the highway ahead and spotted a hazy figure of a man walking along the road in the distance. As his Pete rolled closer to the man a familiar feeling washed over him. The hitchhiker could be seen clearly now, his back to traffic. With his arm extended to his side, his thumb once again beckoned passersby as he strode down the highway at a pace such as a man would have who had no place to go.

The words Mack spoke to Ginger came back to him as he pulled his rig to the shoulder. *God, the Engineer, is still fully in charge.* He turned to his mirror and watched the hitchhiker jog to his truck.

The hitchhiker popped open the passenger door, heaved his bag inside Mack's rig, and then lowered his head to get his footing in order to hop into the truck. Mack leaned over and grabbed the bag's handle before plopping it down between the seats. He looked at the hitchhiker and grinned.

When the man eyed Mack behind the wheel, his eyes widened like those of a cat tossed into the dog pound. He snatched up his bag's handle and yanked it back, but Mack held firm to the other side. A tug-of-war ensued.

Mack glanced at his mirror and caught sight of the black-and-white now parked behind him with lights flashing. "Better hop in, Ricky." He motioned over his shoulder to the approaching state trooper. "Or you can go with him, if you'd like."

The hitchhiker turned to see the state trooper's car behind Mack's truck. He scampered up into the truck and hopped into the sleeper.

Mack grabbed his logbook from the dash, but rolled his eyes and dropped it back down before lowering his window as the trooper approached.

"Everything all right, driver?"

"Yes, sir. I…uh…I just stopped to check on something."

A car zoomed by the trooper. Mr. State Trooper grabbed his hat before it blew off into the wind. He watched with annoyance as the car sped down the highway. "Hang on a minute, driver." The officer walked back to his patrol car and talked on the radio for some time before returning to Mack's truck. "I'm going to catch one of those nutcases one of these days." He motioned his head to the front of Mack's Pete. "Would you mind stepping out here in front of your truck, sir?"

"Be glad to, sir." Mack glanced at the closed sleeper curtain before stepping down from his rig and facing the trooper.

"I just wanted to…" *BLUB…BLUB…BLUB!* Mr. State Trooper turned with Mack to observe a passing truck whose driver flipped on his engine brake upon spotting the trooper's car. The trooper once again grabbed his hat and braced himself for the blast of wind from the semi. He shook his head. "That trucker must have been sleeping and just flipped on his Jake brake out of habit after seeing me."

Mr. State Trooper stared down the highway for some time before returning his attention to Mack. "I just wanted to make sure you're okay. Seems there's been a mini-crime wave going on around these parts." He motioned over his shoulder. "Some characters broke into a truck in Pampa back there." The trooper paused long enough to suppress the grin forming on his face. "Pampa's finest neglected to get the information on the truck before they took off after the bad guys." He eyed Mack in silence for a moment before speaking again. "Can I see your license, driver?"

Mack retrieved his billfold and handed the trooper his license. He turned to look at the sleeper before facing the officer once more.

After eying his license for some time, the trooper nodded. "And then that same driver had one of his tires shot at, which caused a blowout, according to what we heard at the truck stop. Guess the driver was in a hurry. He didn't bother reporting it." The officer glanced toward Mack's rig. "Anyone else in your truck, Mr. McClain?"

"Well...uh...yes, sir. There's someone in the sleeper."

The trooper returned Mack's license. "Well, I'm not going to wake up your co-driver. You guys need all the beauty rest you can get." He tipped his hat to Mack. "Ya'll be safe out there, driver."

"Thank you, sir."

After climbing back into his Pete, Mack watched as Mr. State Trooper walked back to his car. The trooper placed his hand atop his hat and tossed it to the passenger side before easing back onto his seat.

Drumming his fingers across the wheel, Mack stared long and hard at his mirror. When it became obvious the trooper was not going to leave before him, he pulled his rig back onto the highway. He watched as Mr. State Trooper drove out behind him, where he remained for several miles. Mack placed an elbow on his armrest and observed the patrol car in his mirror. *I hate it when they do that.* After some time, the black-and-white pulled out from behind his truck. Mack returned the trooper's wave as he passed.

As the patrol car rolled out of sight he tapped on the sleeper curtain. "Okay, Ricky. You can come out now." Receiving no response, Mack again tapped on the curtain. "Ricky. The coast is clear."

Mack looked over his shoulder. "Ricky!" Seeing a parking area ahead, he pulled in before yanking back the sleeper curtain to see the hitchhiker sawing logs in the back. After dropping the curtain, he shook his head and stared out his driver's side window.

The barbed wire fence around the property across the highway had seen its better days. Mack looked around the property and eyed a yellow-trimmed house. The faded paint peeled off the old home, telling of a lack of care but also suggesting a tale of another, happier time—or at least a time when someone wanted to be seen living in a cheerful place. *Like Georgia's home. Her house was painted yellow like that.*

Mack reached into the compartment where he kept Georgia's bracelet. Not able to feel the bracelet, he lifted himself from his seat and felt around the back of the little cubbyhole. Still not able to feel it, he looked inside and felt around the edges before running his hands along the dash and then across and under the seats.

He jumped down from his Pete and ran around to the passenger side. Flinging the passenger door open, he hopped onto the step and grabbed his trash before scattering the contents onto his floorboard. After rummaging through the papers, he balled them up and stuffed them back into the bag. Mack slammed the passenger door shut with the palm of his hand and banged the other hand onto the door. He dropped his head and stared in silence at the ground beneath his truck.

After shoving himself away from the door, he stormed around the side of his truck and approached a car containing a family, which had pulled off the road, as well. Upon arriving at the rear of his trailer, he yanked up the sight door and eyed the hanging sides of beef. He slapped the door shut and pounded it with the ball of his fist before smacking his forehead against the door.

Pounding and pounding the door with his fists, Mack hit the door with a little more power with each strike. A little girl in the back of the car watched as he banged his fists on the door.

"There's something wrong with that man, Mommy."

Mack turned toward the girl and attempted to smile but displayed something more like a snarl. The car sped off, spraying him with dust and gravel. He cocked his hand back and slammed the door once more with a vengeance. His arms dropped to his side as he walked around to the driver's side of his truck.

He trudged up the steps back into his Pete before plopping down onto his seat with a heave. After raising the sleeper curtain again, he watched the hitchhiker sleep like a baby for some time. He dropped the curtain, shook his head, and turned back to face the highway.

With his elbows resting on the steering wheel now, he massaged his forehead before lifting his phone from its case. He eased back onto his seat and punched in Ginger's number.

"Hello, Mack." Ginger answered the phone like an ex-wife who just found out about another affair.

"Ginger." Mack ignored her tone. "You said Dr. Hashim called and said he'd have someone up here deliver his message for him?" He glanced at the sleeper as Ginger hesitated to answer.

"Yeah...?"

"Is that all he said?" Mack lowered his voice. "Did he say who... or how?"

"That's all, Mack. I was busy and wanted to get him off the phone. That man gives me the creeps."

"Well, if he calls again let him know where he can find me." Mack slipped his Pete into gear and eased back onto the highway. "I have my own message I'd like to deliver."

CHAPTER FIFTEEN

SIN OF OMISSION

Friday, 6:15 P.M.

Mack looked to see Ginger's picture on his phone and raised his finger to hang up when he heard her voice.

"Mack, there's something you probably need to know."

"What is it now, Ginger?" After putting his Pete into high gear, Mack punched the gas and watched his speedometer needle rise.

Ginger hesitated once more. "Maybe I should have told you about this before…"

After setting the cruise, Mack scanned his mirrors, settled back onto his seat, and sighed. "The last time you neglected to tell me something, it was about a deranged killer who, of all people, you let know that I was headed to Pampa to load."

"What are you talking about? Dr. Hashim? I said he gives me the creeps. Who said he's a deranged killer? And you just told me you wanted me to tell him where you are now. What's going on, Mack? Are you feeling okay?"

"I'm fine, Ginger. Just fine. You said you had something to tell me?"

"Well, yeah. I told you there was a lot riding on this load. But I…uh… didn't tell you why."

Listening to deadening silence on the line as Ginger failed to continue with an explanation for some time, Mack spoke up. "Tell me what? What didn't you tell me about this load?"

"There's a lot more to this than I even want to know about. Mack, they don't even run swinging meat from Pampa up there anymore. It seems that taking that load of swinging meat to Chicago is something like a test run to see if it's feasible to do again. The unions are involved, as well as some pretty powerful political figures. They plan to center much of the work up North where their power base is, in order to gain control of the industry. There's a lot of money being thrown around; a lot of palms being greased. It's all part of some kind of greater scheme by agribusiness to consolidate the distribution of food in this country into fewer, more manageable locations."

"How do you know all this, Ginger?"

"Well, as you know, Tom was a sharp guy. He was on his way to building our little trucking company up to where we could compete with the big boys. When he had the accident, I was devastated, of course. And keeping the company afloat has been a real struggle since he's been gone.

"But I still keep in touch with his business connections, who keep me up on trends in the industry. Through them, I learn a lot about what's happening behind the scenes—you know, things the general public would not be aware of. And since Tom was so heavily involved in politics, I still have some of those contacts, as well. By the way, did Tom tell you he was thinking about running for office himself?"

"Oh yeah. He thought it would help him in business. He seemed to have become addicted to politics after being elected as a delegate to the national convention. When he met the President and some high-ranking officials who visited the Texas delegation, that was it. He was hooked."

"He was hooked all right—to the point of obsession. Tom spent every waking moment the last several years building our business and making political friends. This is where my contact comes in. He was one of Tom's political confidants who was helping to groom him for a higher office than what Tom had in mind. The guy tried to hit on me after Tom died.

Boy, are these guys sleazy. Anyway, he had a few too many one night and just kind of started running his mouth. He swore me to secrecy as to the source of the information. The guy may be a sleazeball, but he's a useful sleazeball, so I still have a relationship with him. I learned a lot from Tom."

"I can tell."

"And just what is that supposed to mean?"

"Never mind, Ginger. What did you learn from Mr. Sleazeball?"

"That there are some pretty shady characters involved in all this. Some high-placed, well-known shady characters." Ginger paused for some time before continuing. "Listen, Mack. I just feel like I have to tell someone. But you can't tell anyone. And I mean, not *anyone*. I'm just telling you because you and Tom were friends, and I've been feeling guilty for not letting you know.

"But the really important thing here is that we are going to have a big, fat, juicy contract to haul the stuff up there if it works out—that freight and a whole lot more. If we get this contract, it could be the start of something huge for us."

"Well, thanks for letting me know, Ginger. It would have been nice if you clued me in before I took the load. Do you know how long it's been since I've been out here? I don't need some kind of experimental load my first time out, especially with all these characters you're talking about poking their noses in my business. I have enough drama going on in my life as it is. I'm just out here getting some windshield therapy, remember?"

"You were the only one available after the driver who was scheduled to take the load quit on me, and I know I can trust you." Ginger paused and sighed. She resumed speaking but in a slow, patient tone. "You're not looking at the big picture, Mack. You could eventually own several trucks and lease them through TGN. You can even start your own trucking company. I'm telling you, this is big. There will be plenty of freight to go around. Just help me out now."

"I don't want to own a trucking company, Ginger. And I don't want to *run* a trucking company, either. I want to drive the truck I have and just kind of leave the world behind for a while."

"Tom was right about you, Mack. You don't have any ambition."

"What? He said that?"

"And he was right. You're a talented guy, Mack. Tom told me about the football scholarship you had from Texas Tech. He said you were so good you were a lock for the pros. Think of the good you could have done with all the money you would have made. But you decided to forgo all that to pursue a ministerial degree."

"Did he also tell you I was injured in my senior year? That played into my decision, too. I considered it a sign from the Lord that He was leading me in another direction. I—"

"You quit, Mack," Ginger cut him short. "That's what you did. You quit. Stop making excuses. You could have worked to overcome that, but you didn't. Then after you went into the ministry, you had a number of opportunities for larger churches. A lot of people recognized your talent. You could have had a huge church—like, I don't know—like Joel Osteen, or something. But you got comfortable and stayed with your little church in Kerrville all those years.

"And now that you've changed your profession, you have an opportunity to better yourself." She raised her voice, and hurled one last dagger from her tongue. "But you are content to just drive that one truck you own."

"Listen," Mack shot back at Ginger, "how about I just drive this one truck down the road and lease on with someone else once I dumped off this stupid swinging meat in Chicago?"

"We have a lease agreement, remember?" Ginger paused and softened her tone. "I'm sorry, Mack. You just drive me nuts sometimes. You're so different than Tom."

"Well, I'm just out here hauling freight for you, Ginger. We're not married." Mack raised a hand, looked upward, and silently mouthed the words, "Thank you, Lord," before continuing. "I've got to go. Anything else?"

"All this is kind of scaring me, Mack."

"Scaring you? What's scaring you?"

"I said this whole thing is part of a scheme by giant agribusiness to consolidate control of the food industry, and it is. With all the GMO in our food supply, you can't even reproduce crops from some of the produce we eat. And who knows if we're being told the truth about what's in our food. Now they're taking over the whole distribution process? And consolidating it in areas easier to control?

"I'm getting all this information from reliable sources within the food industry. But my contact tells me our government is manipulating the whole process. They are creating a system whereby certain cities, or even whole sections of the country, could have their food supply cut off. When a crisis comes, real or manufactured, if you don't come to them and be a good citizen, however that's defined, you don't eat."

"I guess you and I will be going on a diet then, Ginger. If it ever comes to that, I think it will be time for the Lord's return."

"That's easy for you to say, Mack. I've got a disabled son I have to feed."

"It's not easy for any of us. We all have to eat. And all of us need to start praying for strength now."

"I don't know how much strength I have left. Tom and I talked a lot about all this before he died. He finally became disgusted by the whole thing and kind of started distancing himself from some of the high-powered politicians he was so proud of associating with. Tom had just begun to step back and rethink everything. But I think he was in too deep."

Mack heard a sob before the line fell silent. "What's wrong, Ginger?"

"Mack... I don't think Tom's death was an accident."

CHAPTER SIXTEEN

SIN OF COMMISSION

Friday, 6:45 P.M.

"Why do you think that, Ginger? A pickup truck crossed the median on I-10 just outside Kerrville and crashed into Tom's Expedition. How could that not be an accident?"

"I don't know. But after Tom's political mentor was murdered..."

"Wait. Tom's mentor was murdered?"

"Supposedly, it was a robbery gone bad. But there was nothing taken, Mack. Nothing. He still had his wallet, cell phone—everything—on him when his body was found. Tom told me this is what powerful people do when they want to leave a message. The police arrested a couple of thugs and charged one with his murder and the other as an accessory after the fact for helping him cover up his involvement. The killer had a...um... an unfortunate accident, I guess you could say, and died before he went to trial."

Mack watched in his mirror as traffic approached from behind. He nodded. "Yeah, I remember reading something about that case. But I never linked it to Tom. I thought he was buddies with that congressman from his district. They didn't say anything in the news about a connection to the congressman. That would have kept jaws flapping in Kerrville for a long time."

"Well, the congressman was the one grooming Tom for high political office. You know what a charismatic guy Tom was…"

"…And he could talk a coon down out of a tree. I can see why they had plans for him."

"But the congressman couldn't be seen as the one working with Tom. So he had his associate meet with him, and he had a little business directed his way, which had the potential to lead to a lot more business. They were working to create a great storyline—a highly successful, self-made businessman desiring to give back to the community by becoming a public servant.

"At first I was ecstatic. I thought this was the break we needed after working so hard to build the company up from that one truck we owned to where we are now. But before his mentor was killed—that's what Tom called him, his mentor—Tom opened up to me about the dark underbelly of the group he was involved with. It turned my stomach. And I don't think he told me the half of it. He made me swear that I would never tell anyone.

"He also made me promise that I would carry on the business if anything ever happened to him. Tom wanted me to eventually pass our business down to Nicky. But Tom is gone now, Mack. And Nicky is in such bad shape he may never recover enough to be able to run the company. I don't know what to do. The only thing I know for sure is getting this contract means everything for the survival of the company."

"Uh-huh. And just how is it that you were offered this big-time contract? Are these the same people Tom were working with?"

"I just walked into the middle of all this, Mack. These things were already in the works when Tom died. What do you think I should do? Just walk away, with no way to cover the expenses for Nicky's care—after I promised Tom I would carry on the business and pass it down to Nicky if anything happened to him? I have some huge responsibilities here. I'm not just some truck driver lollygagging about the country, because I don't want to face reality anymore."

Mack slammed down his phone and looked at Ginger's picture as he prepared to punch the off button to hang up on her. But he took a deep breath instead. "Wash off your war paint, Ginger. I have a right to know these things. I have flesh in this game, too, and Tom was my friend. Who do you think may have killed him?"

"I don't know, Mack."

"Have you told anyone else about this? Have you gone to the authorities?"

"Who could I go to? And tell them what? That I don't think my husband's accident was really an accident? I don't know how high this goes. I've just kept my mouth shut and run my business."

Well, that must have been a challenge, Mack thought. But he just held his piece and, after some thought, asked "What happened to the other guy who was charged in the death of Tom's mentor? It sounds like he may be the only one who may have any knowledge about what happened to him— even if he was an accessory after the fact. Maybe the dots can be connected through him."

"He copped a plea and is doing some time in prison. Tom kept up with what happened to the guy, for obvious reasons. I don't know his name or which prison he is in. But I'll never forget what Tom said his nickname was."

"It wasn't Rocky by any chance, was it?"

"Rocky? No... Why?"

Mack turned and lifted the sleeper curtain. He eyed the snoozing hitchhiker once more before dropping it back down. "Never mind. Listen, Ginger, it's been a pretty eventful day. I know I haven't made much progress since I loaded, but I left just before midnight last night to get up here. And I've still got plenty of time to get to Chicago. I'm going to call it a day and get a little shut-eye. Anything else you need to tell me?"

"Yeah, I just remembered where they put that guy in prison. They call him the Scorpion. Or just Scorpion, maybe. He's up there in the Panhandle near Pampa, where you picked up your load."

CHAPTER SEVENTEEN

STEALING HOME

Saturday, 8:00 A.M.

"Where're we at?" The hitchhiker interrupted the whining of the wheels like a stranger butting in on a private conversation.

Mack leaned toward the sleeper and eyed the head of the hitchhiker now sticking out from behind the sleeper curtain. The mop of hair atop his head was as mixed up as he was. After turning back to check his mirrors and gauges, Mack wondered how long it had been since he had done, either. He resumed his new pastime of watching the rhythmical passing of the white lines. Sitting in silence for some time before answering the man, he shook his head. "Good question."

The hitchhiker crawled out from the sleeper berth and plopped himself onto the passenger seat. "Man." He yawned, brushed back his hair with his fingers, and then peered into the side mirror. "I dozed right off as soon as I hit that nice, air-conditioned bunk. I guess we'll know where we're at when we see those bright city lights of Chicago, huh?" The man turned to face Mack, managing something resembling a half smile in place of his usual smirk. "We *are* still on the way to Chicago, right?"

"Does it really matter, Ricky?" Mack did not return the smile. "You're headed straight back to trouble, as far as I can tell. It doesn't make any

86

difference which direction you go. Me? The road is my home now. This rig will only be pointed toward Chicago for a couple of days."

He turned and glared at his passenger. "Then you and all those swinging sides of beef back there will be out of my hair, and I'll be headed somewhere else." Mack spun his head around, clenched his teeth, and faced the highway as if it were an enemy to be defeated.

The men sat in silence, not speaking to one another for some time, both now watching the lines flying past Mack's truck. The whining of the rig's wheels continued unabated.

"What's wrong with *you*, man?"

"Where is it, Ricky? Or whatever you're called. What did you say they called you?"

"Rocky."

"Uh-huh. Okay, have it your way, Ricky-Rocky. Where is it?"

"What?"

"You know what." Mack barked. "The bracelet." He glared at the hitchhiker once more. "You're fortunate that murder is against my religion. I've decided not to kill you. Just give it back."

The passenger squirmed in his seat and looked out the window for a long moment before turning back to face Mack. "I was going to tell you about it. Really, I was. But I got scared. I was hoping you wouldn't find out that it was gone until after you dropped me off in Chicago."

"Where-is-it?"

"I don't have it."

"Ricky, I will stop this truck and strip you down buck naked if I have to. You took Georgia away from me again and I'm getting her back."

"Are you crazy, man? It was a bracelet. I'll get the money to pay you back. I swear." The hitchhiker grabbed his bag from the sleeper and plopped it down on the floor. "Here," he said, thrusting his hand in the bag's direction. "This is all I own. Keep it. But I can't give you the bracelet back because I don't have it."

Mack hit the brakes, causing the sides of beef to swing forward— *whump!*—as he pulled his truck to the shoulder. The rig rolled to a grinding halt. He popped his brakes, gripped his wheel, and turned to face his passenger.

"Where—is—it, Ricky?"

The hitchhiker snatched up his bag and flung his door open, sending him and the bag flying out of the rig. After sliding down the embankment, he scrambled to regain his footing and then bolted off in the direction of the field beside the highway.

Mack hopped out of his truck and retrieved his hammer from the side compartment before rushing around to the front of his rig. He caught sight of the hitchhiker picking himself off the ground as he headed toward the barbed-wire fence surrounding the property next to the highway.

The man hurdled over the fence and hit the ground running. His arms churned up and down like an athlete competing in the Olympics. He ran past grazing cattle, who chewed their cud at the same slow pace as they watched the men.

Mack grabbed onto a fencepost, leaped over the fence, and set off in hot pursuit of the hitchhiker. He mustered all the will and stamina gained from his days as an athlete and came within spitting distance of the man.

But the younger man gained ground as Mack became winded. Mack threw his hammer, hitting the thief in the lower back. The hitchhiker dropped his bag, stumbled forward, slid across the field, and then pushed himself off the ground, attempting to regain his footing. Bounding toward the man as if aiming for a fleet-footed tailback from his high school days, Mack tackled him, knocking him facedown into the dirt.

"Where is it, Ricky?"

The hitchhiker dug his fingers into the grass, creating ruts in the field as he tried to pull himself away. Mack grabbed the man's arm, twisted it behind him, and then kicked a knee onto the small of his back.

"Are you going to make me strip you down and dump your bag out to find it? Maybe I can go back and get my hammer and aim it a little better next time."

"I swear I don't have it. I gave it to Maria."

CHAPTER EIGHTEEN

DYING TIME AGAIN

Saturday, 8:30 A.M.

"**M**aria?" Mack shoved the hitchhiker's arm up his back and shouted. "Maria from the truck stop? The lot lizard?"

"I met her on work release." The big, bad ex-con façade faded away like a butter on a hot skillet as the man's tears fell onto the field. "Please. I'll pay you back. I swear. I gave it to Maria. She came out to the truck stop and got it."

Mack pushed away from the man, plopped himself onto the ground, and threw his arms across the grass. He watched birds fly across the cloudless sky for some time in silence. "You gave Georgia's bracelet to some..." He breathed in warm air, exhaled, and said to no one in particular, "I don't believe this."

The hitchhiker pushed himself onto his knees and groaned. He swayed his backside right and then left, readying himself for another run, if and when Mack regained his senses. But all he could manage was a crawl. He retraced his steps back toward the fence, pounding his hands onto the ground, feeling for the hammer as he went. He shot his head around in Mack's direction upon hearing his voice.

"Dabda, Dabda, Dabda," Mack said.

The young man continued scampering across the field on hands and knees, pounding the ground with his hands. When a hand slapped onto the hammer, he rolled over and shoved himself up into a sitting position. He watched for any movement from Mack as he wrapped his arms around his legs and gripped the hammer as if it were a lifeline tossed to a drowning man in a raging sea.

"What?"

"Dabda, Ricky. Dabda." Mack rocked his head to and fro like a rowboat on gentle waters, spelling it out with each sway of the head. "D-A-B-D-A." He dropped his head, and continued the same cadence, repeating the letters to himself. "D-A-B-D-A."

"You're losin' it, man."

Mack raised his head and stared long and hard at the dirt-encrusted face of the hitchhiker. "Correction, Ricky. I've already lost it. Lost Georgia…lost my ministry…lost my reason for living…and now I've lost Georgia's bracelet." He rolled on to his side and pushed himself into a sitting position. With his palms flat on the ground, he faced the man in silence. The hitchhiker braced himself with one hand while raising the hammer with his other.

"Know what Dabda is, Ricky?"

The hitchhiker lowered the hammer and waited for his explanation.

"It's an acronym. I used it to remember the five stages of grief. D-A-B-D-A. Denial and Isolation, Anger, Bargaining, Depression and Acceptance. Learned it in my psychology class when I went to cemetery." He paused and grinned before continuing. "I mean seminary. It was a memory aid I used to remember those stages of grief because I needed to know them when ministering to those who lost loved ones."

Mack stared into space, through the hitchhiker, into the eyes of Mr. Hamilton who had just lost Mary, his wife of fifty-two years. He *ministered* to Mr. Hamilton when the septuagenarian sat in his office shortly after the death of his wife.

Mack thought he had listened to the widower at the time, but he knew in reality he was just scanning through the files in his head as the grieving man spoke until he reached the appropriate file. Mr. Hamilton was the last person who came to him seeking ministry before Georgia's death. Mack nodded as he felt the warm summer breeze against the moisture at the edges of his eyes.

"And boy was I good at it. I could nail them every time. I knew exactly what stage they were in." After wrapping his arms around his knees, he grasped a hand around his wrist and let out a long sigh. He focused once again on the young man now sitting across from him. "But you know what, Ricky?"

The hitchhiker pushed himself away before raising the hammer once more upon seeing Mack making an effort to lift himself from the ground.

"Those stages weren't originally meant to describe how someone dealt with the loss of a loved one." Mack turned and pushed himself up from the ground. "Those were the stages the dying experienced when facing their own death."

He brushed his hands on his jeans, dusting off dirt and grass as he continued. "Before I went to cemetery..." Mack glanced up to see the hitchhiker loosening his grip on the hammer, "...I learned how to deal with whatever life threw at me. Growing up dirt poor in the Panhandle, I had to learn to be resourceful. When faced with a difficult problem, I learned there is more than one way to skin a cat."

Mack paused to study the young man's eyes. "Know something else I've learned?" he said, extending a hand. "It's all academic unless you're the cat. C'mon, Ricky, we're burning daylight. We've got to get those babies hanging in that trailer out there to Chicago."

The hitchhiker clutched Mack's hand. He punched a fist to the ground and pushed himself up as Mack pulled him forward. After he released his hand, the man dropped the hammer to his side. "You're a preacher?"

"I was." Mack turned and walked back across the field toward his truck. "Had a church and everything. A church...a wife...a home...a dog..." Grinning like he had horns holding up his halo, he continued. "*And* a cat."

"Whatcha doin' out here drivin' a truck then?" The hitchhiker snatched his bag from the ground and jogged to Mack's side.

"It's the only real job I've ever had. From the time I was knee high to a grasshopper, my uncle Jake used to pick me up when he came up from Dallas to load in the Panhandle." He glanced at his rig parked next to the highway, picked up his pace, and turned to face the hitchhiker. The young man now matched his gait stride for stride.

"When I was a teenager and we were at a place where he could get away with it, he paid me to help him load and unload. I started driving down some old, dusty back roads in West Texas as soon as my feet could reach the pedals. And as soon as I was old enough to belly up to the bar and slap down my money at the DPS, I got my CDL and then drove with Uncle Jake every chance I got."

"But how come you're out here now? Why ain't you still preachin'?"

"Guess God's got other plans for me now. I couldn't… When Georgia was…when Georgia died…" Mack smacked his hand on a fencepost, raised one leg, and then the other over the barbed-wire fence. "Georgia is—*was*—my wife. She was murdered by someone who wanted to kill me—still wants to kill me, it seems."

"Why didn't he just bump *you* off?"

Mack stopped to face the hitchhiker. "Maybe he did, Ricky." After nodding silently for a moment, he managed a half smile. "Maybe he did."

A slight grin seemed to form on the hitchhiker's face but vanished in about one half less than no time.

"What happened to her?"

"My wife was killed with our own shotgun."

The two men resumed walking toward Mack's rig.

"The authorities in Kerr County, where I lived, ruled her death a suicide. But I knew that was crazy." He balled a hand into a fist, flipped over an index finger, and pointed it at his companion. "Number one, Georgia would never kill herself." He flipped over a second finger. "Number two, she was not a large woman. She could barely reach the trigger with her big toe. And—"

"Wait," the man interrupted, "someone just broke into your house and shot her? That don't make no sense."

"None of this makes a lot of sense." Mack looked the man up and down as if sizing him up for the first time. "What were you in prison for, Ricky?"

The hitchhiker tightened his hold on the hammer. "It wasn't for no murder."

Mack eyed the man and his hammer for some time in silence, shook his head, and grinned. "It's still a long way to Chicago. Tell you what. I'll finish telling you my story on the way, and you can tell me yours."

"Okay. But you ain't gonna like it."

"Mine's not very pretty, either."

CHAPTER NINETEEN

INSIDE THE JOINT

Saturday, 9:30 A.M.

The men walked in silence the remainder of the way to the Pete before climbing back into the truck. Mack grabbed his cell, rolled his eyes, and whacked the phone back down onto the console when he saw a missed call from Ginger. He fumbled around beside his seat, found a towel, and tossed it to the hitchhiker.

"Here. Do something about that face of yours. You look about as ugly as a mud fence."

The hitchhiker scrubbed away the grubby mixture of dirt and cow dung on his face as Mack slid his logbook from the dash and plopped it onto his lap.

"Better catch up on my logs. We've got some scales coming up." Mack tapped his pen onto the logbook and stared out the window of his rig for a moment before turning to face the hitchhiker. "I don't get it, Ricky. Why were you with that gal at the back of my trailer at the truck stop? Everyone thought you were breaking in to steal something. But you knew all that was back there was swinging meat."

"Huh?" The hitchhiker lowered his towel.

"C'mon, Ricky. I'm not going to turn you in. They don't have much to charge you with anyway." Mack leaned over and stared down his passenger. "There's nobody out here but us chickens. I'm just curious. What were you doing back there with Maria?"

"What're you talkin' about, man? I wasn't tryin' to steal nothin' from you. I ain't never stole nothin' from you." The man paused for a moment and said in a softer tone. "I didn't even steal no bracelet."

Mack cringed at the mention of the bracelet.

"I saw somethin' shiny on the floor of the truck when we stopped back there. I picked it up and dropped it in my pocket when I reached down to grab my bag. I didn't really look at it until I got inside the truck stop. When I saw it was some kinda jewelry, I called Maria and told her I had a present for her." The hitchhiker shrugged. "I thought it was just some kinda cheapo piece of junk kid stuff or somethin' since it was on the floor of the truck. But I made it sound like it was some kinda high-dollar thing you see high-class rich women wearin' or somethin'.

"I told Maria I would give it to her if she'd come out to the truck stop. Said I was ridin' in a truck headed for Chicago and was gonna hit the road soon. Guess she thought I got it in some kinda major heist or somethin'." Looking as proud and happy as a hog in mud, he continued. "She hightailed it right on out there."

Mack shook his head. "How'd you get hooked up with that gal? She sounds like bad news."

"I met her when I was out on work detail. She gave me stuff to bring back into the joint. One of the guards would make sure I made it back in with the goods." The man rolled his head in Mack's direction and smiled his one-sided smile. "There was some big-time gangster who lived like a king in there. The stuff was brought back to him."

The hitchhiker's face dropped. "Don't say nothin' to nobody, man. I'm dead meat if you do. This dude's some kinda bigshot with the mafia or somethin'. He's as mean as they come. But in a nice kinda way. He'd smile while he slit your throat. They call him Scarface." He drew his eyebrows closer. "I think he was named after some famous old bad guy or somethin'. Anyways, lookin' him in the eye was like tryin' to stare down the devil.

One look at Scarface, and you *knew* what was gonna happen if you ever crossed him."

Mack's passenger changed his tone and continued his story as if spreading gossip to a coworker around the office water cooler. "He had this dude killed for cuttin' him a little short on the goods he brought into prison. Scarface could've had him done in right then and there." He slid an index finger across his neck. "But he had the dude iced *after* he got outta the joint just to make the point there was no place to run an' hide if you crossed him."

"Look, Ricky. I'm not ratting you out to—what's his name, Scarface? I'm not ratting you out to Scarface. I'm not turning you in to the cops. I just want some answers. I want to know the truth. Why were you with Maria at the back of my trailer?"

The hitchhiker raised his eyebrows and leaned away from Mack.

"And why did you run off with her if you weren't trying to steal something? I would have just given Maria money for food if she was so desperate that she had to steal meat from the back of my trailer." Mack leaned in toward the hitchhiker. "Ricky, you don't have to steal from me. I would have helped you and Maria if you needed food or a place to stay."

"What? I don't need nothin' from you, man. Nothin' but a ride outta Texas. Look, Maria took the bracelet an' then we talked about where we was goin' an' what truck we was in an' stuff. Then she just split on me. After I got cleaned up, I started headin' back to your truck an' saw a cop car pullin' into the truck stop. I got scared 'cause I thought maybe the bracelet was worth somethin' after all. So I hid out and waited until after the cops left."

Mack stared long and hard at his passenger. "Ricky, that bracelet *was* worth something. It was worth more than anything I've ever owned. I basically spent my life savings when I was a kid to buy it—everything my uncle paid me for helping him. I had *Bobby Lee and Georgia Forever* engraved on the back of it."

The hitchhiker eyeballed Mack like a calf looking at a new gate.

"Bobby Lee is what Georgia called me," Mack explained. "My uncle Jake called me Bobby Lee, as well. To everyone else I was just Bobby."

"I thought your name was Mack. Oh yeah, that's right, your name's really Robert. I get it. Like ever'body calls me Rocky."

"Sort of. But it's more of a play on my last name, McClain. Or at least now it is anyway. I originally got the nickname because Mack is a generic name for any big rig."

The hitchhiker folded his arms and shifted in his seat toward Mack. "Yeah? Kinda like Pepsi and Dr. Pepper are called Cokes?"

"Yep. Kind of like that. But I think that's just a Texas thing." Mack placed an arm on his armrest, moved in closer to his passenger, and smiled. "When I first started playing football as a kid, I played running back. They called me *Freight Train McClain* because of the way I would charge head first with a full head of steam on every play. In high school, the coach switched me to linebacker, which is the position I played the rest of my time in school. Everyone knew I spent a lot of time in Uncle Jake's truck. They would say that getting hit by me was like getting hit by a Mack truck." He shrugged. "I've been called Mack ever since."

"You look more like a Mack. Bobby Lee sounds kinda like a girl's name or somethin'." The hitchhiker nodded while staring at Mack in silence for some time. "You don't look nothin' like no girl."

"Thanks. I think. But I liked it when Georgia called me Bobbie Lee. I gave her that bracelet to show my commitment to her. We were both too poor to pay attention, but we couldn't wait to be married."

Mack put a hand on his steering wheel, leaned back onto his seat, and sighed. "We were married as soon as we graduated from high school. I found her a wedding band at a pawnshop in Amarillo for fifty dollars." Mack glanced at the hitchhiker and grinned. "Fifty dollars was a lot of money for me then."

The hitchhiker nodded. "Fifty dollars is a lot of money for me *now*, man."

Mack faced the road and stared off into space. He watched the big rigs fly past his Pete, down the highway, until like ships over the horizon they were gone. Speaking in a low voice now, more to himself than to his passenger, he continued. "Georgia wanted to be buried with that ring. The ring and the bracelet were the only jewelry she wore. I buried her with that ring." He turned to face the hitchhiker. "And I kept the bracelet with me after she was murdered. It was like having a part of her with me."

The hitchhiker folded his arms across his chest and sat in silence for some time. He squirmed in his seat before speaking. "I didn't steal nothin' from you, man. It was just layin' on the floor." He flopped his head to the side and faced Mack. "I swear I thought it was just junk."

Mack shook his head and stared down the young man. "But it wasn't junk." He inclined toward his passenger. "Was it, Ricky?"

"I'm sorry I gave it to Maria." The hitchhiker lowered his eyes. "She don't care nothin' 'bout me. She prob'ly found someone else to do her dirty work once I got outta the joint. She didn't get hardly nothin' for bringin' me that stuff to take back in to Scarface, noways." He shrugged and turned away from Mack. "And neither did the guard."

The hitchhiker gazed out his window and watched the cattle grazing in the field. "Maria kept braggin' 'bout some big job she was gonna get that was gonna get her out of the Panhandle." He reclined back onto his seat and sighed. "She hated it there. Said she's got some kin up north somewheres that was gonna help her somehow." He paused for a long moment and brought his brows together once again. "I betcha it was that guard back there with Maria." He nodded and pursed his lips. "Yes, sir." The hitchhiker rolled his head to face Mack. "It was the Boss Man with Maria at the back of your trailer."

CHAPTER TWENTY

COMIC BOOK CAPER

Saturday, 10:15 A.M.

Mack glanced at the red and blue lights reflected in his mirrors. "Now what?" He thrust a thumb over his shoulder. "Hop in the sleeper, Ricky."

The hitchhiker's eyes became like saucers as he tripped over himself heading for the sleeper. He hit the floor and then scampered up onto the bunk.

Mack flipped open his logbook and commenced to scribbling lines on the blank page. Hearing the click of his door as it opened, he looked down with a hand-in-the-cookie-jar expression at a highway patrolman's serious-as-the-business-end-of-a-.45 eyes.

"Everything all right, driver?" Mr. Patrolman inquired. He was a tall man, long, and lanky, with a crease between his bookend eyebrows. "I heard some drivers talking on the CB about a truck on the side of the road so I thought I'd check to see if you're okay."

"Yes, sir. I...um...I just stopped to take care of some business."

"Uh-huh." The officer raised his sidearm hand and pointed a long, bony finger to Mack's lap. "Let me see that logbook."

Mack closed his logbook and sighed. "Yes, sir." He passed it down to the patrolman and drummed his fingers on the steering wheel as the officer thumbed through it.

Mr. Patrolman flipped a page and then returned to the current day's entry. He shook his head. "Looks like you're a little behind, driver."

"I've had a busy day." Mack placed his elbows on the steering wheel and massaged his temples with the tips of his fingers before turning to look down at the officer. "Guess I just forgot to catch up."

Mr. Patrolman nodded and studied the logbook once more. "Follow me down to the scales." He looked up to face Mack. "After you weigh, we're going to take a little trip into town."

"What?" Mack dropped his hands and gripped the wheel. "Into town? The jailhouse? You want me to drive this rig down to the jailhouse?"

"Oh, don't worry." Mr. Patrolman closed Mack's logbook and pointed down the highway. "You're going to drop your trailer at the truck stop down the road and then follow me in your tractor." He stuck the logbook under his arm and extended a hand. "I'll hold your license until we get there."

Mack handed his CDL down to Mr. Patrolman and then eyed his mirror as the officer walked back to his patrol car. He tapped the sleeper curtain. "Better stay in the sleeper, Ricky."

The hitchhiker ripped the curtain open. "We're goin' to the jailhouse?"

"Yeah, but I don't think they'll keep us." Mack steered his rig onto the highway and followed the passing patrol car. "I'm sure they just want to get into my pockets. If you stay in the sleeper, they'll never know you're there." He glanced at the hitchhiker's protruding head. "So don't poke your head out again until I say it's safe."

Mack cleared the scales and then eased off the highway into the truck stop. After parking his rig, he hopped out, cranked down his landing gear, and dropped his trailer. While bobtailing behind the patrol car, he spoke over his shoulder. "Keep your head low when we get there. I'll go in, get my ticket, and come right back."

He pulled into the courthouse lot and stepped down from his Pete.

"Wish I had some stock in Van Camp's. I've got a feeling we'll be eating pork and beans the rest of the way after they're done with me."

Mr. Patrolman met Mack in the parking lot and the two men walked side by side into the old, small-town courthouse building. The officer clicked the door shut and faced Mack.

"Looks like you're a popular fellow, driver. I thought I just nabbed myself a garden variety comic book juggler." He tossed his citation book onto the table and grinned. "But it seems you've got the Texas Rangers looking for you." He paused to study Mack's reaction. "Do you know a Ben Garza?"

"Ben Garza? Captain Garza?" Mack poked an index finger to his chest. "Captain Garza wants to talk to me?"

Mr. Patrolman nodded. "Seems it's rather urgent. We had a little conversation after I ran your tags and discovered there was an alert out for you." With arms crossed, he brought his eyebrows together and stared down Mack. "But he says I don't have to hold you."

Mack grabbed his phone from its case and headed to the door. "Why is Captain Garza looking for me?" He turned to face the officer. "Is that all he said?"

"That's it. Believe me, I tried to get more out of him." Mr. Patrolman eyed Mack's license and studied it for some time. "This could have been the biggest story to hit this town since the cattle hauler lost his load out there on the highway and we had to call out every cowboy in the county to get them rounded up."

Mack cracked the door open. "I'll call him right away."

"Hold on, driver. Aren't you forgetting something?" Mr. Patrolman held up Mack's license. "You may need this."

"Oh. Yeah. Yes, sir. Thanks."

"There's still the little matter of the logbook violation." Mr. Patrolman lowered the license to his side. "Looks like you've got enough trouble. I've decided to be lenient with you. I could shut you down, or hold you until you paid your fine, which is what I planned to do." He flipped open his citation book and offered a pen to Mack. "But I'm just going to give you a little citation and you can be on your way."

Mack snatched the pen from the officer's hand, scribbled his signature on the ticket, and slapped the pen onto the desk.

Mr. Patrolman tore the ticket from his citation book, perforation by perforation, like an OCD patient on steroids, and then smiled as he handed it to Mack along with his license and logbook. "Be safe out there, driver."

Mack flipped over the ticket as he stormed out the door, almost tripping over himself as he read the fine. *Five hundred, eighty-four dollars, and fifty cents!* He spun around on his heels, grabbed the door handle, and prepared to barge back through the door but stopped dead in his tracks.

Captain Garza? Why is he looking for me now?

CHAPTER TWENTY-ONE

CRAZY LIKE ME

Saturday, 11:45 A.M.

Mack walked out to his truck, propped his boot on the step, and punched in the captain's number. After several rings, Mack heard an all business voice answering the phone.

"Captain Garza speaking."

"Captain Garza? This is Mack...uh...Pastor Robert McClain."

"Yes. Of course. Pastor McClain. How are you? I've been looking for you." The captain paused for a moment. "Heard you got yourself in a little trouble."

"My new middle name is trouble."

"Are things not going well for you out there?"

Mack stuffed the ticket into his pocket and patted it in place with his hand. "Long story."

"I called your office over at TGN and left a message for you. Talked to a lady named Ginger."

"How'd you know I leased on with them?"

Captain Garza chuckled. "We have our ways."

Mack grinned and waited in silence.

"That Ginger lady is a pretty tough gal."

"Tell me about it. She's tough all right, and she can be about as mean as a skillet full of rattlesnakes when she wants to be."

"And stubborn, too," Captain Garza laughed. "She wouldn't give me your number. Said you had a private line, and she was not authorized to give it to anyone. I even threatened to haul her in for interrogation, but she wouldn't budge."

"Blame that one on me, Captain Garza."

"Call me Ben."

"Yes, sir. Ben. You can blame that one on me. I all but threatened her with her life if she gave out my number to anyone. She talked to someone else who was looking for me and let it slip that I was headed to Pampa. I was none too happy. I don't think she'll ever do that again."

"I guess not. When she got a little huffy with me, I said, 'Do you realize I'm a captain with the Texas Rangers?' She said, 'I don't care if you're the queen of England!'"

Mack heard laughter on the other end and waited for the captain to compose himself.

"'I don't care if you're the queen of England,' she said, 'I'm not losing my business because my driver up and quit on me out there.'"

"That sounds like Ginger."

"After she refused to give it to me and I couldn't trace it down—by the way, Pastor..."

"Just call me Mack, Ben. That's what most everybody else calls me."

"You really went to great lengths to see that no one could get ahold of you out there, Mack."

"I guess it worked if even the vaunted Texas Rangers couldn't find me." Mack chuckled and then abruptly changed his tone. "But really, Ben, I needed a fresh start. Just wanted to clear my head, get some windshield therapy..." His voice trailed off. "People mean well, but I couldn't take the constant reminders of Georgia."

"I understand. But you might want to think about letting me have that number since we're on a first-name basis now. We may be talking more often. When I couldn't reach you the conventional way, I decided to do it the old-fashioned way and just waited for a cop to run your tags. Haven't had to do that for a while. Modern technology has taken a lot of the fun out of police work."

"Oh, that was a lot of fun, Ben. You just about scared the pants right off me."

There was a long pause. Mack did not want to break the silence.

"Mack, I did a little digging around after I talked to you about your wife's death. I knew something wasn't right about her reported suicide. I felt it in my gut, and I couldn't sleep that night…" Captain Garza sighed and then continued speaking in a serious, professional tone. "We may have a lead in our investigation of…"

Mack nodded and waited for the news.

"Do you know a Dr. Ahmad Hashim?"

"Yes, sir." Mack slipped his boot from the step and crossed his arms when he turned to see Mr. Patrolman leave the courthouse. He nodded as he watched the officer ease back into his patrol car. "I know him. Georgia went to see him when she got sick. She invited him to our church a couple times."

"We've had our eye on him for a while, but we didn't have enough evidence to bring him in for questioning." Captain Garza paused before continuing. "We don't want him skipping out on us."

"Skipping out? What do you mean, skipping out?"

"Leaving the country. We don't want to risk scaring him off. We want to be able to prove that he's a flight risk, but we've got to have enough evidence to revoke his passport. We'll never get him back here if he leaves the country."

"Uh-huh." Mack paced about the side of his rig. "So, uh, so where do you think he might go?"

"Back home. Look, Mack. We need to know everything you know about Dr. Hashim. Anything and everything. We need your help."

Mack looked at the sky and kicked one of his tractor tandems. "Nobody wants to get ahold of Dr. Hashim more than I do."

"I understand, Mack." The Captain's voice softened. "But you have to let us do this. Do you know why Dr. Hashim would want to hurt Georgia?"

Mack raised a hand and massaged his forehead.

Captain Garza broke the silence. "Mack?"

"Dr. Hashim didn't want to hurt Georgia, Ben."

"What do you mean he didn't want to hurt Georgia? Our whole investigation is centered around him now. He's our guy, Mack." Captain Garza waited some time for Mack to respond. The irritation in his voice was clear when he spoke once more. "Mack, I've worked at the DPS my whole career. I worked my way up from a state trooper to the position of a captain with the Texas Rangers. Did it the hard way. I know in my gut he's the one who killed Georgia." The captain paused and softened his tone once more. "I'm not even supposed to be telling you all this. But time is of the essence."

"Dr. Hashim was after *me*, Ben," Mack said almost in a whisper. "He was after me."

"After you? Why do you think he was after you?"

Mack stood alone in the now empty lot, shaking his head for some time. "I knew it all along."

"Why didn't you tell me sooner then? We may have been able to hold him."

"You said you know in your gut that he's your guy. Well, I knew he killed Georgia. I knew it in my gut, too. I knew it! I just didn't act on it. It was too hard to believe that a professional like that—a medical doctor—would be so consumed by hatred...to the point of committing cold-blooded murder"

"Mack, the reason I called you now..."

Mack heard a long sigh before the Captain continued.

"We've lost track of Dr. Hashim. Hopefully he hasn't left the state. We'll try to have him extradited if he has. But we need your help. Tell me everything you know about him. It's imperative that we bring him into custody before he has a chance to leave the country. We'll never get him back. We need to be able to hold him when we find him."

"...And I'm a pastor, Ben." Mack continued as if Captain Garza had said nothing. "Was a pastor. I had my nice little church, a beautiful wife.... If anyone should have known he was capable of that, it was me. I preached about it all the time. About fallen man. About our sin nature. I knew it, Ben. I knew it in my gut."

"Listen, Mack." Captain Garza spoke in a measured tone. "If there is something you know you need to tell me now. If he's threatened you in any way, we may be able to arrest him."

Popping open the side compartment on his Pete, Mack grabbed his hammer before walking around his rig. He pounded his tires as he went. "He was all dressed up, though." *Thump! Thump!* "A professional." *Thump!* "A professional." *Thump!* "Like me."

Mack turned and slumped against his driver tandems. "Like I wanted to be.... Not like some...some truck driver. A nobody." He shook his head and dropped the hammer to his side. "I was almost there. Almost had my doctorate. I was almost *Dr*. Robert McClain." Mack stared at the shops across the quiet, small-town street. He shook his head in silence for some time.

"Yeah, he was like me, Ben."

CHAPTER TWENTY-TWO

STORYTELLING

Saturday, 12:45 P.M.

After climbing into his Pete, Mack banged his phone onto the console before pulling out of the courthouse lot and heading for the truck stop to pick up his trailer. He turned to see the hitchhiker poking his head out from the sleeper curtain.

"All clear?"

Mack acknowledged his passenger, but his eyes remained fixed on the road. "All clear."

The hitchhiker climbed out from the bunk, plopped onto his seat, reclined his head back, and watched the red-brick courthouse disappear from sight in his mirror. He rolled his head and observed Mack in silence for a moment before speaking. "Who's Dr. Hashim?"

Mack turned to face the hitchhiker. He tucked in his chin, raised his eyebrows, and allowed a half grin to form on his face. Although not his usual friendly grin, it was a grin nonetheless and seemed to put his passenger at ease. Mack returned his gaze to the road.

"I couldn't help overhearin'."

"It's called eavesdropping, Ricky."

"Huh?"

"You were eavesdropping. Listening in on a private conversation that is none of your business."

"I wasn't eavesdroppin'. You was talkin' pretty loud out there sometimes."

Mack turned to face his passenger once more. "I guess it did sound kind of loud with your ear stuck to the side of the bunk." His rig threw the men about the cab as they bobtailed along the rough city streets. Mack picked up his phone, which had dropped to the floor, and returned it to the console. "Ricky, have you ever just owned up to anything when you've done something wrong?"

The hitchhiker crossed his arms and hesitated a moment before answering. "If I ever done somethin' wrong, I'd fess up to it."

Mack chuckled. "Yeah. That's me, too. Took me forever to admit guilt for anything. Still working on that one. If it weren't for Georgia, I probably would never admit guilt for anything, either. A wife has a way of making a man humble."

"Yeah? Well, I ain't got no wife."

Mack turned to his window and watched the townsfolk stroll along, tending to the business of their small-town lives. "I don't have one, either." He eyed his passenger. "Who's going to keep us honest now?"

The hitchhiker shrugged.

Mack placed an elbow on his armrest and inclined toward his passenger. "Listen, Ricky, I've told you a little about me. Now it's your turn. Remember the deal we made?" After receiving no response, he reminded him once again. "We were going to tell each other our stories on the way to Chicago?"

The hitchhiker rolled his head and faced Mack. "You don't wanna hear my story, man. Ain't much to it."

Mack pulled into the truck stop, past the packed fuel islands, and headed to the back where he located his trailer. After lining up his Pete, he slipped his rig into reverse. "All of us have stories to tell, Ricky."

Stretching around to view his mirror, the hitchhiker watched as the trailer lined up with the tractor as Mack backed up his rig.

Mack stopped when the fifth wheel reached his trailer. "We all start out as clumps of clay tossed onto the center of a turntable. We don't get to choose what kind of clay we're made of or what sort of turntable we're tossed onto. We go round and round through life; the heat is turned up and then we become hardened." He leaned forward and popped his brakes before facing his passenger. "Know what's so fascinating about all this, Ricky?"

The hitchhiker dropped his jaw. He shook his head for some time before responding, "What?"

"What's fascinating about all this is that we can look at another person and say, 'If I were inside that same piece of clay and was thrown onto that same turntable, I would have turned out better than that.'" Mack reached down to find a pair of gloves beside his seat and tossed them to his passenger. "C'mon, Ricky. Let's hook up that trailer and get back on the road."

The hitchhiker picked up the gloves and looked at Mack like he had left his brains in his back pocket. "I ain't never hooked up no trailer before."

Mack popped his door open, offered a slight nod in his direction, and grinned. "Well, I guess you ain't never gonna be able to say that after today, are you?"

After showing the hitchhiker how to hook up to the trailer, Mack pulled his rig out of the truck stop and back onto the highway. The hitchhiker sat across from him, still clutching his gloves.

The men road together in silence for several miles until Mack pushed himself back onto his seat and rested a hand over the wheel. He faced his passenger. "What are you going to do after I drop you off in Chicago?"

The hitchhiker faced his window and shrugged.

"I mean, how are you going to make a living?" Mack continued with his questions. "What are you going to do for work?"

"I'll get by."

"How? Do you have any skills?"

The hitchhiker turned to Mack, raised his eyebrows, and gave him a one-sided grin.

Mack chuckled and shook his head. "Ever thought about driving a truck?"

"I couldn't never drive no truck."

"Why? It's not so hard. Just put it into gear, give it the gas, and go." Mack pressed on the accelerator and increased his speed to about ten mph above the speed limit before looking about for patrol cars. He eased on his brakes. "And then when you need to slow down you hit the brakes. Just like a car."

He tapped a finger on the gear shift. "You just have a few more gears, that's all. A few more gears, but you do the same thing when you change them. Put your foot on the clutch." Mack placed his foot on the clutch and then put his hand on the gearshift, taking it out of gear. He raised the rpms, clutched it back into gear, and continued. "Then you clutch it again and put it into the next gear. After you do that for a little while, you can do the same thing without the clutch, like you see me do." He repeated the process without the clutch. "So you just have a few more gears, that's all.

"But not to worry, you have plenty of brakes, too." He placed a finger on the red knob on the dash and proceeded to explain the function of the knobs and levers. "Trailer emergency brake." He tapped the yellow knob. "Parking brake." Pointing to the trailer hand valve, he said, "Trolley brake.

"And last, but not least…" Mack pointed to the floor while pressing on his brake. *Psssst.* "Your foot brake." He pointed to each brake once more. "One, two, three, four. Four brakes. One gas pedal. Four brakes. Plenty of brakes to stop this baby if she gets out of hand.

"Oh!" Mack flipped a switch on his dash and took his foot off the accelerator—*blub, blub, blub.* "You even have an engine brake to help slow you down on hills. Anybody can drive a truck."

"Ain't nobody gonna hire me if I did learn how to drive one. Who's gonna hire an ex-con to drive a truck?"

Mack stared in silence at his passenger for some time before speaking once more. "Ever hear about the paralyzed man at the pool of Bethesda?"

"Huh?"

"It's in the Bible—the book of John. Think you have problems? This guy had been paralyzed for thirty-eight years. He waited by that pool for an angel to come and stir the waters so someone could dip him into the water in order for him to be healed. He had to be the first one in, but he said every time the angel stirred the waters, someone else went down ahead of him."

"Sounds like that dude had my kinda luck. What's that gotta do with me drivin' a truck?"

"Everything. Jesus came and met him at the pool. Know what He asked him?"

"Uh-uh."

"He asked this man if he wanted to be healed. Do you believe that? Here's this man who's been paralyzed for thirty-eight years and Jesus asked him if he wanted to be healed. Why do you suppose He would ask him that?"

"I dunno. Don't make no sense to me."

"If you want something to happen in your life, if you want a miracle to happen, if you want to change your condition, you have to first believe it's possible. Nothing's going to change before that. When Jesus asked the man if he wanted to be healed, the man responded by explaining why healing had been impossible in his life in the past. But Jesus was bringing him to faith. That's why he asked him that question. Know what Jesus told him to do after that?"

"What?"

"He told him to get up and walk. Do you know what that man did then?"

The hitchhiker shook his head. He stared at Mack in silence.

"He got up and walked. After being paralyzed for thirty-eight years the man just got up and walked. Listen, Ricky, you're not even thirty-eight years old yet. You don't have to spend any more years explaining why change is not possible because of things that happened in the past."

"I ain't got no money to go to no truck drivin' school, noways."

"There you go again. I'll make a deal with you. If you decide you want to turn your life around, I'll teach you how to drive and help you get a job. How about that?"

"I'll think about it."

"You do that. Just remember, the offer is on the table."

The hitchhiker nodded, turned to the window, and looked down to watch the pavement roll by. Mack turned his own focus to the highway as the two men became lost in their thoughts. After some time, Mack placed his hand over the wheel, pushed himself back in his seat once more, and sighed before speaking to his passenger again.

"So, Ricky. All I know about you is that you were just released from prison and you spent four years or so there."

The hitchhiker held onto the gloves as he crossed his arms. "Yeah? Suppose you wanna know 'bout the terrible thing I done that got me thrown into the joint?"

Mack turned to watch the young man and then faced the road. "Where are your parents? Ever see your mom and dad?"

The hitchhiker laughed. "Las' time I saw the ol' man he was fallin' down drunk, runnin' outta the door in his underwear, hollerin' at the cops. The cops came out to haul me in for questionin' 'bout some job my brother done. That was the only time I remember the ol' man stickin' up for me." After pausing for some time, he shrugged. "He's prob'ly dead by now."

Mack looked out his window and nodded. "How about your mom?"

The man sat in silence for some time, watching the road go rolling by.

Mack left the man to his thoughts and watched the road go by as well—the same road he watched as a passenger when Uncle Jake came to take him from the Panhandle. Mack's passenger jarred him back to the present when he broke the silence.

"Mama was taken off to the loony bin one too many times." He rolled his head and faced Mack. "She come home that las' time, but her head was still in the nuthouse."

"You must have been pretty young. How did you take care of yourself?"

"My brother showed me how to make it out on the streets. We picked up some money here and there."

"Uh-huh. So where is your brother now?"

"He's doin' some hard time, man. My brother's goal in life was to make the FBI's ten most wanted list." The hitchhiker shook his head and smiled. "He almos' done it, too." He turned to face Mack once more. "You know when the ol' man ran out in his underwear when the cops come out to question me 'cause o' somethin' my brother done?"

"Yeah?"

"Know what my brother done that time?"

"Is that the time he got caught?"

"Naw, man. That was later, after he got outta Texas again 'cause things was too hot for him there. Anyways, he made the mistake o' comin' back to Texas an' robbin' a groc'ry store." The hitchhiker shifted in his seat and leaned in toward Mack. "My brother broke his leg while he was out in California. After he come back home he needed some money. So he went into the store with a sawed-off shotgun, an' robbed the place.

"He stuck up that store, an' then hobbled outta there with a *broke leg*, man. My brother's got some…" The hitchhiker paused. "I almos' forgot you was a preacher, man. Anyways, I wish I had guts like that."

"What difference does it make whether I'm a preacher or not? You never seemed to care before."

"No one never cared 'bout hearin' my story, neither. Only other preacher I ever met was in the joint. An' I didn't never care nothin' 'bout goin' to hear him preach. Not after watchin' my cellie go down there an' take a dive after the preachin' was done."

"Your cell mate took a dive?"

"Yeah. You know how, at the end o' the preachin', when they talk about Jesus an' stuff an' then tell you to say somethin' back to 'em?"

"There's a little bit more to it than that, Ricky."

"Yeah? Well, after my cellie took a dive an' said what the preacher tol' him to, he got all kinds o' extra priv'leges. He rode that horse till he got out."

"Why didn't you do the same thing if it was so beneficial?"

The hitchhiker shrugged. "I dunno, man. I jus' decided that if I ever done it, it was gonna be real. Besides, I never thought it was smart to play around with that kinda stuff. Remember the dude I tol' you about that Scarface had iced after he got outta the joint?"

"Yeah?"

"That was my cellie, Scorpie."

CHAPTER TWENTY-THREE

STUNG BY A SCORPION

Saturday, 2:00 P.M.

"Scorpie?"

"Yeah. That's what we called him. Scorpie. Short for Scorpion. Scorpie had jus' barely got locked up an' was suppose' to be there longer 'n me. An' he had already got put on some easy work release job an' was workin' for Scarface. But someone hired a high dollar lawyer for him an' this lawyer dude got Scorpie out on some kinda technicality or somethin'. Scorpie went around braggin' about it before he got out. Word was that jus' before he got out, he shafted Scarface on some of the goods that was brung into the joint for him. An' we thought he got away with it. But I guess Scarface was jus' waitin' till Scorpie got out before he had him iced on the outside. Ever'body knew after that there wasn't no place to hide from Scarface.

"That ain't never made no sense to me, though. Scorpie was scared to death of Scarface, just like ever'body else there. I think he got set up, man. Anyways, after Scorpie got out, before I knew it, I was bringin' stuff in for Scarface."

From the corner of his eye, Mack caught the image of a blue car whizzing past his Pete followed by a black sedan. He shook his head. *Can't*

116

be. I've got to get more sleep. "Did Scorpie ever tell you what he was in prison for?"

"Scorpie's problem was he liked to talk too much. He bragged about how he helped some guy who bumped off a congressman or somethin'."

"I heard about that. He worked for a congressman."

"Scorpie worked for a congressman?"

"The man who was killed. He evidently worked for a congressman in some capacity. What about the other guy—the one who killed the congressional aide? Know anything about him?"

"Scarface had him done in, too. At least that what Scorpie said. That's why it didn't make no sense to me when I heard about how Scorpie ripped off Scarface."

"What was this other guy's connection to Scarface—the one who killed the congressional aide?"

"I dunno what he had to do with Scarface. But according to Scorpie, the dude worked for the government or somethin'."

"The government?"

"Scorpie made it sound like he was involved in some kinda under-cover work for the FBI or somethin'. Like he hung around some big-time hit men and was workin' on some important job for 'em. He bragged to me before he got out that he was gonna do another job for 'em on his own."

Mack pointed to a rest area sign. "I'm going to pull off here and check things out. After that we're going to get some miles under our belt and make up for lost time."

The hitchhiker yawned. "I'm gonna hop in the bunk then."

After parking his rig, Mack hopped out, grabbed his cell phone, and punched in Ginger's number.

"Hello."

"Ginger. Just got to thinking again about Tom."

"Yeah?"

"Do you know anything about the man who ran into him?

"According to the cops, he was just some drunk in an old pickup with no insurance or anything."

"Did you have your lawyer look into it?"

"I did. But he wasn't able to find anything out. The feds jumped right in and took over because of Tom's connection to the congressional aide who was murdered. Before we knew it, the guy was cremated and buried in a pauper's grave."

CHAPTER TWENTY-FOUR

RUDELY INTERRUPTED

Saturday, 9:00 P.M.

The sun dipped into the plains over Mack's shoulder, pulling down the curtain on another day in this new life of his. Having studied philosophy in college and the Bible in seminary, he could always wax philosophical and find an appropriate quote when events in life threw him for a loop. As a pastor, these quotes usually came from Scripture. But a quote from that famous philosopher John Lennon seemed fitting for this moment: "Life is what happens while you're busy making other plans."

A canopy of stars dotted the sky. The stars increased in number as that sky darkened. They were Mack's only company now, save for the trucks and thinning ranks of cars left on the highway. Driving along an increasingly lonely road, he watched as car after car exited. The drivers returned to their lives, leaving only the truckers who often sought, but never seemed to find, an exit ramp to take them away from the only life they knew.

But Mack knew there was no exit for him. Listening to that old siren song about the freedom of the open road, he allowed the seductress, now his mistress, to tighten her hold on him.

As if on cue, the hitchhiker crawled out from the sleeper and slumped onto his seat, interrupting Mack's quiet time. But the man just turned to his mirror and watched the reflector posts vanish into the night.

Mack leaned on his armrest and laid his hand atop the wheel. He turned to watch his passenger staring into the mirror with his arms folded across his body. The hitchhiker's limp body moved with the Pete as it rocked in rhythm with the highway. Shaking his head, Mack scanned his mirrors before speaking. "Ricky, I remembered something you told me just before we got busted and went to the jailhouse back there. And there's something I've been wondering about."

The hitchhiker brought his hands to the sides of his seat, pushed himself upright, and stiffened his body before turning to face Mack. "What?"

"The man you said was at the back of the trailer with Maria. What did you call him? The Boss Man?"

"Yeah...?"

"Well, just who is this Boss Man and why do you think he was at the back of my trailer?"

The hitchhiker squirmed in his seat before answering. "Boss Man is jus' what we called the guards back in the joint. The Boss Man I was talkin' 'bout was the one that got me back in with the goods for Scarface. You know—the stuff I got from Maria."

"So this guard, the Boss Man, facilitated the transfer of illicit goods from the street into the prison?"

After staring at Mack in silence for some time, the hitchhiker nodded.

"And you said he got a cut—which you said wasn't much. And Maria got a cut—also not much. What did you get out of the deal?"

"I got to stay alive, man. That's what I got." The hitchhiker plopped his head onto the headrest with a thud and let out a deep sigh. "I didn't wanna end up like Scorpie. After Scorpie got out, I got the best jobs on work release. I met Maria while I was out workin' an' she sweet-talked me into bringin' stuff back inside for Scarface. The Boss Man made sure I got back in with it."

Turning to watch his mirror, Mack shook his head and waited for the man to continue.

The hitchhiker rolled his head in Mack's direction and furrowed his brows before speaking once more. "I think Maria may have had somethin' goin' on with the Boss Man all along."

Mack turned to face his passenger and nodded. "What do you think they were doing at the back of my trailer?"

"Beats me. Like I tol' you before, Maria kept braggin' 'bout some job that was gonna get her outta the Panhandle. Maybe they was gonna steal somethin' from your trailer."

"We're hauling a load of swinging meat, for crying out loud," Mack chuckled. "What were they going to do? Open up a barbeque stand and raise the money to get out of town?"

"I dunno." The hitchhiker shrugged. "All I know is that as soon as I tol' her 'bout the bracelet, an' 'bout where we was goin' an' stuff, she run right out an' met me at the truck stop."

Mack turned his attention to his mirror once more and watched as the car following him for miles pulled around to pass. He returned his focus to the highway until the car pulled next to his rig and rode beside him for some time. The car's passenger window was to the rear of his window now.

He scanned his mirrors to see there was little traffic in sight. From the corner of his eye, Mack watched as the car's window lowered when the black sedan pulled dead even with his truck. He turned as the window rolled all the way down to reveal a man leaning to the driver's side of the car.

"My God! Hang on, Ricky!" he shouted, after staring into the man's face and looking down at the business end of the gun pointed in his direction.

CHAPTER TWENTY-FIVE

TIME AND ETERNITY—THE ROUGH WAY

Saturday, 9:30 P.M.

M ack leaned in toward the hitchhiker and steered his wheel to the shoulder. Time slowed to a crawl. The blast turned a still, quiet night into a crackling cacophony as the rig's window glass shattered like a cheap vase. Projectiles shot through his cab as Mack's world went blank.

Saturday, 9:31 P.M.

He felt his body leaving his rig and then lost all sense of direction as he spun away from his Pete and descended into a wide hole. Mack clawed his hands into the side of its wall and slid to an abrupt stop. He listened as dislodged rocks bounced off before falling silently into the abyss. Casting a glance into the chasm, he watched the murky grey about him darken into a coal-black nothingness.

Mack looked up to see a piercing, bright light that stabbed into the darkness. He scratched and scraped as he struggled to reach the light but lost a step for every one gained on the slippery surface. As he stared into the light, he caught the image of a body plunging down into the hole.

The hitchhiker tore at the face of the glaze-like surface as he descended. Mack grabbed the man's hand while digging his own fingers into the wall with his free hand. The momentum of the falling man pulled Mack down with him until his hold stopped the fall.

The two men hung suspended between the darkness below and the ray of light from above for some time. Silence filled the void now, save for a faint wheezing sound as the men gasped air and then exhaled with a woeful noise of men without hope.

The hitchhiker looked at Mack as his fingers slipped away one by one. His hand spread open toward the light as he descended. Mack watched the man turn as if drawn into a vortex. It was not the face of the hitchhiker he saw, but the face of his father, spinning around and around until lost in the depths below.

Mack grasped his hand back onto the wall and brought his forehead to the wall with a thud. He sobbed. But he stopped at once upon hearing a sound like steps coming from beneath him. He felt the wall shake in cadence with the sound until fingers like serpents slithered around his ankle. He turned to look at the hand, followed the arm to the body of a man, and then stared into the face of Dr. Hashim.

Dr. Hashim smiled when Mack caught his eye. But his face melted away as if made of wax, revealing another face: a face that was not smiling, could not smile, a face devoid of all compassion and mercy. The creature (for it was a creature and could not rightly be called a man now) returned Mack's stare from eyes of wrath filled with fire.

Mack's grip gave way, sending him spiraling into the void. He shot his hand upward as if reaching for a lifeline and looked at the light. The light shrank in size to a pinhead and then disappeared, leaving Mack enveloped in darkness. He continued his descent alone, fighting to slow his fall, but could not maintain a grip on the slimy surface.

"Ugh!"

He slammed onto a rock-hard surface, hitting it like a sack of sand, knocking the wind from his body. Mack drew in hot air to catch his breath but gagged upon tasting the sulfur-like atmosphere.

Pushing up from the ground, he braced himself on all fours and listened to a far-off sound of mournful cries. After rising to his feet, he felt around in all directions for something, anything, but there was nothing and no one there with him.

The cries mounted, becoming louder as he stood alone in the darkness for some time. The voices wailed a woeful, sorrowful sound that reverberated all around him, as if in an echo chamber, before fading into silence. Mack stared into the stone-cold blackness about him.

When the voices fell silent, he heard cries far more terrifying coming from below. Although horrified by the awful sound, Mack sought a way to find the source of the cries. He stretched out his hands and moved about until he found a wall to guide his way. A ridge led to flickering red and yellow lights, which illuminated the underworld and brightened as he made his way downward.

At first grateful for the light, he felt another of his senses assaulted as he descended. The souls he passed now were not alone but shared their space with hideous creatures, like the one that pulled him down into the pit. The dreadful, unanswerable screams for mercy from the lost souls mixed with the cruel, otherworldly sounds of the creatures sent rivers of revulsion rolling through Mack's soul.

"Argh!"

A dull thud like a strike from a bat sounded as a shock of pain shot through Mack's shoulder. He dropped to the ground as talons thrust into him with a fierceness that tore at his flesh. Mack turned to face the creature now dragging him from the path into one of the caves along the side of the ridge.

The beast bore numbers seared into its flesh above its eyes. Mack smacked his hand onto the floor of the cave and clutched a rock. He thrust it toward the beast, striking the creature in its eye. The beast lost its grip and shrieked as it scurried to the back of the cave.

Mack crawled back to the ridge and continued his trek downward. The scenes increased in horror as he made his way toward the cries from below. He recognized some of the tortured faces of famous and infamous men from ages gone by, as well and those who perished in his time. These souls were great sinners, evil rulers, and mass murderers, as well as unknown cowards, revilers, and deceivers of men. The light brightened as he neared the end of his quest.

Continuing his descent to the bottom of a great slope, Mack stopped dead in his tracks, awestruck by the sight of an enormous, fiery lake spreading out before him as far as his eyes could see. He looked down the precipice of a cliff above the lake where men and women were herded like cattle. Mack also recognized some of these damned souls.

He watched as men once followed by throngs of adoring crowds during their time on earth were brought forward away from the crowd to stand alone. The men wore the same fine garments of hypocrisy and deceit with which they cloaked themselves as they deceived men great and small, leading many of the beguiled souls to spend eternity in the upper reaches.

Mack looked on in horror as great religious leaders were stripped of their garments, exposing ugly, vile hearts of pride and greed for all to see before they were shoved off the precipice of the cliff into the lake. The lost souls screamed in terror as they descended. But their cries could no longer be heard when their bodies neared the lake as they were drowned out by the sound of all the souls who came before them.

The souls swirled about the lake from the outside around toward the center of an immense vortex. A grotesque creature at the center of the vortex tore at the damned souls as they neared him before tossing them aside like rag dolls. The souls grasped rocks in an attempt to scale the cliffs surrounding the lake but dropped back into the great spiraling current, which pulled them toward the creature once more.

Mack turned away in revulsion, unable to look upon the monstrous creature. He sought a way upward, out of the pit, but there was none. His body slammed against the wall as he squeezed his eyes shut and clapped his hands over his ears. He fell to the ground, shouting out a one-word cry that shook the foundation of the underworld.

"J-E-S-U-U-U-U-S!"

CHAPTER TWENTY-SIX

ETERNITY—THE HIGH WAY

Saturday, 9:31 P.M.

Mack breathed in and enjoyed the priceless scent of pure, clean air. His eyes opened as a cleansing wave inside him washed away every impurity of body and mind. A sense of peace and serenity flowed like a river through his body, permeating his soul. He was once at rest, yet vibrant and alive.

He arose with the ease of a child to observe a vast expanse of sheer beauty spreading out before him like a carpet woven from the most precious, finely crushed emerald gemstones. A luminous, crystal-clear blue sky covered the green as far as he could see.

A gently flowing stream carved a meandering path from the center of a glowing light in the distance. The stream brought a burbling song of peace and harmony as it delivered life-giving water to the land. Majestic trees rose from the earth and offered noble branches as resting perches for songbirds that presented their rendition of praise throughout the land.

Mack walked toward the light at the center of his new world. Silk-like grass yielded to him and then resumed its slow dance in the breeze, as unmolested as the sea after the passing of a fish. A feeling of unrestrained joy heightened with each step as he watched the light pulsate with the same pit-a-pat, pit-a-pat beat of his own heart as he approached.

A whisper of music rising from the center of the light, followed by a chorus of angels joined together in praise sent Mack to his knees. A billowing wave of love swept over him, wave after wave, like the mighty ocean's never-ending swell at the shore of a welcoming land.

Two forms separated from the light like slow-moving embers. Mack lifted himself from the ground and focused on the approaching forms. The figures appeared hazy as a mirage. But the bodies, enveloped by a lesser light, could be seen as human forms.

The couple continued without haste in his direction. Silhouettes of a man and a woman became distinct as they walked farther away from the greater light. A sense of recognition came over Mack as the man and woman came into view.

"Georgia! Uncle Jake!" Mack rushed forward and embraced them, weeping tears of joy. A great surge of love and energy flowed like a current from Georgia and Uncle Jake. "What a beautiful place!" he exclaimed with the exuberance of a child. "I'm so happy I'm finally able to be with you!"

After some time, Georgia and Uncle Jake separated themselves from Mack's embrace before Georgia placed her hands upon Mack's arms. She ran her hands along the length of his arms, grasped his hands in hers, and smiled. Georgia looked through his eyes into his soul, past the opaque barrier that separates one soul from another and prevents one from being seen or known in truth.

Her smile looked the same to Mack. That is to say, he recognized the smile he had seen hundreds of times. But her smile was radiant now: a pure, joyous, and loving smile, a smile that would make his worries disappear like the sun dispels darkness.

"Bobby Lee," Georgia said, "you will see beauty and feel love like nothing you can imagine now when we see you again. There is no way to describe what it will be like when you get to be with Him." She lifted her hand, turning it upward toward the light. "When you come back it will be as if you never left. There is no time here."

"What do you mean when I come back? I don't want to ever leave."

Uncle Jake placed an arm over his shoulder. "He needs you somewhere else, son."

"Needs me where?"

Turning to face Mack, Uncle Jake smiled. "Do you remember how excited you were when I taught you how to drive a truck when you were a kid?"

"Of course, I remember. I could barely reach the pedals. And you let me drive that truck like I was operating a giant Tonka toy. I still can't believe you did that."

"You just wait until you see what He has in store for you. That was nothing." He chuckled, and slapped Mack's arm. "Believe me, that was nothing."

"But why can't I stay now, Uncle Jake?" There was a pleading tone to Mack's voice as he sensed after the arm slap he was about to be left alone. "Why can't I stay and experience it *now*?"

"He's got work for you to do first."

"What? What am I supposed to do?"

Uncle Jake spoke to Mack as he had when the two were in his truck together when he first introduced him to the Lord. "I said He has work for you to do, and He does. But it's not about the doing, son. It's about the being. The doing flows from the being. Just focus on the being. The doing will come as you do."

He allowed Mack to ponder what he said for a moment before he continued. "Sheep don't worry about the future. When they hear the Shepherd's voice, they follow Him."

Mack stared in silence into his eyes. He became aware of the sound of his own breathing as he waited for more.

Uncle Jake spoke once more as he turned to leave. "Just listen for Him. You know His voice."

Georgia squeezed Mack's arms. "It will all be worth it, Bobby Lee.

All your trials, a thousand times over, will seem like nothing when you come to be with Him." She eased her arms to her side and turned to join Uncle Jake.

The two strolled off toward the light. Mack attempted to follow, but sensed a barrier separating them. He placed his palms upon a clear, glass-like surface as he watched their bodies once again become surrounded by light. Like a film reversed to show embers returning to the fire, the light around them intensified with each step.

Georgia and Uncle Jake walked step for step with one another toward the greater light. A pulsating, blinding flash of light came from its center as a door opened, welcoming their return. The two became engulfed in the light as they entered through the door.

CHAPTER TWENTY-SEVEN

BACK IN TIME

Saturday, 9:45 P.M.

Mack raised his head from his steering wheel and felt the warm summer breeze blowing on his face from where his window had been. He pushed himself back against his seat, scanned the inside of his truck, and eyed broken glass scattered throughout his cab. While reaching to pull back the sleeper curtain to see if the hitchhiker remained in his truck, he caught the image of a highway patrol car barreling down the highway behind him. The car's lights turned the darkened landscape into an alternating sea of red and blue as it approached his rig.

The car rushed past his truck and veered off onto the shoulder before skidding to a stop in front of Mack's rig. With his window gone now, he heard the screeching of the car's wheels and smelled the burning rubber from its tires. The officer raced back and slammed on his brakes just inches from Mack's bumper.

Another police car careened off the highway behind him, sending a cloud of grass and dirt into the air as it fishtailed to a stop beside his rig. Mack turned back to his driver's side mirror and eyed another patrol car rolling up to the rear of his rig. That car came screeching to a halt so close to his bumper that its lights were all that could be seen at the rear of his trailer.

Mack's head shot back around as his passenger door flew open, revealing a police officer standing as still as a statue beyond the door. The officer stood with his legs spread for balance, arms raised, aiming his weapon toward Mack. His face was firm and lined with deep crevices, as if carved from stone.

Officer Stone Face watched for movement from Mack, like an animal sizing up his prey before a strike. With dead-on precision his trigger finger pointed at Mack's chest, a knuckle bend away from firing off a Promised-Land-sending bullet to pierce his heart.

Another officer released the passenger door and ducked for cover, losing his hat in the process. That officer's firearm could first be seen rising above the Pete's hood, before the officer's hatless head poked up to face Mack. His hair remained tightly pressed against his head where the hat had been, except for the fuzzy, balding top of the head, which was beaded with sweat. That officer gripped his firearm with one hand, while attempting to steady his aim with the other. His firearm, if discharged now, could send a projectile anywhere from into Mack's brain to his belly. Officer Shaky squinted his eyes and stared catlike into the rig.

"Put your hands on the wheel!" Officer Stone Face shouted. "Put your hands on the wheel!"

"Yes, sir." Mack gripped his hands onto his steering wheel as he turned away from watching Officer Shaky to focus once again on the officer standing at his open passenger door. "Mind telling me what's going on here?"

"Is there anybody in there with you?"

Mack turned toward the sleeper and lifted a hand to pull back the curtain.

"Get your hands on the wheel!" Officer Stone Face shifted his stance and barked orders with an even more forceful tone. "Put your hands back on the wheel! Now!"

"Yes, sir." Mack grabbed his steering wheel once more as if hanging on for dear life.

"Is there anybody else in there?"

"I don't know."

"Listen to me, driver. Look at me!"

"Yes, sir."

"Keep your eyes on me. Don't move!"

As he concentrated his focus on Officer Stone Face, Mack heard a *click* and felt his driver's side door open. The officer nodded in the direction of the driver's door. Mack turned to view a smiling officer with a .357 zeroed in on him. He did not return the officer's smile.

Officer Smiley stared Mack dead in the eye before turning away to survey the interior of the truck. He tilted his head to view Officer Stone Face, before casting a glance toward Officer Shaky, who still worked at steadying his weapon. Officer Smiley eyed Mack once more, grinned, and offered a slight wink. He holstered his weapon and tapped it into place.

"Okay, driver. You're going with me. You're going to slowly lift your hands from the wheel, turn your back toward me, and then exit your truck backward. My partner and I will help you down."

"That may be a challenge without my hands, sir."

"Get out of your truck now!" Officer Stone Face shouted.

"Yes, sir." Mack twisted around in his seat, still gripping the wheel as he eyed Officer Stone Face.

Officer Smiley placed a boot on the step, pushed himself up, and patted down Mack. He gripped the back of Mack's shirt and proceeded to explain what was going to happen next in a level, no-nonsense tone. "You're going to take your hands off the steering wheel, raise your hands above your head, and then we're going to help you down out of your truck." The officer leaned around to view Mack's face. "Got that?"

"Yes, sir."

Officer Smiley stepped back and nodded to Officer Shaky, who strode around the patrol car in front of Mack's truck to stand at his side. Officer Smiley yanked Mack down from his truck before he and his partner dragged him across the shoulder and wrestled him facedown to the ground. Officer Smiley drew Mack's arm around to his back, slapped a handcuff onto his wrist, pulled the other arm back, and clasped the second cuff.

Stomping over from his post at the passenger door, Officer Stone Face stood before Mack and holstered his weapon. "Listen, driver, if someone else is in that truck, you need to let us know now." He nodded to Officer Shaky.

Officer Shaky stepped back, raised his weapon, and aimed his gun at the center of the Pete's sleeper. He moved his fingers about as if playing a flute and steadied his aim.

"Is there anyone else in there?" Officer Stone Face said, returning his attention to Mack once more.

"There was an angel, I guess—or someone in there with me." Mack plunked his head to the ground and rolled his forehead in the dirt. "The last thing I remember, a car pulled up and blasted a gun in my direction. I don't know how I got the rig stopped."

He raised his head in an attempt to make eye contact with Officer Stone Face but grimaced in pain when he lifted his head past the officer's shined, standard-issue boot. After easing his head back to the ground, he sighed. "There was a hitchhiker in there with me but I'm sure he's long gone by now."

Officer Stone Face nodded to his partners, pulled his handgun from his holster once more, and bolted up into the Pete. He shoved the sleeper curtain to the side and scanned the bunk. The officer turned to his comrades and shook his head before stepping down from the rig and walking over to the patrol car.

"There's no evidence of anyone else being in the cab of that truck."

Officer Smiley wrapped a hand around Mack's arm and pulled him from the ground. "C'mon, driver. Your angel and the hitchhiker seem to have taken off on you." He continued speaking as he marched Mack over to his patrol car. "So did Tinker Bell and the Tooth Fairy and whoever else you had in there. How long have you been driving?"

After opening the back door, he placed a hand atop Mack's head and guided him down onto the seat. The officer smacked one hand onto the top of his car and the other onto the open door as he leaned in. "Just have a seat here and sit for a spell while we have a little chat." He eyed Officer Stone Face and shook his head for a moment before slamming the door shut. The two officers turned and walked toward the approaching Officer Shaky.

Officer Shaky thrust a thumb over his shoulder in the direction of Mack's rig. "Couldn't find any weapons in his truck."

Officer Smiley stormed back to his car, flung the door open, and banged a hand down onto the roof of the car once more. He placed his other hand on his sidearm and sighed. "Okay, driver. What happened? We got a call from someone who said some crazy trucker shot at him. He said he fired back and took off."

"I was driving down the road minding my own business…" Mack took a deep breath before continuing in a calm, level tone. "The hitchhiker I picked up had just crawled out of the sleeper. We were minding our own business when a car that had been following me for some time pulled around and came up beside me. The car's passenger window rolled down and a man in the car pointed a gun at me. I was so shocked by the sight, I barely turned away in time before he fired. After that I blacked out."

"You didn't fire shots before?"

"I don't have a gun with me. You heard the other officer say there was no gun in my truck."

"How did you get your rig stopped and pulled to the side of the road after he fired at you? You said you blacked out."

"I don't know how it stopped." Mack turned to his Pete and then glanced at the officer's hand, which still rested on his sidearm. "After I was shot at, the next thing I knew I was looking down the barrel of a .357."

Officer Smiley lifted his hand from his weapon, crossed his arms, and eyed Mack in silence for some time before speaking. "Listen, driver." He let out a long sigh. "We'd like to help you here, but you have to cooperate with us. I'm going to give you one last chance to tell me the truth. What in the heck happened here?"

Mack grinned. "Do you believe in God, officer?"

The officer looked at the ground before returning Mack's grin. "So God put an angel in your truck. And then that angel parked it for you after someone tried to kill you?"

"Got a better explanation?"

Officer Smiley shrugged. "I've been a cop for twenty-one years. If I didn't believe in God, I would have quit a long time ago. You wouldn't believe some of the things I've seen people do out here. But I've never had anyone tell me an angel parked their truck for them."

He motioned his head in the direction of Mack's rig. "My partner said there's no evidence of anyone else being with you in that truck. But you said there was a hitchhiker riding with you when the shot was fired. What happened to him?"

"Your guess is as good as mine. I don't think he likes the police very much. I'm sure he hightailed it out of here as soon as he saw your lights flashing."

"Uh-huh. And just who is this hitchhiker? Where did you pick him up?"

"I picked him up after I loaded in Pampa, Texas. Out near the Jordan state prison. He said his name is Ricky. That's all I know." Mack shook his head. "His name is Ricky, and he just got out of prison—I think."

Officer Smiley nodded. He observed Mack in silence for some time before responding. "So your angel is a hitchhiking ex-con?"

Mack chuckled. "Remember that old movie they play at Christmas time? Uh…"

"*It's a Wonderful Life*?"

"That's it—*It's a Wonderful Life* with Jimmy Stewart? You know…he got the second-class angel?"

"Yeah…? So…? What? You got, like…a third-class angel?"

"Guess that's how I rate." Mack shook his head. "No, that hitchhiker is no angel. I don't know what he is. But he is no angel. God doesn't send angels in the form of hitchhiking ex-cons." He turned to face the front of the patrol car. "I don't think."

"Well, I've picked up a lot of hitchhikers, some ex-cons and a few hitchhiking ex-cons. None of them seemed all that angelic to me. Look, driver, you seem to be a reasonably intelligent guy. Why in the world would you pick up a hitchhiker who you think may have just gotten out of prison?"

Mack spoke in a careful, measured tone. "I picked him up because I felt that was what God wanted me to do."

Officer Smiley pursed his lips and nodded. "Got any enemies who might like to harm you? Did you have any altercations with anyone on the highway?"

"I haven't had any altercations with anyone. At least not until now. But I do have one enemy who would like to kill me." Mack paused for a long moment and sighed. "Listen, my wife was recently murdered. You can talk to Captain Ben Garza with the Texas Rangers about my situation. If you can take off these handcuffs, I'll give you his card."

"Hang tight, driver." He closed the patrol car door and walked over to his partners. The officers chatted with one other for some time before Officer Shaky broke away and entered his patrol car. They all huddled together once more when he returned. Mack watched as the men spoke in a much more relaxed manner. Officer Smiley walked over, opened Mack's door, and grabbed his arm.

"Okay, driver. Up and at 'em."

With the help of the officer, Mack stepped out of the patrol car.

"Turn around."

Mack turned his back to the officer, who unlocked his handcuffs before placing a hand on Mack's shoulder and nudging him around to face him.

"We called the Texas Rangers. Talked to Captain Garza and confirmed your story. By the way, he wants you to call him in the morning. Early in the morning—like daybreak. Says he's an early riser. Why didn't you tell us earlier that you were buddies with a captain with the Texas Rangers? We may have been able to wrap things up a lot sooner than we did."

"I didn't know I was. We've talked a few times."

"Well, he spoke pretty highly of you. Said you were a pastor who decided to hit the road in a truck, looking to find some peace of mind." The officer folded his handcuffs and clutched them in his hand as he tried but failed to suppress a grin. "So how's that working out for you, Pastor?"

Mack returned his grin. "Still looking."

Officer Smiley nodded. "I think we've got enough pictures of your truck. I'll give you my card. We'll be in touch." He lifted an arm and pointed to the highway. "There's a truck stop at the next exit. You can spend the night there and see about having your glass replaced in the morning."

Mack rubbed his wrist. "Thanks."

"One thing before you go. My partner said he didn't see any evidence of anyone else being in the cab with you. I know angels don't leave calling cards or anything. What about the hitchhiker?"

"Like I said, if he saw you guys coming he's long gone by now. I have no idea where he may have gone."

Officer Stone Face walked up with a greeting card in his hand and slipped the card from its envelope before offering it to Mack. "Any idea what this may be about, driver?" He thrust a thumb over his shoulder in the direction of Mack's rig. "We found it in your truck lying on top of some broken glass."

Mack scanned the outside of the card. "Eid Mubarak?" He flipped the card over and read the note written within:

"After the time of five
Is there a time of rest?
No! Not until all heed the call times five
Until then there shall be no rest
Because those who ignore the call
Keep peace from the land
For now, there is no peace at all
But when those have died, peace will be
at hand"

CHAPTER TWENTY-EIGHT

SAYING GOOD-BYE

Saturday, 10:45 P.M.

Mack climbed back into his Pete, plunked himself onto his seat, and let out a long sigh before easing his truck onto the highway. The three police cars streaked by him, single file, as if shot from a rocket. Officer Smiley leaned across his seat and waved as he passed. After returning his wave, Mack exited and found a spot for his rig at the truck stop the officer told him about.

He pulled his curtain around, hoping no one would notice his window was missing, crawled into his bunk, and plopped his head onto the pillow. Mack chuckled to himself as he thought of the story about the driver's experience in the Windy City. *If I can't get the glass replaced, I won't have to worry about rolling my window down in Chicago. At least the thieves can't break it if I have to leave my truck.*

As he stretched out in the sleeper, he rested his head on an arm and stared into the darkness while his eyes adjusted to the dim light. His thoughts, as always, turned to Georgia. *Why did she have to die?* His inquiries, as they had for some time, seemed to rise no farther than the roof of his cab. He closed his eyes and sighed. *Why couldn't I have died out there, and gone to be with her?*

Mack focused his eyes on the shattered glass. Georgia stood with the last of their finest wineglasses before throwing it onto the kitchen tile. Listening to the sound emanating from the fracturing pieces of glass spreading across the floor, as if in slow motion, Mack returned his attention to his wife.

Georgia placed her hands on the counter before bending her knees, sliding her back down the kitchen cabinets and plopping onto the floor. A red bandana covered her head. She looked into her husband's eyes and asked a simple question: "Why?"

After easing himself down onto the floor Mack sat across from his wife and wrapped his hands around his knees. He stared long and hard at Georgia's sunken cheeks and eyes. *Lord, that woman is beautiful.* Replying with an answer as simple as her question, he responded, "I don't know."

"Bobby Lee." Georgia softened her tone. "I want you to get married again."

After staring across the kitchen into Georgia's eyes for some time, Mack shook his head and grinned. "Not a chance, Gorgeous. You know you're the only one for me."

Georgia picked up a stem from one of the broken wineglasses and threw it at the cabinet beside Mack. "You big brute," she said, returning his smile. "You know you can't take care of yourself. I was the one who kept you out of trouble. You need to find another woman to take care of you or you'll be in trouble all the time."

"Sorry I've been so much trouble," Mack chuckled. "You should have married Johnny Redd. Then you would be Mrs. Dr. Redd, and you could have had a bunch of red-haired babies and lived happily ever after."

"Johnny Redd? Johnny Redd may have become a doctor, but he couldn't fix a broken heart. And that's what I would've had—a broken heart—if I didn't get to you before that hussy of a cheerleader did."

"Who?" Mack asked, poker-faced.

"Who?" Georgia laughed. "Who, he says. It's a good thing you became a preacher rather than going into politics. You don't lie very well. You know who."

Mack maintained his poker face for some time before he blinked. "Brandy?"

"I saw those goo-goo eyes ogling the star linebacker of Pampa High." Georgia raised a hand and then pointed a finger at her husband as if aiming a gun. "And I saw that star linebacker looking back. She brought her hand to the floor and continued staring into Mack's eyes. "Just think, you could have married her instead. Y'all would have made a great couple: Bobby Lee and the Bimbo."

Mack chuckled once more. "Bobby Lee and the Bimbo?"

Georgia nodded. "And I could have married Johnny Redd and been a broken-hearted doctor's wife. I would have been so heartsick sad I couldn't do anything but become a country singer." She paused before continuing. "You've got to admit Georgia Redd is a pretty good name for a country singer."

"So I've been nothing but trouble, and I ruined your chance at stardom?"

"And I wouldn't change a thing. All I ever wanted is to be with you."

Her words hit hard and seemed to reverberate inside of Mack, as if in an echo chamber. *"All I ever wanted is to be with you."*

"I'm sorry..." Mack sighed a long, deep sigh. "I'm sorry I never received my doctorate after working on it for so many years. I wanted to do it for you. I wanted us to be introduced as Dr. and Mrs. McClain. I always wanted the best for you. Seems like I can never finish what I start."

"Bobby Lee McClain." Georgia shook her head and sat before her husband for some time in silence before speaking once more. "I swear you can be so dense at times. Didn't you hear what I just said? I never cared anything about any of that. I would have been just as happy riding around the country with you in your uncle's truck.

"But you couldn't be happy driving a truck. You had to prove that you're better than that. That whole stupid Dr. McClain pursuit was for *you*, not me—for you, and for your uncle because he bankrolled your education."

Georgia picked up another glass fragment and tossed it onto the floor beside Mack. "Your father died in prison a long time ago. You're going to die in a prison of your own making if you don't free yourself. You've been trying all these years to prove you're better than your drunken father, that you're not white trash anymore. And all along, you had a wife who adored you for who you are. You never had to prove anything to me. You've wasted too many years, Bobby Lee. Just be *you* from now on. Just be you."

Mack and Georgia's eyes locked together as a lifetime of memories rolled by like a movie before Mack's eyes, like a man drowning at sea.

Georgia looked away and stared instead at the shattered wineglasses on the kitchen floor. "I'm sorry I made a mess."

Mack choked back the words he wanted to say. *I never got to say good-bye*, he thought. But he just forced a smile and said, "I'll have the maid clean it up."

"We don't have a maid."

"I'll get one. I'll have to. I can't take care of myself. Remember?"

Georgia stared once more into the eyes of her husband. "You have to let me go, Bobby Lee."

"I can't let you go. Ever. You didn't have to leave me. I would have taken care of you. Maybe you could have been cured. Why didn't you go to another doctor after seeing Dr. Hashim? Cancer isn't necessarily a death sentence these days."

"Cancer?" Georgia tore the bandana from her head, revealing her luscious head of red hair. The color returned to her face as she shook her head to and fro. Her face became fresh, vibrant, and full of life. "I never had cancer."

A tap, tap, tapping on the door as Georgia spoke became louder and louder until it could no longer be ignored. Georgia smiled, and spoke in a soft voice that sounded like a whisper above the noise.

"Good-bye, Bobby Lee."

The intruder now pounded on the door. Mack turned his eyes away from his wife and faced in the direction of the voice heard from behind the door.

"Mack!"

CHAPTER TWENTY-NINE

SOUL JOURNER AND THE CO-JOURNER

Saturday, 11:45 P.M.

"Mack! It's me!"

Mack stared into the darkness. "Ricky?"

"Can I come in?"

Propping himself on an elbow, Mack rose from his bed, pulled back the sleeper curtain, and blinked his eyes. "What happened to you out there? Where did you go?"

The hitchhiker eased the door open, looked about at the glass on the floor of the cab, and then faced Mack. "I thought you was dead."

Mack pushed himself into a sitting position and pointed an upturned hand toward the passenger seat. "Get in, Ricky."

The hitchhiker stepped into the cab and spoke as he brushed off his seat. "I did. I thought you was dead, man. Your head was just lyin' on the steerin' wheel, an' you wasn't movin' or nothin'. When I seen the car stopped after they shot at us, I jumped outta the truck an' took off into the woods."

He plopped onto the seat and let out a deep sigh. "I ain't never been so scared in all my life. I thought they was gonna shoot me, too. Anyways, the car backed up an' some dude jumped out an' run up an' throwed somethin' into your truck. Then the dude ran back to the car, an' barely got in before the car took off like a bolt o' lightnin'. I didn't know what to do. I just stayed there in the woods till the cops got there." The man shook his head, turned toward Mack, and grinned. "Man, I thought them cops was gonna shoot you again, until I seen them drag you outta your truck."

Mack returned the man's grin. He nodded and stared at the new arrival for some time before asking, "How did you get the truck stopped?"

"When we got shot at you was leanin' in toward me and the truck started runnin' off the road. I grabbed the steerin' wheel, an' then pushed down on this brake thing." He pointed to the trailer hand valve before turning to face Mack once more. "What'd you call this thing?"

"The trolley brake."

"The trolley brake. I pushed down on the trolley brake an' then hit the gearshift till it popped outta gear. Man, the truck was goin' all over the road. I just kinda kept easin' on an' off the trolley brake an' steered the truck onto the shoulder. When I finally got it stopped..." he pointed to the yellow button on the dash, "...I pulled on this thing like I seen you do when you stopped."

"The parking brake."

"I pulled on the parkin' brake, an' then, like I said, I ran off into the woods when I seen that car stopped ahead of us. An' then when I seen them cops comin', I started runnin' again, but I came back an' watched when I seen they wasn't comin' after me."

"You took quite a chance coming back. You could have gotten yourself into a lot of trouble if they caught you and got the wrong idea about why you ran off."

"I been in trouble all my life, man." The hitchhiker shrugged. "I just had to come down here an' see what happened to you. When you got back on the road, an' the cops took off behind you, I ran outta the woods, an' seen where you got off."

"Listen, Ricky." Mack scooted to the edge of the bunk, clasped his hands together, and leaned toward the hitchhiker. "There's something I need to tell you. Or rather, there's something I need to ask of you."

"Shoot, man. Ain't much I can do for you, but I'll try."

"I need to ask for your forgiveness."

"Huh?"

"I'm asking you to forgive me. I've wronged you in many ways."

"What're you talkin' about, man? You ain't never done nothin' wrong to me. You picked me up an' you're givin' me a ride to Chicago. You didn't have to do that."

"Ricky, if I had stuck pins on a map to mark the places I would have liked to go first in my new truck, there would be a hole the size of Brewster County around Pampa, Texas. But since I was there, I went off route to visit my old homestead and saw you hitchhiking on my way to the slaughterhouse.

"I didn't want to be there in the first place and I *sure* didn't want to pick up a hitchhiker. I wanted to be alone, but I felt compelled to pick you up. I heard from God then but just went on about my business—tried to go about my business anyway. If there is anything I've learned through all this, it's that God's business *is* my business."

"I don't get it. Why would God want you to pick me up? That don't make no sense to me."

"It didn't make sense to me, either. You were not even headed in the same direction I was. And you were not on the route I was going to take. And talk about signs…" Mack grinned. "Remember that sign? The 'Do Not Pick Up Hitchhikers' sign?"

The hitchhiker returned Mack's grin. "I tol' you I didn't read the sign, man."

"Well, I did. They put those things on the highways near prisons for a reason. I didn't know what to think. But I had to go back to see if you were still there after I got loaded. When you weren't, I was actually relieved. But when I saw you hitchhiking down the road from there…"

"I jus' about give up on gettin' a ride when I seen your truck pull over."

"And I'm sure you wished I hadn't stopped after I almost killed the both of us. Anyway, the rest is history. We only turned around to go back to that truck stop because I realized I might not have all the time in the world. I wanted to visit the place my uncle Jake took me to as a kid since I was so close by. I don't understand why any of this happened, Ricky." Mack shrugged. "All I know for sure is that I heard from God but didn't trust Him."

"What?" The hitchhiker raised his brows and leaned away from Mack. "You didn't trust God? An' you was a preacher?"

"Guess I've still got a lot to learn, huh?"

"Sounds like that's between you and God. What's that gotta do with me? You ain't got nothin' to ask forgiveness for from me."

"Yes, I do. I thought from the time I picked you up that I was better than you. And I treated you like you were inferior to me."

"You *are* better 'n me. An' ever'body knows it."

"There's only one Person's opinion of you that you need to worry about. A wise man once wrote a book in which he said: 'There are three people living inside of you: one, the person you think you are; two, the person others think you are; and, three, the person God knows you are.'"

"Then God knows I ain't a very good person. I ain't never done nothin' but get into trouble. Ever'where I been trouble seems to just follow me around."

"It doesn't matter where you've been, Ricky. It's where you're going that's important."

"But you're a preacher. You're smart. You went to college. I even heard you tellin' that cop on the phone that you almos' became a doctor."

"I *did* almost become a doctor. Almost had my doctorate. Almost became Dr. Robert McClain…" Mack shook his head and drifted off into silence.

The hitchhiker spoke after Mack did not continue for some time. "So what happened?"

"…But for the first time, I thank God that I didn't." Mack lifted his head and looked the hitchhiker in the eye. "What happened? God had other plans for me, that's what happened. If I had continued on the road I was on, I may have been so filled with pride I may never have been able to hear from God again—I mean *really* hear from Him.

"I was already so filled with pride I considered myself better than you just because you were in prison, and you're not educated like me. But I was wrong. And you're wrong about the way you think about yourself. You're no different than me. If God had not put my uncle Jake in my life, who knows how I would have turned out? He led me to the Lord, helped get me through school—everything. And even after all that, God still had to put Georgia in my life to keep me anchored." He paused and shook his head. "Georgia was right. I can be so dense at times. I'm just now getting it—I mean, *really* getting it."

Mack stabbed a finger to his chest. "It's what's here that matters." After a couple of taps to the side of his head, he continued. "Not here. I knew this—even preached whole sermons about it. But the sermons came from here." He tapped his head once more. "From everything I learned in cemetery—I mean seminary." He lowered his hand, leaned in toward the hitchhiker, and asked, wide-eyed, "Know what Jesus did for a living, Ricky?"

"Jesus had to work for a livin'?"

"Well, no. Not really. He didn't *have* to. But He did." Mack chuckled. "You know, come to think of it, maybe He *did* have to work for a living. I've spent my whole ministry worrying about high-minded theological questions instead of spending time getting to know my savior.

"Jesus must have had to work for a living, at least before the beginning of his public ministry. You ask good questions. I'm going to have to think about that one." He raised his hands with his palms facing the hitchhiker. "Know one of the things Jesus had that I don't have?"

"What?"

Mack pushed his hands forward for emphasis. "Calluses." He nodded in silence for a moment. "Yep. Jesus must have had calluses on His hands from working with them since He was a kid in His dad's shop."

"Wait. I thought God was His father. God an' Jesus had a shop?"

"God *is* His father. But Jesus had an earthly father, too. You know, like a stepfather, an adoptive father. He worked with that earthly father in his shop." Mack smacked his hands onto his knees and grinned. "Jesus had calluses, Ricky. The omnipotent, omniscient creator of the universe had calluses on His hands."

"The creator of the universe?" The hitchhiker pointed to the field across from the truck stop. "Jesus made all this stuff? I thought God did."

"He did. God, the Son. God made all things through His Son, Jesus Christ."

"Sounds like there's two Gods to me."

"Actually, Ricky, there are three. Not three Gods but three Persons. One God. Three Persons. God the Father. God the Son—Jesus. And God the Holy Spirit."

The hitchhiker brought his eyebrows together. "I don't get it."

"If you don't understand that, join the crowd. That God is three persons, yet one God, has made learned theologians write two-inch thick door stopper books in an attempt to make us understand it, and they haven't pulled it off yet. I know, I had to read them in cemetery—seminary.

"Listen. It's like this." Mack balled a fist and flipped a forefinger over before using his free hand to tap his other forefinger over it. "I am my father's son." Flipping a second finger over and then a third, he continued. "I am my wife's husband, and I'm my children's father. In all of these relationships, I play a different role. All of them see me in very different ways. I am, in a sense, three persons. But really, I'm still just one person. It's nowhere near a perfect analogy, but it's the closest I've come to being able to understand the Trinity."

The hitchhiker sat nodding in silence for some time before speaking. "So Jesus is God. He made all this stuff. And then He came here as kinda like—a human God?"

"Couldn't have said it better myself. That's actually pretty close to quoting Scripture. But we'll read the whole story in John when we hit the road again."

"So Jesus was, like, God when He died on the cross?"

"You got it, Ricky. God in the flesh. He stretched out those callused hands of His and let them nail Him to the cross. All to atone for our sins."

"What does that mean?"

"That means that Jesus was a blue-collar worker. A blue-collar worker died for my sins." Mack shook his head once more. "And I thought I was going to be better than that."

"No. Atone." The hitchhiker clarified his question. "What do you mean atone?"

Mack grinned. "Sorry. Sometimes I talk like I'm still behind the pulpit. Atone is not a word you hear very much. It just means to pay for. To pay one's dues. You see, Jesus paid our dues for us. He paid a debt we can't pay. He died for your sins and mine."

The hitchhiker stared out into the field and remained silent for some time.

Leaving the man to his thoughts, Mack stared in silence toward the field as well before interrupting their shared quiet time with a yawn. "Let's get a little shut-eye while we can, Ricky. It'll be daylight before we know it. As soon as we get the window glass replaced, we'll hit the road again."

Mack eased himself off the bunk, plopped down onto the driver's seat, and motioned a thumb back toward the sleeper. "You might as well sleep back there. I'll have to get up and see about fixing that window as soon as I can. Hopefully we can get it done in the morning."

The hitchhiker glanced over his shoulder at the sleeper and then faced Mack. "Okay. Thanks." After crawling onto the bunk and laying his head onto the pillow, he stared into the darkness for some time before breaking the silence. "Can I call you Mr. Mack?"

"Works for me, Ricky. I've been called worse." Mack paused. "Funny. I haven't heard that in years. Haven't even *thought* of it in years. But that's what my father called me after I started being called Mack in school." He turned and looked into the sleeper. "You can call me anything you like. Just don't call me late for supper."

The men stretched out and settled in for the night. The only sound in the cab came from the wind blowing through the open window until the hitchhiker spoke once more.

"I'm sorry I stole from you, Mr. Mack."

CHAPTER THIRTY

THE SOURCE

Sunday, 7:00 A.M.

Mack bolted up into a sitting position at daybreak and viewed his watch. *Should be able to see about getting that glass replaced soon.* After raising the sleeper curtain, he observed the hitchhiker sleeping like a baby for a moment before dropping the curtain back down. He shook his head and yawned.

Upon climbing down from his rig, he stretched to work the kinks out, popped open his side compartment, and pulled out his hammer. As he thumped his tires the words from the card thrown into his truck after the shooting came to mind. *After the time of five…*thump!…*is there a time of rest?…*thump!…*No!…*thump!

When he made it back around to his truck, he tossed the hammer onto the step. *Well,* he reasoned after glancing at his watch once more, *Captain Garza did say he wanted me to call him early.* Mack kicked a boot on the step and punched in the captain's number.

"Captain Garza speaking."

"Hello, Ben. This is Mack."

"Mack. How are things going out there? Better than last time we talked, I hope."

"I know you heard about my latest run-in with the law."

"I did. They said someone shot at your truck." Captain Garza paused for a long moment. "Are you okay? It seems to me you've had more trouble than a run-over dog since you've been out there on the road."

"I'm fine, Ben. Listen, I think I may have a reason for you to hold Dr. Hashim if you find him."

"For what—attempted murder? You think he was the one who shot at you? I'll do anything I can to haul that scoundrel in, Mack. But you're out of state now. My authority ends at the Red River."

"I'm out of Texas now but I'm not sure where Dr. Hashim is. I don't know if he hired someone to shoot me or what, but there were two people in the car where the shot came from, the driver and the shooter. It's going to take some time to sort all this out. But you may be able to charge him with falsifying medical records. That's a start."

"Falsifying medical records? What records?"

"He was the one who diagnosed Georgia with cancer, remember? Did anyone examine her body or other health records to see if she actually had cancer?"

"That's not something we would normally look into if there is no suspicion of a crime being committed. When I started to check Dr. Hashim's background..." Captain Garza paused. "What makes you think she didn't have cancer?"

"Remember when I asked you how you found out about me leasing on with TGN? You laughed and said you had your ways?"

Captain Garza chuckled. "I do."

"Well, I have my ways, too. I think you will find she did not have cancer. It seems to me that falsifying the medical records of a woman who supposedly committed suicide after learning of her diagnosis would be enough to hold him since he's a flight risk. And he's a suspect in her murder already—the *only* suspect, right?"

"It's him, Mack."

"Well, now we know that once you get your hands on him, he'll never see the light of day again."

"You seem awfully confident of your information. How did you find this out?"

"You have your sources, I have mine."

"The difference is if we find out he did falsify those records, we can have your source subpoenaed, and we can make them tell us everything they know."

It was Mack's turn to chuckle now. "Good luck with that. Look, let's keep this friendly, now. We both need each other, and we both want to bring Dr. Hashim to justice."

"You're not telling me you're going to try to go it alone, are you, Mack?"

"Ben, if you can get justice for Georgia, I'll let you know what's going on at my end."

"Of course, I want justice for Georgia. I'll do everything I can to bring in Dr. Hashim."

"You're an old-fashioned kind of guy. Just give me your word that all of our conversations are confidential. Everything said between us is off the record from now on."

"Okay, Mack. You got it. But that works both ways. Right?"

"That works both ways. I give you my word." Mack took a deep breath. "Dr. Hashim has evidently been keeping track of me since I left Kerrville. I don't know what's going on, but I've received a couple of notes from him."

"He left you notes? He threatened you? You've been holding notes from Dr. Hashim and you didn't let anyone know about it?"

"I just got one of the notes last night. And I wasn't sure who I could trust. Until I talked to you after being stopped by that cop and got a ticket for the log violation..."

"You got a ticket? The officer didn't tell me you were getting a citation. How much is it?"

"Five hundred something—almost six hundred dollars."

"Six hundred dollars! For a log violation? You haven't been on the road for years, and you probably just forgot. That's ridiculous."

"That's what I thought. Anyway, I wasn't even sure I could trust *you*. I found out that night you were looking at Dr. Hashim as a suspect, remember? Up until then, as far as I knew, even *you* didn't believe me when I told you Georgia didn't commit suicide."

"We don't want any vigilante justice done, Mack. That's why we often don't tell the family everything—especially before we're sure we have the right guy. I told you about Dr. Hashim then because I thought you may be of help finding him once we lost track of him."

"Well, we better start communicating more because I decided I was going to find out what happened on my own and see justice done one way or the other. After I determined for sure he was the one who killed Georgia, I planned to lure Dr. Hashim to me."

"Leave the justice to us, Mack," Captain Garza snapped. He continued in a softer tone. "Get those notes to me, and I'll have more ammo to bring to a judge to issue a warrant for his arrest. And send me that stupid ticket you got. Maybe I can help, even though it's out of state. Listen, has anybody ever told you that you have an unusual knack for getting into trouble?"

"Actually, the person who told me Georgia never had cancer said something to that effect."

"They know you well, don't they? You need to call me when these things happen in the future. I have a feeling this is not the last incident you'll have before you get unloaded in Chicago."

"I'll send to you the ticket along with the notes. But Dr. Hashim didn't threaten me specifically, at least by name or anything. And he didn't sign the notes, either."

"Sounds like the notes are kind of cryptic. Are you sure they're from him?"

"The notes are from him, all right. Seems to me he's letting me know the reason he's doing what he's doing. And he wants to be sure I know before he kills me."

"Before he kills you?"

"Listen, the guy's on a mission. And I think he was on a mission before I ever came along. But I'm at the point where I'm not worried about what he may do to me. He won't stop with me, though. I'm just the first on his list. I think he feels he needs to take care of me next because he thinks I'm evil and tried to pull him away from whatever it was he was going to do."

"You don't seem like such a bad guy to me, Mack. What did you do to him that was so evil?"

"Remember when I told you Dr. Hashim came to hear me preach after Georgia invited him?"

Captain Garza waited a moment for Mack to continue before he replied. "Uh-huh…um… You're going to have to help me here. I've heard some pretty bad sermons before where the pastor just droned on and on until it got to the point where I wanted to kill him. But I never followed through with it. And I've never heard of anyone else doing it, either."

Mack chuckled. "I've never been that bad—I don't think. No, it wasn't me. It was God, the Holy Spirit drawing him. When he heard me preach the gospel he was almost persuaded."

"And…?"

"That's it. He was almost persuaded, Ben. I've never seen anything like it, never seen anyone so resistant to the gospel. He was almost pulled away—literally pulled away from the grip of evil. But he's become so hardened now; I don't know that anything can deter him."

"Mack, I…" Captain Garza paused. When he spoke once more it was in a no-nonsense, professional tone as he fired off questions in rapid-fire succession.

"You said there were two people in the car that shot at you. What kind of car was it? Did you get a good look at the shooter? How about the driver? How can you be sure one of them wasn't Dr. Hashim?"

"I'm sure, Ben." Mack answered the captain in his best, slow Texas drawl. "As far as the car—I don't know. A black one. A black sedan. But I'm sure Dr. Hashim was not in that car. The note was from him, but he wasn't the shooter, and he wasn't driving."

"Who else could be involved then? Is there anyone else you suspect?"

Mack glanced at his truck, walked to the back of his rig, and leaned against the rear of his trailer. He rested a boot on its bumper and let out a deep sigh. "I don't know, Ben. But it has something to do with someone from the prison outside Pampa. I haven't figured that part out yet."

The line fell silent for some time before Captain Garza spoke. "Pampa? The Jordan Unit?"

CHAPTER THIRTY-ONE

SHARING NOTES

Sunday, 7:30 A.M.

"Yes, sir. The Jordan Unit. I don't know what's going on there… Listen, somebody tried to break into my trailer when I was parked at a truck stop in Pampa."

"And that's somehow connected to the Jordan Unit?"

"It has some kind of connection. Evidently there's a smuggling operation going on in that prison that is controlled by some kingpin who's imprisoned there. Seems a couple of characters involved in the smuggling were the ones trying to break into my trailer."

"Uh, Mack… How did you learn of this smuggling operation?"

"Good try, Ben. Remember the deal we made? Keep it confidential?"

"Uh-huh. Just tell me this. It wasn't the feds, was it?"

Mack chuckled as he shook his head. "Not even close. It took me awhile to trust *you*. I sure as heck can't trust the feds. At least not until I sort some of this out."

"Look, I can tell you this much. I was a little taken aback when you mentioned the Jordan Unit. We've been aware of the smuggling going on there for some time now. But we haven't made a bust yet because we're still collecting evidence to make sure we rope in everyone who is a part of it. What makes you think it was someone involved in the smuggling there who tried to break into your trailer?"

"Some truckers ran the guys off who tried to break into my trailer and then called the cops. A couple of Pampa police officers responded and were able to catch them. But they likely let them go since the would-be thieves ran off when the truckers showed up. They never actually broke into my trailer.

"I found out later the culprits were a couple who had been smuggling in contraband for this big-shot criminal. The couple consisted of a lot lizard—a truck stop prostitute—and a guard at the Jordan Unit. The Pampa cops nicknamed them Bonnie and Clyde. Only they didn't know anything about the smuggling—still don't, to my knowledge."

Captain Garza chuckled. "Bonnie and Clyde, huh? I like that. Bonnie and Clyde. That's their new nickname for us, too. We've had our eyes on those two for a while now. Unfortunately, this sort of smuggling into our prisons is not all that uncommon. But this is Texas, and we discourage that sort of thing. We don't like the bad guys, no matter how powerful they are, acting like they're in some third-world country.

"Since you said you don't trust the feds, I'll tell you this: here we were investigating what we assumed was a run-of-the-mill prison-smuggling operation, except it involved a really big-shot crime boss. And then along came the feds sticking their noses into it.

"First it was the FBI. Before we knew it, a whole alphabet soup of agencies came down here and started snooping around. Then they began to push their weight around, trying to nudge the Rangers out of the way.

"Well, that dog don't hunt with me. This isn't the movies where you see the feds come into town flashing their badges and telling the locals to get out of the way. You said I was an old-fashioned kind of guy, Mack, and I am. I know who has authority in this kind of situation, and it ain't them. The State of Texas has authority here. They answer to us. That's how the legal system is designed. I went into this thing with my head held high, and that's the way I'm going out. I'm about to retire anyway. I'll walk through hell and half of Texas if I have to, but I'm going to get to the bottom of this before I do."

Captain Garza fell silent for a moment before speaking once more. "Tell me what you know. I give you my word I'll do everything within my power to see that Dr. Hashim is brought to justice."

"That's about it, Ben. Like I said, Dr. Hashim has written a couple of notes to me. Three, actually—all in the form of poems. Pretty weird, huh? I received the first note in the mail after he killed Georgia. But I wasn't sure it was from him. I was still in denial then until I read the one attached to my windshield, which I discovered after I had a tire replaced due to a blowout. Turns out the tire blew out after someone in a passing car shot at my truck with a low-caliber gun. The note from last night was thrown into my truck after someone shot at me through my window. It's only by the grace of God that I survived that one."

"It was a miracle you got your truck stopped all right. Whoever shot at you was pretty brazen. They evidently intended to finish you off then."

"It was, literally, a miracle all right. Do you believe in God, Ben?"

"When you've seen all the evil I have in my career, it's enough to make a believer out of you. A lot of cops are like that. You come to think there must be a counterbalancing good or we couldn't survive. Sure, I believe in God."

"Well, the reason I didn't go to join Georgia last night is because I had someone in my truck who got it stopped for me when I blacked out after I was shot at."

"Someone else was in your truck? I thought you were driving alone. You have a co-driver?"

Mack peeked around the trailer and looked at his truck. He leaned back once more and shook his head. "Not a co-driver. I picked up a hitch-hiker in Pampa who claimed, or at least implied, that he was just released from the Jordan Unit."

"A hitchhiker? Why in the world would you pick up a hitchhiker, especially near a prison?"

"Long story."

"But he wouldn't be in Pampa if he was just released from the Jordan Unit. Prisoners are sent to Huntsville before being released."

"And then they're given fifty bucks and a bus ticket before being told to get the heck out of Dodge. I know, Ben. But wherever he came from, this hitchhiker saved my life, and he's just beginning to really open up to me. I'm going to let him do it in his own time. I'm not going to press him for more information—at least not for a while. I think he's pretty much told me what he knows about what went on inside that prison anyway. Whatever happens, I'm not going to do, or say, anything to get him into any more trouble. He's been through enough."

"Just be careful, Mack. You can't trust those guys. They're all a bunch of con artists."

"So I've heard. But this one just likes to eavesdrop—probably out of habit from when he *was* conning people. He seems to be having a change of heart, though."

"Let's hope so. He certainly seems to be a good source of information. Speaking of information. What about those notes? Can you send them over to me?"

"I'll scan them and get them over to you this morning. I've got your card. Want them sent to your email on the card?"

"Uh… How about sending them to my private email? I'll text it to you as soon as I get off the line."

"Okay. You got it."

"One other thing, Mack. What is the hitchhiker's name? Maybe I can dig up some info about him."

"Remember, Ben, I don't want him to get into any more trouble."

"I'll keep him out of it. You have my word. We have bigger fish to fry here."

"Like Scarface?"

Captain Garza paused and chuckled. "Like Scarface. You're pretty familiar with the characters in that prison, aren't you? We have a database with all the inmates in our prison system matching them up with their prison nicknames and street names. Helps us apprehend these guys and also helps with undercover work.

"I'm not concerned about your hitchhiker. We'll leave him alone. But we'd certainly like to keep Scarface locked up as long as possible. He's one bad hombre. We don't want him out terrorizing the citizens of Texas again. But whatever is going on may go even above his pay scale. The way the feds are snooping around, who knows? I don't like the way this looks. Some of those guys are so arrogant they could strut sitting down. But they tried to push aside the wrong guy this time. We have our own ways of getting information from inside of our prisons."

"Okay, Ben. This doesn't go past you, right?"

"It doesn't go past me."

"All I know is that the hitchhiker's name is Ricky. His name is Ricky, and he goes by Rocky."

"That's it?"

"That's it. Oh yeah. His cell mate was called Scorpion. Or Scorpie. Supposedly, Scarface had him killed once he was released from prison."

"Scorpion…? Hmmm… I think he was one of the characters involved with the mugging of that congressional aide around Kerrville. The one who was killed not too terribly long ago?"

"Accessory after the fact. Only it wasn't a mugging…"

Captain Garza did not respond for some time.

"Ben?"

"Just thinking. Trying to jog my memory. Yeah. Nothing missing… cash, credit cards—everything still on him. Uh-huh. The feds were all over it."

"Listen, Ben…"

"What is it, Mack?"

"There was another death not too long after that. You remember Ginger, the lady who owns the trucking outfit I'm leased to?"

Captain Garza chuckled once more. "How could I forget? You haven't killed her, have you? I can get you a good lawyer if you have."

"No, I haven't killed her—not yet. But her husband Tom was a friend of mine. He died in a car crash out on I-10 near Kerrville. Ginger doesn't think it was an accident, but she's scared to death to talk to anyone about it."

"Why? Was there something suspicious? I can have some of my guys look into it."

"I don't know. Ginger seems to think something's suspicious about it. Tom was heavily involved in politics. This congressional aide—whoever, or whatever he was—was Tom's mentor. The guy was grooming him for high political office, but Tom soured on the whole deal. Evidently he wanted out. Ginger thinks their deaths may be connected. And I think she's right. This Scorpion guy? If I were a betting man, I'd bet my bottom dollar he was involved in it."

"I…uh…I better look into that one myself."

"Don't put too much on your plate at one time, Ben. My number one priority is getting justice for Georgia. I want to see Dr. Hashim arrested for her murder."

"Oh, don't worry, Mack. I can walk and chew gum at the same time. You'd be surprised at how often one investigation will lead to information in another when you're working in the same area. We'll get those medical records, and you're sending me the notes. That should give us enough to hold Dr. Hashim once we find out where he's at. Can you think of anything else that may be helpful?"

The line fell silent for some time before Mack heard Captain Garza's voice once more. "Mack?"

"Ben…this can't get out to *anyone*."

"What?"

"If any of this is true, you're not going to be able to find out about how Tom and the congressional aide were killed, not without bumping into the feds at every turn. They're not going to let you find out."

"Who? If any of *what* is true? Who's not going to let me find out? Who is *they*?"

"I only half-believed it myself at first. The feds. The feds and some cabal they're part of involving giant agribusiness. They also have some factions of organized crime working with them."

"Listen, Mack. I'm sure I don't need to tell you we'll both hang if it becomes known that we know anything about what these guys are doing in secret. Ours will be the next mysterious deaths in the news. Just tell me everything you know, and I'll try to get to the bottom of this. Better yet, I'll try to put you in contact with someone who may be able to help us with this. You can tell him."

Captain Garza paused. "Good Lord help us all if this is what I think it is."

CHAPTER THIRTY-TWO

FIX-IT MAN

Sunday, 8:30 A.M.

Mack headed to the coffee shop to grab a cup while he waited for the shop to open. After seating himself, he rested his elbows on the table and rubbed his eyes as a waitress strolled over.

"Can I get you some coffee, sir?"

Mack yawned and looked up to focus on the server. "I'm sure I look like I need some. Sure, I'll have a cup…uh…" He paused after reading her name tag. "Sam. Short for Samantha, I presume?"

"That's what they say. I've been called Sam all my life. I think my father added the rest after I was born. He was sure I was going to be a boy."

"What time does the shop open, Sam?"

"On the weekend? Whenever our mechanic decides to crawl out of bed. Depends on how many he had the night before." The waitress winked. "Don't tell him I said that. Although I suspect you may guess that anyway when he comes staggering in here with breath so strong you could hang out the washin' on it."

"If he can fix my window, I don't care if his breath smells like turpentine."

"Your window? What's wrong with it? Won't roll up or down?"

"It won't do anything. I don't have one. I…uh…I had a little accident."

"You all right?"

"I'm fine. Will you let me know when he gets here?"

"He should be along any minute now. The cops were all busy dealing with some kind of incident with a trucker on the highway last night, so they didn't have time to throw him in the hoosegow, I'm sure. Guess who gets to bail him out when he does?

"He always stops by here and grabs some coffee before he opens the shop. You'll know him when he shows up. But don't let his looks scare you. He's as handy as rope at a hanging. He could fix the gridlock in congress if he'd sober up. That's why they keep him around. I'm telling you, that man can fix anything."

The door to the café opened to reveal a disheveled man. The man held the door open for a time as he looked about the restaurant until he spotted the waitress. Mack turned with Sam to face the new arrival.

"Hey, Beautiful. How about some coffee for the most handsome man in town?"

"Look at him." Sam returned her focus to Mack and shook her head. "He's such a liar; he'd beat you senseless and tell God you fell off a horse."

Mack chuckled. "I assume that's the mechanic?"

The server nodded. "Yeah. But don't bother him until he's had his coffee. You think he's ugly now…?" Sam faced the man at the door and scowled. "Keep your pants on, Romeo. Comin' up." She turned back to Mack and winked once more. "That's really what we call him. Romeo."

Mack waved the man over to his table and motioned his hand to the empty seat across from him. "Sir, would you like to have a seat? The coffee's on me this morning."

Romeo closed the door before wobbling over to Mack's table. He faced the waitress as he pulled up his britches, before smoothing out the wrinkles on his shirt. "At least someone in this place has some manners."

Sam leaned forward and stood nose to nose with Romeo. "At least someone around here can walk a straight line this morning. Do you want your coffee mainlined or in a cup?" She turned and stormed off to get the coffee.

Romeo plopped himself onto the seat across from Mack and stared at the backside of the waitress as she left before turning to face Mack. "Women," he said, "if she didn't keep me in coffee in the morning and the best iced tea this side of Tulsa in the afternoon, I'd give her the what-fer." He pointed to a scar above his eye. "This is what happened the last time I tried that, but I still think I can take her. That woman is not as mean as she looks." Romeo whacked his hand down onto the table and grinned. "Thanks for the coffee, driver."

"Anytime. Listen, I've got a broke truck out there I'd like to talk to you about getting fixed once you've had your coffee. No hurry. I need to have a cup or two to wake up myself."

"You've got a broke truck? What's the matter with it?"

"Just need to replace the window glass on the driver's side."

"The window? How did you manage to break your window?"

"Long story. Had a little accident on the highway last night. Can you fix it?"

"That was you?" Romeo pointed a finger toward the highway. "Just down the road from here? Man, the cops had the road around your truck lit up like it was the Fourth of July last night. I was on my way over to the Do Drop In when I passed by. I figured they wouldn't bother me since they had some drug-hauling trucker or something pulled over. Guess they couldn't find anything, huh? What'd they do? Bust your window and drag you out of there?"

Mack grinned. "No, someone else broke it before they dragged me out. Listen. Can you fix it?"

Sam returned and placed a cup of coffee in front of each of the men.

"Thanks," Mack said.

"Yeah. Thanks, Beautiful," offered Romeo, accompanied by an exaggerated wink.

The waitress glowered at Romeo, turned on her heels, and left.

Romeo shrugged and returned his focus to Mack. "I can order one for you. 'Course this being the weekend, it may not get here until Monday."

"Monday? I can't wait until Monday. I've got to be in Chicago by then. Maybe I'll just have to do it the old-fashioned way. With some plastic and duct tape? It may look tacky, but I have to be there on time."

"Hmm… What're you driving?"

"A Pete. A new Peterbilt 389."

"A new Pete, huh? I'm not supposed to do this…"

"I'll pay you what I have to get it done. I've got to unload in Chicago Monday, or I'll never hear the end of it. I'll drive there without a window before I'll sit here until Monday."

"I'm not going to gouge you, driver. The owner of this truck stop has a new Pete parked out back that I could…uh…borrow one from. I'll replace it with the one I order for you. It should be here Monday, no problem. He'll never miss it."

"You won't get in trouble, will you? I don't want you to get fired or anything."

"Fired? No, he'll never fire me. Too hard to find decent mechanics. I'll use the plastic and duct tape on *his* window." Romeo leaned back and threw an arm over the back of his booth. "But you have to tell me what happened. If the cops didn't break out your window, who did?"

"I'm sure the news will be all over town soon anyway. Can't keep something like that quiet. Someone shot at me last night. There were a couple of guys in a car that pulled up to me last night—the driver, and a man in the passenger seat who fired the shot.

"By the grace of God, I survived. And fortunately, I wasn't killed by the cops afterward. They didn't know what they were dealing with. All they heard was that there had been a shootout on the highway."

"You were in a shootout with those guys?"

"No. Someone called in and said I shot at them and they returned fire."

"So why did they shoot at you? Road rage? Did you do something to tick them off—like driving too slow or something? Doesn't take too much to put people over the edge these days."

"No, I was just driving along minding my own business, talking to a hitchhiker I picked up in Texas. I noticed this car had been following me for some time. When there was no traffic in sight, they just pulled around, rolled down their window, and opened fire."

"You picked up a hitchhiker? They weren't after him, were they? I've had to hitchhike myself a time or two when someone took my keys so I couldn't drive. I left behind a whole bar full of people who wanted to shoot me."

"No, they were after me. I don't know if they even knew the hitch-hiker was with me. He actually saved my life. It was the hitchhiker who steered my truck off the road and got it stopped."

"Where's this guy at now—the hitchhiker?"

"He's snoozing away in my sleeper. Couldn't handle all the excite-ment, I guess."

"I'll probably wake him up when I put in the window."

"Don't worry. He's a pretty sound sleeper."

"So...uh...so what were these guys driving?"

"A black sedan. I don't know what make or model. A newer one. I was too focused on the barrel of the gun pointed in my direction to be sure."

"A black sedan? A Caddie, maybe?"

"Could have been. I'm not sure."

Romeo nodded in silence for a moment before speaking once more. "Well, I don't think they're driving it anymore."

CHAPTER THIRTY-THREE

DÉJÀ VU RENDEZVOUS

Sunday, 9:15 A.M.

"How do you know?"

"I thought those guys looked out of place. Never seen them around these parts before. But I just thought they were having a little rendezvous, if you know what I mean."

"No, I don't know what you mean. You think you saw the guys in the black sedan?"

"A guy and a gal. Over by the Do Drop In. They got out of a black Caddie and walked over toward another car. Didn't really get a good look at them. I just figured they were coming back from having a little hanky-panky."

"Do you know what kind of car they got into?"

Romeo shook his head. "Not sure. I didn't think that much about it at the time. I just headed to the bar and minded my own business. But the Caddie was still there when I left and they were nowhere in sight."

Mack stared at Romeo in silence for some time. "Do you know the cops around here?"

"Are you kidding? I'm on a first-name basis with all of 'em. 'Course most of the conversations I've had with them were from the back of a patrol car or from the wrong side of the bars down at the jailhouse."

"It...um... It might be best for you if you didn't let them know about that right now. You know, that you saw those guys get out of the car?"

Romeo looked inside his cup and turned it in his hands before eying Mack once more. "You threatening me, driver?"

Mack chuckled. "No, I'm not threatening you. Just looking out for you. The guys in that car *did* try to kill me, remember? If they hear there's someone in town who may be able to identify them, things may not go well with you."

Romeo pursed his lips and nodded.

"If you think of anything else..." Mack dug out his wallet from his jeans, pulled out a card and handed it to Romeo. "If you think of anything else, please give me a call. I know someone who may be able to trace that Caddie to see who it belongs to if it's still there."

"You got it." Romeo held the card at arm's length. "You got it, Mack. So where's your truck? I'll go rob the window off the boss's truck and put it on yours. You'll be out of here in no time. You've had enough delay for one trip."

"You don't know the half of it. Thanks." Mack pointed out the window of the café. "It's over there by the field."

Romeo took one last sip of coffee before tapping his cup onto the table. "Thanks for the coffee, Mack. Sit tight. I'll let you know when I'm done."

"Thanks."

Romeo placed a hand onto the table, eased himself up, and walked past the approaching waitress. "Hate to disappoint you, Beautiful. But I've got a wench—I mean a wrench—out there calling my name."

Sam rolled her eyes and continued to Mack's table. "More coffee?"

Mack tilted his cup back and swirled around the remaining coffee. "How about a cup to go?"

The waitress turned her head as Romeo exited through the back door. She faced Mack once more. "I've never seen him so anxious to get to work.

He usually lounges around shooting the breeze and drinks a pot of coffee or two before he finally decides to go to work."

Mack nodded. "It's amazing what a little motivational talk will do sometimes."

Sam stared at Mack in silence and nodded, as well. She shrugged, walked back to the counter, grabbed a to-go cup, and poured Mack's coffee. Other waitresses gathered about as she poured his drink. Sam placed her pot on the counter, cast a thumb over her shoulder, and shook her head as the ladies gabbed.

After some time, she returned with Mack's coffee. She placed the cup and the bill in front of him. "Okay, we gotta know. How did you get him motivated?"

Mack glanced at the waitresses still gathered about the counter and then faced his server once more. "I told him loose lips sink ships." He dug out enough money to cover the coffee and tip before handing it to Sam. "Thanks for the great service."

After walking out the door, he pulled his phone from its case and sat on a ledge outside the café. Mack sipped his coffee and watched as Romeo left the shop with a tray of tools in hand. He rested his cup on the ledge and punched in Captain Garza's number.

"Captain Garza speaking."

"Ben, I've got some news you will be interested in."

"You haven't had another incident, have you, Mack?"

"No. But I may know where you can find the car that those guys were driving when they shot at me."

"You do? Where? What kind of car is it?"

Mack heard the buzz for an incoming call. He checked his phone and saw Barb's number. After making a mental note to call her back, he returned his attention to his conversation with Captain Garza. "Sorry. Had another call coming in. An old friend."

"No problem." Captain Garza waited for some time for Mack to continue before prodding him. "The car...?"

"A Cadillac. A black Cadillac sedan. It's parked at a bar called the Do Drop In just down the road from where I'm at now."

"How did you find out about the car?"

"Remember our deal about sources? He may be in danger if it's known the information came from him."

"Mack?"

"Yeah?"

"I've done this sort of thing before."

"Sorry, Ben. This is all new to me. I know you'll protect his identity. It's the mechanic who's working on my truck. He saw them get out of the car at that joint while he was out barhopping. He said he didn't really get a good look at them. Thought they were out having a little...um... rendezvous, as he called it. They walked over to another car, but he didn't see what it was."

"It was a man and a woman then? A couple?"

"Yep. Must have been a woman driving the car."

"Hmm... You haven't told anyone else, have you?"

"I don't know anyone else I can trust, Ben. I told you I would keep you informed as to what's going on with me. I know you don't have any authority here, but I thought you would know who to contact."

"Uh-huh. I might. My...uh...my contact you're meeting? He may know someone in the area. I'll let him know so he can look into it."

"Wait. I'm meeting him? When? We just talked about this earlier this morning. You said you would try to put me in contact with him. I assumed I was going to talk to him over the phone. When do you think I have time to meet with him? This load has to be delivered tomorrow."

"I just got off the phone with him. He's already in Chicago, looking into something that's related to what we're dealing with. He's going to meet you at a truck stop just south of there tonight. I'll send you a message with the time and place when I get off the line.

"You said you don't know who else you can trust? Well, you can trust this man with your life, Mack. He knows everything that I do about what's been going on. You can be as open with him as you are with me. Tell him what you know and all that's happened to you. And he will be just as open with you. Things are moving pretty fast, so we don't have time to hide things from one another.

"I know I don't have to tell you this, but…" Captain Garza paused, "… keep a tight lip about it. He's with the FBI."

CHAPTER THIRTY-FOUR

FAME AND FORTUNE

Sunday, 10:15 A.M.

Mack stared at his phone for some time once Captain Garza got off the line. *The FBI? I thought Ben didn't trust the feds.* He sipped the remainder of his coffee and then looked down at the missed-call notification. After punching in Barb's number, he listened to several rings before hearing her message. Her voice sounded as clear as a loudspeaker announcing a special at the end of aisle nine.

"Howdy. This is Barb. If this is a bill collector, I died. If this is my Casanova, get lost. I've heard it before. Anyone else can leave a message and I'll call you back as soon as I can sneak out without my manager seeing me." Beep.

"Uh, Barb, this is Mack. Still working on getting to Chicago. Just returning your call."

"Mack? Mack! Hang on, honey. Let me step outside, away from Big Ears."

"Who?"

"My manager."

"Okay…um… Want me to just call you back?"

173

"You stay right on that phone, honey. I don't get to talk to famous people very often, so no way am I going to let you go now."

"I'm famous?"

There was silence on the line for a moment before Mack heard Barb exhale with a heave after catching her breath. "Okay. I can talk now. You *are* famous. You're the biggest story to hit Pampa since the oil boom of '26."

Mack chuckled. "That's not saying much. Nothing much ever happens around Pampa. I remember stories about that oil boom, though. That's when Georgia's grandfather moved to the Panhandle to find work. Her grandmother used to just pine away about how she missed her home in Georgia. That's where my wife's name came from."

"Well, all people have talked about around here since you left is the story about this trucker who had his trailer broken into and then had his truck shot at, causing a blowout, which led to him coming back to the same place to have it fixed. This story has it all—crime, sex, intrigue."

"It does?"

"First we have the crime—or crimes. Someone tries to break into your trailer. Then someone shoots at your truck…"

"Wait. How did you know that's the reason I had the blowout—that someone shot at my tire?"

Barb cleared her throat.

"Sorry."

"By the way, honey, did you ever figure out why they did all that?"

"Still working on that one, Barb."

"I didn't want to tell you all this if you already know. Anyway, the sex part comes in with the affair between Bonnie and Clyde. You know who Bonnie is—she's Maria the lot lizard. You're not going to believe who Clyde is."

"You know Clyde, too?"

"Listen, honey. Pampa is not that big. I knew if I thought about it long enough, I would figure out who that polecat was. Remember when I told you I thought I recognized the guy in the back seat of the patrol car

174

when it was parked outside the truck stop? But I couldn't be sure because I didn't get a good look at him?"

"Yeah...?"

"Well, I don't know why it didn't dawn on me before. I just caught a glimpse of him. But there's no mistaking that prettied up hair of his, all slicked back, perfectly parted on the side. You know—like Cary Grant."

"Cary Grant? Haven't heard that name in a while. You must like classics."

"Honey, I *am* a classic. Anyway, he's a guard at the Jordan Unit. Can you believe that?"

"Uh-huh. That's something all right. Any idea what he was doing with Maria?"

"After going out with him, I do. She's probably the only woman who will put up with him. For a price, of course."

"You went out with the guy?"

"Don't say that so loud, honey. Just one time. Listen, the pickins' are pretty slim around here. And I'm not a spring chicken anymore. A woman my age has a better chance of winning the lottery than finding a good man."

"I didn't mean to insult you, Barb."

"Well, he came in the café and pestered me so much, that in one of my weaker moments, I said yes. What a mistake that was. He wouldn't leave me alone after that. He kept calling me all the time and tried to get me to go out with him again. I kept telling him no, but he was persistent. I think he's in love with me. Obsessed, even. Yuck."

"He *was* so persistent? He stopped calling you?"

"No. It's just that once I figured out who the guy was, I decided to do a little detective work on my own. *And*...since some cowboy came into my café and got me so curious and then wouldn't finish telling me his story... Anyway, so I called this guy up and told him I'd thought about it and would like to see him again if he could pull himself away from Maria long enough.

"He told me Maria didn't mean anything to him. Said he just did a few jobs with her. He was out on the road somewhere when I talked to him and he said he couldn't go back to Pampa to live. But he promised me he would come back for me and take me out of the Panhandle, too. I had to keep it quiet, though, since he was on some important job. There would be plenty of money for both of us when he was done, he said.

"Honey, I just got so excited. I told him I'd been waiting for him to ask me to leave with him and played right along as he drew me into his scheme. That's when he *really* started opening up to me."

"Uh-huh… And what did he tell you, Delilah?"

"Delilah?"

"Never mind. What did he say?"

"Well, one thing I found out is there is a smuggling operation going on at the Jordan Unit. Do you believe that? Right there in a state prison. He bragged about working with some big-shot gangster in there or something."

"Um… Barb… You haven't told anyone else about this, have you?"

"No. You're the only person I've talked to about this. Why?"

"Do me a favor?"

"Anything for you, honey."

"Please don't tell anyone else about this. I know about the smuggling operation, too. It could be very dangerous for you if the wrong people find out you know about it."

There was silence on the line for some time before Barb spoke once more. "How did you know?"

"Know what? About the smuggling operation?"

"No. How did you know that my hair is dyed?"

"Well…um… I suspected it was…since you're…um…you know…"

"An older woman?"

"I wouldn't say you're an older woman. You're younger than me, I'm sure… Wait. What does dying your hair have to do with what we were talking about?"

"I knew you had to know that I was a blond before. Well, maybe I was blond *and* a little grey when I dyed it. But I was all blond before. You had to know I was a blond to think I would be dumb enough to go blabbering to everyone in town about what's going on. You're the one who just fell off the turnip truck, remember?"

"Now you're playing me."

"I'm only telling *you* because when I found out about what's going on, I started to worry about you."

"Don't worry about me, Barb. I'm a big boy. I can take care of myself."

"Oh, and you've just been doing a great job of that so far, haven't you, honey? First, you pick up a hitchhiking ex-con. He calls a lot lizard to get her to come see him, which is what got you involved in this thing to start with. And then the second thing…"

"How did you know about the hitchhiker calling Maria to get her out there? Uh… Never mind."

"The guard—Clyde. He told me about the big heist the two of them were involved in. That's what I was talking about when I said he opened up to me and started spilling the beans about what they were up to. They planned to load some high-dollar contraband into your trailer that they got from the big-time bad guy he worked for. And then they were going to follow your truck to Chicago. That way, if they got stopped, they wouldn't have to worry about getting busted since they wouldn't have the loot on them.

"And *you* didn't know anything about it, so you wouldn't be nervous and make the cops suspicious if *you* were stopped. They planned to break back into your trailer and get the stuff out before you unloaded. And then they were going to fence the goods."

"Fence the goods?"

"Yeah, you know, when goods are sold for cash or swapped for other commodities that can then be sold for cash that can't be traced. Kind of like the modern-day banksters do."

"I know what 'fence the goods' means, Barb. You've been watching too many old gangster movies."

"Listen, if I'm going to play detective, I'm going to have some fun with it."

"And you've been doing a pretty good job of it."

"Thanks, honey."

"You know, Barb, their scheme might have worked too if not for a couple of truckers who spotted them trying to break into my trailer. It all makes sense now. They weren't trying to steal anything out of the trailer. They were going to put something *inside* the trailer."

"Yep. And if the Pampa police hadn't tracked them down, we may never have known about any of this."

"Where's the stuff now?"

"What stuff?"

"Whatever it was they were going to put inside my trailer. Where is it now?"

"Maria has it. She double-crossed Clyde. Kept the loot for herself."

"You keep talking about *the loot*. What is this *loot*?"

"Isn't that what they call it? The loot? Remember those old movies we used to watch? That's what they called it—the loot. I don't know what she has—or had—but it was pretty valuable."

"What she *had*? She doesn't have it anymore?"

"He said she sold it and wired the money off ahead of her before she took off."

"What a pair. By the way, Barb. You said there was a second thing I did?"

"Huh?"

"When I said I could take care of myself. And you basically said I haven't been doing such a great job of it? First I picked up the hitchhiker...?"

"Oh yeah. Honey, has anyone ever told you that you can be pretty dense at times?"

Mack chuckled. "Actually, I have heard that somewhere before."

"That's the main reason I called you. You're about to get yourself into some more trouble. Big trouble. Haven't you learned your lesson yet?"

"What do you mean? Learned my lesson about what?"

"After all the grief the hitchhiker caused you, why did you pick up Maria?"

CHAPTER THIRTY-FIVE

ROMEO AND WHO DONE IT

Sunday, 11:15 A.M.

"Maria?" Mack looked up to see Romeo approaching with his tool tray in hand. "Gotta go, Barb."

"Honey, if you leave me hanging again, I'm going to put some ghost peppers on your burger when you come back to Pampa."

"Sounds good, Barb. The hot sauce you had there wasn't hot enough for me. Have to take care of some business. I'll call you back when I'm done." Mack placed his phone on the ledge and waited for the news about his truck.

"Okay, Mack." Romeo stopped and pointed in the direction of Mack's rig. "You're good to go."

"That was quick."

"Still gotta patch up the boss's Pete. Hopefully, it won't rain before Monday when I'll get the new glass in. If you come back this way and I'm not here, you'll know he found out."

"I thought you said he'd never fire you. I wouldn't have let you do it if I knew it would cost you your job."

"Oh, he won't fire me, but I could have an affair with his wife and he wouldn't be as mad as he'll be if he finds out I've been messing with his pride and joy out there. He's going to kill me if he does."

Romeo dropped his tool tray onto the ledge beside Mack. The tray landed with a clang as his tools settled. Mack glanced down at the tools.

"I've been thinking," Romeo said. "I was three sheets to the wind already when I got to the Do Drop In last night."

Mack looked up toward Romeo. "Did you remember something else?"

"Maybe." Romeo shrugged. "Can't trust my memory after a night like that. When I got there, that couple getting out of the Caddie caught my eye. Like I said, I assumed they just got together for a little hanky-panky—not my business. But I remember thinking, 'They sure don't look like the kind of people you'd see driving a Caddie like that.' Then it hit me."

"What?"

"I got to thinking about it while I was putting your window in. One of the good things about being a mechanic is you fix people's problems—you know, you make their lives better. So there I was, looking through that glass, thinking about how nice it will be for you to have a clean, clear window to look through now."

Romeo shook his head. "I was so focused on the couple and that Caddie they were driving… You know, that's not something you'd expect to see at that dive. Anyway, the car parked out back really didn't register with me. But there was only one car parked back there—an old blue car with a cracked window."

"An old blue car? A Chevy, maybe? Chevy Malibu?"

"Could have been. I was drunk when I got there and drunker when I left. No, you're right. Come to think of it, that's what it was. I've worked on enough those things in my time. Anyway, the car was gone when they kicked me out of there."

"They kicked you out?"

"They always kick me out of that place. It's a tradition." Romeo paused and stared at Mack in silence for a long moment. "How did you know what kind of car was parked behind the Do Drop In?"

"Remember when you told me you often left the joints with a whole bar full of people who wanted to shoot you? Guess you're not the only one who has made some enemies."

"But mine never followed through with it. Think I might stay out of the beer joints for a while."

"Might be a good idea. Listen, how about the guy and the gal who got out of the Cadillac? You said you didn't get a good look at them. Do you remember anything about them at all now that you've...um...?"

"Sobered up?"

"Now that you've had some time to think about it. You said it just hit you when you were repairing my truck—you know, about the car? What about that couple?"

"Like I said, I really didn't get a good look at them. The gal had a ponytail, I think. She carried herself more like a streetwalker than some high-class broad you'd expect to see driving a car like that—she was driving, by the way. That's what made me kinda do a double take when I saw that couple, even if I was drunker than a skunk at the time. They just looked out of place in that car."

"And the man?"

"Just noticed his hair, really. That dude prettied himself up, too—like he was trying to make himself look all high class." Romeo ran his fingers through his hair and struck his best pose, as if preparing for a photo shoot. "Like Brad Pitt, maybe, when he used to slick back his hair?"

CHAPTER THIRTY-SIX

GARZA AND McCLAIN

Sunday, 12:15 P.M.

Romeo snatched up his tools. "Why couldn't I have been born so good looking *and* be rich like Brad Pitt?"

"Try putting your money into index funds instead of the beer joints," Mack advised.

As he walked off toward his shop, Romeo muttered, "Good point. Index funds, huh? Maybe I'll just do that."

As he watched Romeo walk away, Mack picked up his phone from the ledge and punched in a number.

"Captain Garza speaking."

"More news, Ben."

"What's up now, Mack?"

"The guys in the car? The ones who shot at me? I think I may know who they are."

"Who?"

"It's the guard—and Maria. You know, the guard from the Jordan Unit and the lot lizard who were involved in the smuggling there?"

"Bonnie and Clyde. What makes you think it's them?"

"You're checking into that Cadillac I told you about?"

182

"It's stolen. Stolen and abandoned at the beer joint you told me about. They're checking it out now, but I'd be surprised if they found anything. I've seen this a number of times. The car was stolen just to be used in this crime, so it couldn't be traced to anyone."

"I'm impressed, Ben. You found all that out already?"

"A lot of this investigation has been…um…expedited. What about our suspects?"

"The mechanic I told you about? He saw them get out of the Cadillac and walk toward a car just like the one used by that couple when they were caught at the back of my trailer."

"That's not enough to go off chasing down a rabbit hole over. That's a pretty big leap to make—from being a couple of thieves to cold-blooded murderers. And it had to be pretty dark out there. It was late at night, and the guy was headed into a bar. He could've been drunk already."

"Look, you know how it is, Mack." Captain Garza paused before continuing with his explanation. "You get a new car and suddenly you see those cars everywhere. He told you about a car like our suspects have and now you're jumping to the conclusion that it's them. Could be a coincidence. You didn't even see the car either time—when they tried to break into your trailer, *or* at the bar."

"Yeah, I know how it is." Mack rose from the ledge and paced in front of the café as he spoke. "It's called frequency illusion. The Baader-Meinhof phenomenon. You're talking to someone who graduated college and cemetery—seminary, remember? I just about had the good sense educated right out of me.

"Listen to me, Ben. It's them. The mechanic didn't get a good look at them, but from what he told me, I know it's them. I'm sure of it." Mack balled a fist before extending a finger and shoving it forward for emphasis. "You need to get on this thing. I don't know where they are, but there's a good chance they're not far from here. They have to sleep sometime."

He plopped down onto the ledge once more, crossed his arms, and let out a deep sigh. "There's something else I need to tell you."

"I'm all ears, Mack."

"This couple—Bonnie and Clyde? They stole some high-dollar ship-ment from Scarface. You know when they were caught trying to break into my trailer? Well, they weren't trying to steal anything. They were planning to put whatever they stole from Scarface into my trailer to get it up to Chicago. Then they planned on breaking back into it before I delivered there."

"Uh-huh. Okay, Mack. I don't know how you do it, but as usual your information is dead on. Want to come to work with me when I retire, and you decide to get off the road? Garza and McClain has a pretty good ring to it."

"No, thanks, Ben."

"McClain and Garza?"

"Police work is not for me."

"Well, you seem to be doing some pretty good detective work on your own. As you know, we've got our eye on those characters in that prison. Something's been in the works for a while. And things have really been heating up around there. Of course, the feds are all over it as usual. But I've got my own guys in there, and we're not sharing anything with them until I sort all this out. Do you have any idea as to where the contraband might be since they were unsuccessful in breaking into your truck?"

"According to my source, Bonnie has it."

"Got any idea why they would want to shoot you?"

Mack shook his head. "I don't know, Ben. This doesn't make sense to me. They got caught before they were able to break in, so they don't have any reason to kill me. And they wouldn't shoot me anyway if they were able to get the goods—uh, contraband—into my trailer. They would just wait until I stopped somewhere and break back in to take it out of there."

"You said Bonnie still has the contraband. What happened to Clyde? They were a team. He was there, too, right? I thought he was the shooter."

"That's the part I don't understand. Supposedly Bonnie double-crossed Clyde. She stole the stuff for herself and then sold it and wired the money up ahead of her. But they were together last night."

"So Bonnie stole the shipment from Scarface?"

ROUGH WAY TO THE HIGH WAY

"Looks like it, Ben."

"Where was it between the time they got caught at the back of your trailer and then brought back to the truck stop so the witnesses could identify them? There wasn't anything found in their car."

"Good question, Ben. I don't know. But…"

"But what? Anything else you need to tell me?"

"This is moving so fast. There's one other thing I just thought about that may be important."

"What?"

"Somehow they think Bonnie is with me."

"Mack…?"

"Yeah?"

"There's no one around there eavesdropping is there?"

Mack eased himself up from the ledge and walked to the end of the building. He scanned the area before answering Captain Garza. "No. I'm outside the café, away from my truck. There's nobody around."

"Good. I think I know why someone tried to kill you last night."

185

BLACK AND WHITE

Sunday, 1:00 P.M.

"It had to be Scarface. It's his modus operandi. If he thought Bonnie stole something from him she would be dead in no time. No way would he let some lot lizard get away with that. He probably thought you ran off with her, so he decided to kill you both. And he likes to be dramatic with his hits. Something spectacular like that fits his style to a T.

"By the way, I had someone look into your friend's death for me. It has all the earmarks of a Scarface hit, as well. My guy was investigating the death of that congressional aide—your friend's mentor—before. Remember how I told you how one investigation will often lead to discoveries in another? Looks like these deaths are connected in a more direct manner than we suspected.

"This thing is getting uglier all the time. The feds are used to state police agencies stepping aside when they come into an investigation. My guy keeps running into roadblocks set up by them. But we keep digging right under their noses anyway—all under the guise of conducting other investigations they're not interested in.

"This thing stinks to high heaven. I've spent my whole career trying to live up to the code of honor of the Rangers. I'm not going to bow down now and kiss the rings of a bunch of ol' boys who are about as full of air as a stall of corn-eating horses.

"You were right about your hitchhiker's roommate Scorpion. He was involved in your friend's murder, as well, in a more…um…hands-on way than he was with your friend's mentor. He stole from Scarface and—"

"Scarface had him killed."

"By having him run head-on into your friend's truck. Scorpion killed himself while doing a hit for Scarface. So Scarface killed two birds with one stone, I guess you could say. The stone in this case being the old pickup that was provided for him. He probably threatened Scorpion's family with a fate far worse than death if he didn't do it. Scarface can be pretty persuasive that way.

"In any case, this Scorpion character guy got drunker than Cooter Brown and ran across the median of I-10 before crashing into your friend's car. Seems Tom's main crime was that he knew too much about the congressional aide's death—knew too much about the whole sorry mess he was involved in."

"But I heard Scorpion's body was cremated and that he was buried in a pauper's grave right after the accident. How do you know for sure it was him?"

"I'm not even going to ask how you knew that, Mack." Captain Garza chuckled. "It wasn't him who did it. That is to say, it wasn't the man buried in that grave who killed your friend.

"We suspect after Scarface got the pictures of Scorpion's body that he wanted, Scorpion's body was swapped for some poor homeless guy they bumped off and could blame for the accident. Someone without family or insurance to sue over. Someone who would soon be forgotten. Happens more often than we like to think."

"What happened to Scorpion's body then?"

"You don't eat sausage, do you?"

"Not anymore."

"We obtained conclusive DNA evidence we snuck out from under the noses of the feds. And a little birdie from the Jordan Unit filled us in on what was going on there. It was definitely Scorpion who was driving that pickup."

"What is someone that dangerous doing in the Jordan Unit? I didn't think that place was for big-time criminals like him."

"It's not. He got arrested for jaywalking, or something. Don't remember the original charge. But at least for now, we've got him safely locked up in the Jordan Unit while we're expanding our investigation. He's pretty much run the place since the time he was incarcerated. So I don't think he minds too much."

"Something sounds fishy about this, Ben. This Scarface character is as tough as stewed skunk. Why would these two people, who *knew* how mean his is, steal from him knowing what would happen to them if he found out?"

"Good question, Mack. Some folks would stick their hand into a rattler's nest if they thought there was gold in there. I suppose they considered the reward worth the risk. In any case, the investigations are still ongoing. And we just learned about Bonnie stealing from Scarface. We'll find out."

"What about your friend? What's he doing?"

"Who?"

"The FBI agent. The one I'm meeting."

"He's up there tracking down Bonnie and Clyde, among other things. I'll call him up and let him know it's them when I get off the line. Knowing who those characters are may help him locate them."

"What's going on, Ben? I thought you didn't trust the feds."

There was silence on the line for some time before Mack spoke again.

"Ben?"

"Listen, Mack, I might as well tell you this now." Mack heard a deep sigh before the captain continued. "This is a lot worse than I originally imagined. No, I don't trust the feds. At least not the ones who have been snooping around the Jordan Unit."

"Then why am I meeting with an FBI agent?"

"Not just an agent, Mack. He's one of the highest-ranking members of the agency outside of the director. The highest ranking White Hat anyway."

"White Hat?"

"Do you remember the conversation we had about Dr. Hashim? You said he was almost pulled away from the grip of evil?"

"He was almost persuaded. Sure, I remember."

"And you said he was probably so hardened he would never be deterred from his mission now? He was totally given over to evil? Well, I didn't really want to listen at the time. Thought I had to focus on the more important police work at hand. But I've thought a lot about that since that time. There are people like that at the highest levels of our government. They've given themselves over to the control of nefarious forces and they now believe the evil they do is good. At least that's how they rationalize it sometimes—or maybe they just think they're on the winning side. They like being close to power while enriching themselves in the process."

"Black Hats?"

"You got it, Mack. It was the Black Hats in the agencies involved with Scarface in the Jordan Unit. They've been coordinating things with him and the agribusiness giants you talked about. Scarface has been paying off some relatively minor figures in the underworld as he consolidated control. They're working together to bring all this about."

"To bring what about?"

"Control. Control of our resources and control of the population. The Black Hats, the crime bosses, and the big corporations are all on the same team. This has been in the works for quite some time."

"How did you discover all this?"

"You got me started on this hunt, remember? And I've been working with my buddy at the FBI. He's the one you're meeting. Sharpest guy I've ever known. Clean as a whistle, too. We've been friends since college. He was recruited by the Bureau while we were in college. Me? Nobody recruited me. I went to work at the DPS as a state trooper."

"You seem to have done pretty well for yourself, too, Ben."

"We both got what we wanted."

"You wanted all this?"

"This is what I live for. If we don't stand up to these guys, who will? Remember that quote from the Irish philosopher, Edmund Burke? 'The only thing necessary for the triumph of evil...'?"

"'Is that good men do nothing.'"

"It will be a pretty dark world if these guys win."

"Uh-huh. So how are things looking for our side? The White Hats?"

"The battle's still raging, Mack. Could go either way."

CHAPTER THIRTY-EIGHT

THE MESSAGE

Sunday, 2:00 P.M.

Mack walked back to his rig. After cranking it up, he lifted the sleeper curtain to check on the hitchhiker, who still slept like a log. He knew from experience now he could roll the truck over and not wake the man up. So after pulling his truck onto the highway, he set the cruise when he reached the speed limit and punched in Barb's number.

"Hello, stranger. Thought you forgot about me."

"You know I could never forget about you, Barb. Listen… about Maria—"

"Honey, I know you have a big heart, and she probably conned you into helping her. But she's going to get you in big trouble if you don't get rid of her. If you'll drop her off, I'll let it be known that she's no longer with you."

"Barb, I didn't pick up Maria. I've never even *seen* that woman. I don't even know what she looks like. The drivers who identified her when she was in the back of the patrol car at the truck stop blocked my view."

"Hmm… That dirty dog."

"What? Who?"

"Clyde. Mr. Smarty Pants, who thinks he can outwit everybody. After I started playing along with him, I told him about talking to you at the café, and he actually seemed kind of jealous. Is that weird or what? Anyway, he took off after Maria to collect his part of the cash after she stole the goods from him, or at least that's what he said anyway."

The line fell silent for a moment before Barb continued. "Dang it! I had this all worked out and now I don't know what's going on. Where is Maria if you didn't pick her up?"

Mack grinned. "Who's being played now?"

"I know. Maybe I'm not cut out for detective work after all."

"Sounds like you've been doing a pretty good job of it. Remember, it even took Sherlock Holmes a while to piece things together."

"Thanks, honey. Before Clyde left, he said he needed to get the word back to that big-shot bad guy in the Jordan Unit that Maria had stolen the goods from him. And that she took off with a truck driver afterward—the same driver who was hauling up the stuff there for him."

Barb paused. "Wait. *Now* I know what that skunk was doing. He was using me because I have a certain reputation."

"You have a reputation?"

"Not *that* kind of reputation, honey. He thought I would blab it all over town that Maria had stolen the goods and sold them and then taken off with some handsome truck driver. He was using me to confirm his story to the bad guy in the Jordan Unit and take the heat off him—I think. Who knows what part of his story was true?"

"So, you...uh...you thought this guy—this crime boss in the Jordan Unit—was going to harm me because he thought Maria was with me?"

"As far as I knew Maria was in your truck with you. That's why I called you as soon as I found out—to warn you and to let you know you needed to get that woman out of your truck ASAP."

"Thanks, Barb. You may have been on to something."

"What do you mean?"

"I'll let you know later. Listen, do you have any way of getting ahold of Clyde?"

"Not since he left after saying he was going to chase down Maria. I have to wait for him to call me from another phone that has some kind of hidden number or something. He's become almost as secretive as you now, honey. You finally gave me your number to contact you directly, but Clyde evidently doesn't want anyone to be able to find *him*."

"Well, I'm about to leave here, and I'm not stopping until just south of Chicago not too far from where I'm delivering tomorrow. If you hear from Clydey-boy tell him I'm alive and well and would like to have a little get-together with him. Tell him I said Scarface knows everything."

"Scarface?"

"He'll know who I'm talking about."

CHAPTER THIRTY-NINE

Face-to-Face with the Fed

Sunday, 9:00 P.M.

Mack parked his rig at the truck stop south of Chicago, hopped out, and walked over to the designated meeting location under a broken security light. A man with a trench coat approached with head bowed. The man's fedora cast a long shadow across his face.

The man stopped before Mack and scanned the lot. "Mr. McClain?" His voice was like run-over gravel, spoken almost in a whisper.

Mack looked about the lot and spoke in a matching tone. "Yes, sir."

The man lowered his hat across his brow before raising his head to reveal his face for the first time. Although still obscured by shadows, his firm features could now be seen. He placed his hands to either side of Mack's torso. A slight grin came to form on his face as he eyed Mack and spoke once more. "Just a precaution."

Mack returned the man's grin as he lifted his arms. "I understand."

After patting down Mack, the man took a small step back. "You're not carrying?"

"No, sir."

"Not even in your truck?"

"No, sir."

"Why not?"

Mack shrugged. "Just never thought I needed to carry a weapon."

The man motioned his head toward Mack's truck. "And the hitch-hiker? Is he still with you?"

Mack stared at the agent in silence for some time before answering. "He's…um…he's asleep in the bunk. But he doesn't have a weapon, either."

"We haven't been able to confirm the identity of your passenger. Maybe he hasn't been completely honest with you about his history. You know these men—"

"Are all a bunch of con artists."

"Yes, sir."

"Well, the hitchhiker saved my life. If not for him, I wouldn't be standing here talking to you now."

"In any case, you might want to rethink the weapon thing, Mr. McClain."

"Just call me Mack."

"I'm sorry, sir, but I like the old-fashioned formalities. If something happens to you…"

Mack nodded. "So what should I call you then? Mr. Spook?"

The man shook his head. "That's the CIA, Mr. McClain. They have the spooks."

"Well, you-know-who didn't tell me your name."

"Just call me G-Man."

"G-Man?"

"Yes, sir. There are a lot of bad guys out there. That's why I say you may want to rethink the weapon thing. The world's gone crazy, and the bad guys are getting badder every day."

Mack looked about the truck-stop lot. "So I'm finding out. I think I might have to sleep here with one eye open tonight."

G-Man nodded. "You know you could be in a lot of danger, Mr. McClain."

"Tell me something I don't know. Someone tried to break into my trailer in Pampa, Texas. Then I had a tire shot out when I left there and had to come back and have a new one put on. I finally made it out of there and then someone shot at me and almost killed me. It's only by the grace of God that I made it here at all. This has been the load from hell. But I'm unloading it tomorrow in Chicago, and this nightmare will be over. Hopefully things will go a little smoother on my next load."

"Yes, sir." G-Man pushed back the lapels on his coat and slid his hands into his pockets. "We're looking into some of the...um...problems you've experienced. You will be interested to learn that we have arrested the individuals who attempted to break into your trailer. The couple code-named Bonnie and Clyde?"

"You arrested Bonnie and Clyde?"

"We had reliable information about their whereabouts. But it turns out they were caught speeding back in the direction of where you were. They were in a full-blown panicked state and seemed almost relieved to be in our custody when they were apprehended."

Mack nodded. "Must have made a phone call."

"A phone call?"

"Just thinking out loud. Did they admit shooting at my truck, too? That had to have been them that shot out my tire not far from Pampa. And it was definitely them who almost killed me when they shot at me near the truck stop where I had my window fixed."

"They haven't confessed as yet, but there is an ongoing investigation in regard to all of that. The good news is they are not going to be released due to what we found in their possession."

"So Bonnie didn't really sell the goods they stole from Scarface?"

"No, sir. What Bonnie and Clyde took was an item that replaced the one Mr. Scarface was planning to ship in your trailer."

"Replaced? Replaced by who?"

"I'm not at liberty to say, sir. But Bonnie and Clyde thought what they had contained something so valuable they risked their lives for it by scheming to outwit Mr. Scarface. But they were unable to open the container they were carrying. It's a good thing for them. The container was relatively small but carried enough explosives to kill them and everyone else in the vicinity had they been able to open it."

"Bonnie and Clyde were trying to load a bomb into my trailer?"

"Yes, sir. But they didn't know what they had. When they were caught attempting to break into your trailer they were going to load it into there then. Evidently they schemed to take it back out before you unloaded in order to keep the contraband for themselves."

"What was in the original shipment that was replaced?"

"Seems the individuals responsible for replacing the original shipment with the explosive device have been outwitted by a rather clever law enforcement officer in Texas. He took it right out from under their noses in Pampa and has it in safekeeping until all this is sorted out."

"A law enforcement officer in Texas? Captain Garza?"

G-Man grinned. "I'm not at liberty to give out that information, either, but the shipment contained a veritable treasure trove inside of it, sir—enough for Scarface to have consolidated his control of trucking and food distribution in the Midwest. More importantly, it contains evidence to prove that Mr. Scarface was working with some…um…elements in our government."

"Black Hats?"

"Yes, sir. I know you've talked to Captain Garza about them. It seems that Mr. Scarface was double-crossed by the Black Hats."

"Aren't you worried about me knowing all this?"

"Sir, you're aware that most species of roaches are nocturnal creatures?"

Mack nodded for some time as he processed the information before responding. "I assumed as much. I remember them scattering when I turned on the lights in my kitchen when I was a kid."

"One of the reasons the Black Hats have been so successful in the past is because we have allowed them to operate in darkness for fear of what their activities may do to the reputation and security of the country."

"*We* allowed them? The White Hats?"

"For the lack of a better term, yes, sir. There has been a battle raging in the shadows between the Black Hats and White Hats for decades now. Yes, I'm concerned for your safety, but light needs to be shed on these creatures. And the light needs to stay on, so they will remain hidden away in their crevices where they can't do any harm."

"Darkness and Light. I shouldn't be surprised by any of this considering the business I've been in most of my life..." Mack drifted off into silence.

G-Man eyed Mack for some time as he waited for him to continue. He nodded. "I understand you were a pastor for many years?"

"Most of my adult life. I preached on good and evil but in an abstract kind of way, it seems to me now."

"Hard to see things as abstractions when a gun is pointed at your head, sir. Metaphorically speaking, of course."

"Agreed... So they—the Black Hats—took the contraband that Scarface had and replaced it with the bomb that Bonnie and Clyde were going to load into my trailer? Why? What was their end game?"

"Apparently some high-level Black Hats decided they had their ducks all lined up in a row in a sufficient manner to do a false-flag attack on a major city."

"A false flag?"

"They would set off the bomb and blame it on enemies foreign or domestic in order to declare martial law and put their plan in motion."

"What plan? What is this all about?"

"Control, sir. That's what it's always about. Control. They want to control the economy, our lives—everything. Whether it is hardened communists or greedy capitalists with ice water in their veins, they seek to gain control and bring about their version of utopia, which is really a hell on earth for most of us.

"While you and I are working, raising our kids, and eating hot dogs at the ballpark, these people are plotting to build an empire that will reach to the heavens. This has been in the works for a very long time."

Mack glanced at his truck and then turned back to face G-Man. "I guess so. Since Babel."

"Babel?"

"As in the Tower of Babel. You remember the biblical story? A tower would be built to reach the heavens—God's domain?"

"But God confused their language to put a stop to it before man destroyed himself. Of course." G-Man stared in silence for some time. "The code..."

"The code?"

G-Man focused on Mack once more. "Computer code, sir. The language programmed into computers for communication. The Black Hats have their own code, which we haven't been able to break."

CHAPTER FORTY

DARKNESS AND LIGHT
Sunday, 10:00 P.M.

G-Man walked away into the night. The sound of his footsteps on the gravel beside the parking area faded away to silence. Mack watched his image darken until only a fedora-topped silhouette of the man could be seen in the dim light.

Mack returned to his rig and lumbered up the steps as if carrying a sack of sand before plopping down onto his seat. After pulling his curtain around, he flopped his head back against the headrest and sighed long and hard. The stress built up in his body like a rag rung dry released and vanished along with the light in his truck as the curtain shut out the world around him.

When Mack pulled back the curtain he once again became captivated by the scene inside the slaughterhouse. Strong, bloodstained men trudged along like weary soldiers who long ago lost heart for the battle they faced. The grim-faced men with blood-spattered white coats smacked the last sides of beef onto hooks hung from rails on the ceiling of Uncle Jake's trailer.

He stood alone now, hidden behind the curtain next to a dock as he waited for the men to finish loading. His uncle allowed him to watch the men load after he begged him to do so.

"Okay, Bobby Lee," Uncle Jake said, "but don't let them catch you, or they may load you up, too."

When Mack glanced over to see his uncle walking away to tend to business, fear tightened its hold on him like a vise. But his fascination with the scene at the slaughterhouse overrode his fear as he turned to watch the men once more.

One of the men, by far the largest and strongest of all, had a face like a dragon. Dragon Man clutched a side of beef with his massive hands. He lifted the hulky slab like a gladiator's vanquished foe before slamming it down with a thud onto a hook.

Mack grimaced when the hook stabbed into the cold chunk of meat before he watched it dangle as if on a hangman's noose above the trailer's floor. Droppings from the red carcass and those loaded before it formed rivers of blood in the crevices below.

Another man worked alongside Dragon Man and followed him wherever he went. The man's hands dripped with blood, but his face was that of an angel. Mack watched as Blood Angel and Dragon Man turned upon seeing him hiding behind the curtain.

Mack trembled behind the curtain, unable to move as Blood Angel approached. The man ripped back the curtain, leaving him exposed for all the men to see. Blood Angel slapped his hands to Mack's sides and carried him to the waiting arms of Dragon Man.

Dragon Man lifted Mack above his head like a trophy. Blood Angel and the other men laughed at the sight of the boy in his hands. The man threw Mack over his shoulder and walked with him toward the hanging sides of beef. Mack beat the back of Dragon Man and screamed as the man marched toward the last hook, which hung like a steel dagger above the blood-washed floor.

Dragon Man ripped Mack away from his shoulder and raised him above his head as he prepared to slam his back upon the hook.

"Stop!"

Light flooded the slaughterhouse as the door opened. Uncle Jake stood and faced Dragon Man. Blood Angel and all the men turned to face him, as well. But all shielded their eyes and sought to hide, for none could look upon the light.

"Let him go," Uncle Jake commanded. "He belongs in the light."

Dragon Man cursed and threw Mack to the floor of the slaughterhouse. Mack ran and took cover behind Uncle Jake.

Uncle Jake took Mack by the hand and led him to the light. He brought him outside to see a funnel-like image coming down from the sky. The smaller end faded into the heavens while the larger part opened before him like a horn of plenty. Mack stood before the funnel unafraid.

"You may enter now, my son," said a voice from above the clouds. "Or you may stay and face an uncertain future upon the earth."

No words were spoken by Mack when he answered the voice. But he knew the Source heard his unspoken reply. He chose to stay.

CHAPTER FORTY-ONE

IT IS WELL

Monday, 6:30 A.M.

Mack stared at the ceiling of his cab for some time upon awakening. *I haven't had that dream since I rode in Uncle Jake's sleeper when I was a kid. Too bad I didn't decide to leave then. Don't know what I've been kept around for.*

After grabbing a cup from the coffee shop Mack drove into the Windy City and parked his truck near an old brick warehouse. He snatched up his paperwork, hopped down from his rig to check the address, and eyed an old mailbox with faded numbers on it, confirming he was at the right location. Seeing a dumpster in front of the warehouse, he walked back to his truck, gathered some trash, and returned. He knelt to pick up trash scattered about the dumpster and spotted some shoes before tossing his garbage.

Sneaking a look around to the back of the dumpster, he discovered the shoes were attached to the feet of a man. Mack squeezed into the space between the dumpster and the wall behind it, bent down, and peeked under the cardboard covering the man. He knelt onto the sticky garbage goo the man's head rested on to see if he still breathed. After verifying he was indeed alive, Mack removed his own shirt, rolled it up, and eased the man's matted hair onto it.

Now in his sleeveless white undershirt, Mack walked back to his rig wiping garbage goo from his hands onto his jeans. He popped open his side box, retrieved some hand cleaner and rags, and wiped his hands before stepping into his truck. After some digging he found snacks, stuck them into a bag, and started to leave. But he returned to his rig and snatched up the blanket from his bunk before tossing it over his shoulder and heading back to the dumpster.

"Hey!" *Scr-e-e-e-ch!*

Ice-cold soda thrown from a car hit Mack's body as he turned upon hearing the noise.

"Get a job, ya bum!" the car's passenger shouted. He tapped his door with the soda cup and turned to the car's driver. The two men laughed as the car sped off.

Mack stared down the road as the car turned out of sight. "I have a job!" Upon looking down at his soda-covered clothes, he muttered to no one in particular, "But I'm thinking about giving it up."

After patting down his face and arms with the blanket, he took a deep breath and continued to the dumpster. He placed the bag of food next to Dumpster Man, lifted his cardboard covering, and tossed it into the dumpster before easing the blanket over him.

"Hey! What're you doin'?" The man raised his head from the shirt, which now served as his pillow.

"Just putting my blanket over you. I took your cardboard and thought I needed to replace it." Mack bent over and placed his hands onto his knees, allowing the man to focus on him before he continued speaking. He pointed to the shirt. "That shirt is kind of old. I felt bad leaving it. Would you like a new one to wear?"

Dumpster Man propped himself onto an elbow and squinted at Mack. "I've got a shirt. What do I need a new one for?"

"Good point." Mack eased onto the pavement, leaned against the wall, and wrapped his hands around his knees. He stared at his rig parked on the street, still running, before returning his focus to Dumpster Man. "We tend to burden ourselves with a lot more stuff than we need to in this life, don't we?"

Dumpster Man nodded.

"Still, a new shirt may be useful when you're out looking for a job, so it is kind of a necessity."

For the first time, Mack noticed an empty bottle as Dumpster Man pulled it to his side and placed it upright next to him. The man glanced down and shook the bottle before easing it back onto the ground. A breeze carried the scent of liquor mixed with garbage goo to Mack's nostrils. He rubbed his nose with the back of his wrist and coughed as the man spoke.

"I had a job once. A good one. Had plenty of money and a fine house in one of the better neighborhoods in all of Chicagoland."

"And...?"

"And what?"

"So what happened? What's the rest of your story? It usually takes a pretty dramatic event to make a man give up all that to take up residence behind a dumpster."

"I need another drink." Dumpster Man raised the bottle and rubbed his eyes with his forearm before tapping the bottle to the ground with a clink. He focused once again on Mack. "Hey? Are you a driver? You said something about a job. Let me shine up your wheels or something for you. Some of the drivers who unload here give me a few bucks for cleaning up their truck for them."

"Finish telling me your story and I'll see what I can do to help you out."

Dumpster Man pushed himself onto his hands and knees and wobbled to one side and the other before he crawled out of his space. He eased onto the pavement and plopped back against the wall next to Mack. The man stared straight ahead in silence for some time before he spoke.

"That fine home I had?"

"Yeah?"

"It burned to the ground."

"You could have just bought another house. Didn't you have insurance?"

The man nodded. "With my wife and four kids inside. Would that be enough to send you to the dumpster?"

Mack faced Dumpster Man before turning with him to focus on his truck idling in the street.

"Probably," Mack agreed. "It probably would if I didn't know the Lord. I recently lost my wife and that just about did me in."

"I'm sorry." Dumpster Man turned to face Mack. "So you're religious, huh?"

"Religious?" Mack offered a slight grin and shook his head. He continued eying his rig in silence for some time before answering the man's question and his own. "No. Not me. Not anymore. I'm just a truck driver. A truck driver who knows the Lord, that's all."

He returned his focus to Dumpster Man. "Ever heard of Horatio Spatford?"

Looking as if Mack just asked him to name the capital of Botswana, Dumpster Man responded with a question of his own. "Horatio who?"

"Spatford. Horatio Spatford. He was from Chicago—like you. And he suffered through something very similar to what happened to you."

"I'm sorry to hear that. Did you know him well?"

"No." Mack shook his head. "He lived in the nineteenth century. Around the time of the Great Chicago Fire. First, he lost his two-year-old son and then he was financially ruined by the fire."

"That's terrible."

"It was. But that was only the beginning of his troubles. Not long after that he planned to take a trip to Europe with his wife and four daughters. But he had to stay behind to tend to some business, so he sent them off without him. Their ship sank on the way, and all his daughters drowned. He found out about it when his wife sent him a telegram that said: 'Saved alone.' Shortly after that, he got on another ship to meet his wife. Know what he did when the ship passed near where his daughters died?"

"Jumped in?"

"No. Ever heard of the song 'It Is Well with My Soul'?"

"'It Is Well'? Yeah." Dumpster Man motioned a thumb toward a building across from the warehouse. "I've heard it at the mission across the street where I've stayed a time or two."

"Well, Horatio Spatford knew the Lord. That's how he survived all that. He looked down into those waters and was inspired to write the words to that song. Those words helped to comfort him and countless others after him."

Mack laid his head against the wall and began to sing in a soft tone.

The voice of Dumpster Man joined in the refrain. Mack saw tears streaming down his face like a cleansing river as the tears washed grime away before falling onto his chest.

"It is well…"

The two joined together, sounding as a chorus as they closed their eyes and leaned their heads against the wall.

Dumpster Man lifted himself from the pavement before offering a hand to Mack.

With his help, Mack arose from the ground, as well, and dusted himself off. He pulled some bills from his jeans, stuffed them into the man's torn shirt pocket, and placed his other hand on his shoulder. Mack gave it a firm squeeze before he spoke. "Spend that on booze and I'll pray that the Lord breaks both your legs, so you'll have to drag yourself to the liquor store to buy another drink."

The man patted his shirt pocket. "If I spend this money on alcohol it will be for the kind that helps to heal wounds."

After scanning the rough Chicago neighborhood surrounding the warehouse, Mack said, "Certainly no shortage of wounded people around here."

The man cast a glance toward the mission he spoke of earlier. "Y'know, I think I may go back to that mission over there to get cleaned up." He raised the shirt that served as his pillow. "Thanks for the shirt. Thanks for everything, driver."

After watching him walk across the street and enter the mission, Mack headed back to his rig.

A large sedan pulled in front of the warehouse and came to a stop beside Mack. A man built like a bear emerged from the vehicle and slammed his door shut. His torso and arms, as well as his demeanor, seemed to belong to one best suited for the ripping and tearing of flesh. The man cast his eyes toward Mack's truck before he faced Mack. He thrust a thumb over his shoulder.

"That the Texas load, driver? Outta Pampa, Texas?"

Mack nodded. "Yes, sir."

The man planted a cigar between his lips before moving it to the side with his teeth. He took a deep draw, breathed out a stream of smoke, and offered a hand to Mack.

"I'm the president of the local here." The men shook hands before Mr. President pulled out his stogie and used the wet end as a pointer. "Back into that first dock there."

"You got it." Mack glanced toward the dock before walking to his rig.

Mr. President stuck the cigar back between his teeth and rubbed his massive paws together. "Yes, sir. We've been waiting for this one."

CHAPTER FORTY-TWO

SPECIAL DELIVERY

Monday, 8:45 A.M.

After backing his rig, Mack hopped down to open his trailer doors before bumping the dock. As he walked to the rear of his trailer, a door next to the dock eased open, revealing a white-clad dockworker, clipboard in hand. The man lowered his head as he trudged down the steps before walking toward Mack and Mr. President.

The man's shaved head glistened in the light as he approached. White stubble dotted the wrinkles and folds atop his bare head, causing it to resemble a large sugar dumpling. Upon arriving at the back of Mack's trailer where the men now stood, he retrieved a pencil from the fold of his ear and examined the paperwork attached to his clipboard. Sugar Dumpling studied his paperwork for some time while Mack and Mr. President waited.

Mr. President chomped on his stogie and snatched the clipboard from his hand. The man stepped to the side and watched as he scanned the seal and the paperwork.

"Break it," Mr. President ordered as he handed the clipboard back. The man broke the seal and clipped it onto his paperwork.

"Yes, sir. This is going to be the best thing that's happened to our union in a long time. We're going to be stepping in high cotton again. Isn't that how you boys say it down South?" Mr. President smacked Mack on the side of his arm as he motioned for Sugar Dumpling to open the door.

The dockworker popped open the trailer door before swinging it around and locking it open onto the side of the trailer. As he walked around to the other door, Mr. President stuck a hand to his midsection and nudged him to the side.

"Looks like they sent all the documents for us. Lot bigger than I'd thought it would be," Mr. President said as he pointed to a large box resting on the trailer floor. He pulled keys from his pocket, popped open his trunk, and looked at Sugar Dumpling. "Put it in the trunk of my car."

Sugar Dumpling yanked at the box, which didn't budge. He tugged at it again. "What the…"

Mr. President shoved him to the side, tilted his head, and looked at the bottom of the box. "Velcro." After removing his stogie, he pointed it toward Mack. "I guess they weren't taking any chances with this cowboy, in case he couldn't handle the load." He stuck the cigar back into his mouth, rolled it to the side, and said through clenched teeth, "This your first rodeo, Tex?"

"Let me see that seal." Mack reached for the clipboard. "I didn't see that box back there when they closed the door and sealed it back in Pampa."

The dockworker balled his fist and faced Mack. He glanced at Mr. President, who stepped forward and pushed him away.

"Show it to him."

"Here you go, driver." Sugar Dumpling shoved the clipboard into Mack's midsection.

After taking the clipboard, Mack smiled and offered a wink to the man. He separated the seal and compared its number to the paperwork. Mr. President took the worker's arm, pulled him to the dock behind Mack's trailer, and shoved him against the padding surrounding the door. He spoke in a low voice, but could be heard nonetheless.

"Do you want to keep your job?"

After glancing toward the men, Mack returned his focus to the paperwork. Unable to hear the man's mumbled response, he listened as Mr. President continued to berate him.

"Then get back over there and just do your job. This is too important for some stupid dockhand to mess up."

A dull thud followed by a groan sounded as the union president slammed the worker against the padded dock once more.

"Any more trouble out of you, you'll be out of a job, and your wife will be working the streets on the South Side. Go open the other door for Tex, put the box in my trunk, go back inside, and get back to work."

As the men walked back, Mr. President stuck his stogie in his mouth and grinned as the dockworker slinked past and opened the second trailer door. After struggling to remove the box from the last bit of Velcro, he fell backward as it came loose. The man hit the ground with a clump as the box crashed on top of him.

Oomph!

Mack and Mr. President dodged him and the box as he fell.

"This thing's a lot heavier than I thought it would be," Sugar Dumpling said as he turned to face the men.

"Sorry, driver. Hard to find good help these days." Mr. President grinned as he pointed to the dockworker struggling with the box.

Sugar Dumpling pushed the box to the side and grunted as he lifted it from the ground. He waddled over to the car before dropping the box into its trunk and tapping the lid shut.

As the man walked back toward the rear of Mack's trailer, Mr. President pulled him aside and pointed to the material that held the box onto the trailer floor. "Get that junk out of there and make sure it's destroyed."

The dockworker removed the materials and placed them at his side. He did not look at the men as he passed, but lowered his head once more as he slogged up the steps leading into the warehouse. After opening the door, he walked into the cool blast of air, leaving Mack and Mr. President alone at the rear of the trailer.

Mack climbed into his Pete, backed up, and bumped the dock before hopping down from his rig. As he walked to see that he was lined up with the dock, Mr. President grabbed his arm. "You're good." He motioned a thumb toward the warehouse door. "Sorry about the knuckle dragger."

The men turned to watch the trailer shake as workers began to unload the rig. Mack glanced down at the man's grip on his arm.

"Some of these guys couldn't pour water out of a boot if the instructions were printed on the heel." Mr. President relaxed his grip. "They're lucky to have a job. Sometimes they need to be reminded of that." He released Mack's arm and motioned to the clipboard. "Everything in order there, driver?"

"The numbers match." Mack handed the clipboard to Mr. President, who offered a quick nod in his direction. The clamoring noise of the men unloading his trailer was the only sound heard before Mack spoke once more as he motioned a thumb toward the warehouse.

"Are ya'll running a packing house or a pretzel factory in there?"

Mr. President shifted his stogie and clenched it between his teeth.

"Because there are more twists here than in a pretzel factory. I know there was no box in the back of my trailer after I loaded in Pampa."

After glancing toward Mack's truck and then the warehouse, Mr. President leaned in, lifted open hands, and shrugged. "What box? I didn't see no box."

Mack crossed his arms and nodded.

"If anyone wants to come and talk with the knuckle dragger in there…" Mr. President pointed to the warehouse door. "There's a good chance he could have a very unfortunate accident. And if you tell the police or anyone some crazy story about an imaginary box you brought up from Texas… Who do you think they're going to believe?" He punched his fingers to his chest. "A fine, upstanding citizen of Chicago who contributes to the outstanding representatives running our fair city and to the police organizations?" The union president removed his cigar from his mouth, pointed the wet, chewed end at Mack, and held it there for a moment. "Or some lowlife truck driver?"

After dropping his cigar onto the pavement, he crushed the remainder of the stogie with one of his spit-shined leather slip-ons. He pulled out the lapel of his jacket and grinned.

Staring into the man's eyes, Mack watched as he slipped a hand into his jacket.

Mr. President eased out his hand and produced another cigar. After biting off its end, he spat it onto the pavement before firing up a match and cupping it in his hands to guard the fire from the wind as he lit the cigar.

He took in a long draw of the fine tobacco, rolled the smoke in his mouth, and raised his face toward the clouded Chicago sky. The man blew out a long stream of smoke and then faced Mack once more. He lifted the cigar to shoulder height and rolled his stogie between his fingers in silence.

"Cohiba Singlo. Cuban," he said, after some time as he studied the layers of tobacco. "Some truck drivers work hard all week just to earn enough money to buy maybe two boxes of these." He pulled another cigar from his jacket and offered it to Mack.

Mack shook his head.

"You have chutzpah, driver. That's what my grandmother used to call it. Chutzpah." Mr. President slipped the cigar back into his jacket and patted it into place. "I like that. I need men with chutzpah to work for me. You come to work for me and you'll earn enough money to buy ten boxes of these every week."

Mack shook his head once more.

"Know what else my grandmother told me?" Mr. President shrugged before staring down Mack. "She said your chutzpah can get you killed if you're not careful." He walked toward his car, opened the driver's door, and placed a hand on top of the door. He turned back to face Mack. "Suit yourself, driver. After you get unloaded, you might want to get out of Chicago as fast as that truck of yours will take you." He slid onto the seat of his car, rolled down his window, and pointed a finger in Mack's direction. "Don't come back to one of my warehouses again."

CHAPTER FORTY-THREE

CHATTERBOX

Monday, 9:15 A.M.

"On the road again..."

Mack heard the new ring tone for his phone as he stepped back toward his truck. He lifted the phone to see Barb's number.

"What's up, Barb?"

"Mack!"

After pulling the phone away from his ear, he listened as Barb continued.

"Mack! Where are you?"

"Chicago... I finally made it to Chicago. Why?"

"Honey, you need to get in that truck of yours and get out of there as soon as you can."

"Oh, don't worry, Barb." Mack looked over his shoulder to see Mr. President still parked in the street, waiting for him to leave. "I'll be out of here just as soon as I get unloaded. They're about done with me. I've already let it be known I want out of here ASAP."

"Well, you need to just leave that load and get out now."

"I can't just up and leave the load. I told you they're about done with me anyway. What's the hurry?"

"There's a lot of chatter going on about Chicago, that's what."

"Chatter?"

"That's what they call it. Chatter."

Mack listened as Barb took a deep breath and exhaled before proceeding with her explanation.

"You know, when bad guys are talking about doing some really bad things? That kind of chatter."

"Uh-huh. So what does that have to do with me?"

"They're going to hit Chicago, Mack. That's what. And soon."

"Who's going to hit Chicago?"

"Remember me telling you about my son Billy? His wife's family is from there."

"Yeah… I remember you telling me that. Your son Billy, the Navy SEAL. His wife left him for another man. But he remained close to her family, you said."

"And I told you Billy was about to come home on leave? Well, he came to see me and then flew up to Chicago to see that everyone in her family gets out."

"Barb, if he's right, people should have been warned. Why haven't we heard anything about this?"

"I don't know. Maybe there's not enough time. What are they supposed to do anyway? Tell everyone to get out of town because Chicago is going to be hit somewhere and cause some kind of stampede or something as everyone tries to get out? And then they wouldn't be able to deal with it—whatever it is—since they don't know exactly where they're going to hit.

"Listen to me, Mack. I can't do anything about the rest of the people there, but I've talked to him about you. He said to tell you to get as far away from Chicago as you can, as fast as you can."

"You talked to your son about me?"

"That's how he found out you were going to Chicago. I don't know a lot about what Billy does, but I do know that he knows a lot about intercepting communications that our government may be interested in. So I asked if he could trace a number that someone was trying to hide."

"So you've gone from playing detective to espionage?"

"Just this one time. I didn't think Clyde would call me again. And from the tone of your voice the last time we talked, it seemed like it was really important to you that I relay your message to Clyde about that Scarface character. So, I...um...I helped things along a little."

"Uh-huh. Don't get yourself in trouble. But your little trick was what...uh..."

"Was what did what?"

"Was...um...was what got me to thinking. You said Billy came up here to get his wife's family out. Where is he now?"

Barb fell silent for some time. The next sound Mack heard was a sniffle on the line before she spoke again. "I'm hoping he's with them. I haven't been able to get back ahold of him."

"He's a SEAL, Barb. He knows how to take care of himself. I'm sure he's gotten himself and his wife's family to a safe place. As for me, even if something bad is going to happen here, Chicago is a big town. Likely as not, I won't be anywhere near where it happens anyway."

Mack surveyed the area around him and caught the eyes of Mr. President, still focused on him like a laser. He turned, leaned against his rig, and propped a boot on a step. "Nothing around here but a bunch of warehouses and worn-out old buildings. Not the kind of place that's likely to be attacked. And I'll be leaving here soon anyway."

"Mack, if you don't call me when you get out of town, I'll do something worse than put ghost peppers on your burger when you come back here." Barb softened her tone. "By the way, honey. I have something for you when you do make it back to Pampa."

"That may be awhile, Barb."

"Well, if you don't want to come see me, I'll send it to you. You're probably going to want to get it back as soon as you can, though. One of the drivers who saw Bonnie and Clyde out there by your rig said he picked it up near where you had been parked. Guess my manager waited to see if it was worth anything before he threw it into the lost and found since I just saw it in there."

"What is it? What makes you think it's mine?"

"Well, there aren't many women named Georgia out there, so when I saw it was a bracelet with Georgia engraved on it…"

"What?" Mack slipped his boot from the step and pushed himself away from his rig. Mr. President pulled out his stogie and stared open-mouthed at the sight of the sudden moves. Mack ignored the man. "You have Georgia's bracelet?"

"It says *Bobby Lee and Georgia Forever* on it. Took me a while to figure that one out. But then I remembered someone had called the truck stop that morning before you got there. He was looking for a TGN driver named Robert. Remember me telling you that?"

Mack eased back against his truck and propped his boot onto the step once more. "Uh-huh."

"That was you, wasn't it? Did you used to go by Bobby Lee?"

"When I was a kid. But Georgia never stopped calling me that. I've been called Mack most of my life by everyone else."

"Do you want me to send it to you? One of the big truck-stop chains bought the land this truck stop and café sits on, so I may not be around here too much longer anyway."

"That's terrible. What are you going to do?"

"Since my prince charming isn't going to come back here and sweep me off my feet anytime soon, I guess I'll have to find another job. By the way, did that doctor ever find you?"

"What doctor?"

"The person who called looking for a TGN driver named Robert something?"

"Yeah…?"

"It was that doctor. He came to the café and talked to my manager just before you got there. I didn't think anything about it. I didn't even know you worked for TGN until after Bonnie and Clyde tried to break into your trailer. I forgot about it in all the excitement. Didn't think it had anything to do with you anyway. Once I learned your name is Mack, I thought it was some other TGN driver. Since you were so mysterious, I didn't know it was you he was looking for until after I saw the bracelet. The doctor had some kind of weird name. Hashee or something."

"Dr. Hashim?"

"Maybe that was it. It's none of my business, honey, but what did that doctor want with you? After seeing those eyes of his, I thought, 'That man looks like someone who'd steal the flowers off his grandma's grave.' If someone like that was looking for me, I'd get out of town and never come back. Anyway, Dr. Doom left before you showed up. You just missed him."

"Barb..."

"Yeah?"

"You...um...you said you have a certain kind of reputation?"

"I do. Honey, I know you think I've got a ten-gallon mouth, but I know when to keep it shut, too."

"Well, I'm going to trust you to be tight-lipped on this one. You've been so kind to warn me about Maria—and now this. But you have to promise me you won't talk to anyone else about this."

"Wild horses couldn't drag it out of me. You're the only one I've told about what's going to happen in Chicago, you know. Listen, don't you think my own son knows about my reputation? He wouldn't even tell *me* if he thought I was going to blab it all over town and put myself in danger."

"I know, and I know your son is a good guy. I also know other good guys in our government are working to stop it—whatever it is that's going to happen in Chicago." Mack paused and shook his head. "I hope."

"So why was Dr. Doom looking for you?"

"Dr. Doom...uh...Dr. Hashim..." Mack let out a deep sigh. "Dr. Hashim is the man who killed Georgia, Barb."

"What? I thought you said they didn't know who killed her?"

"I said they haven't caught him yet. And they still haven't, but there have been some...um...developments since I left Pampa. Hopefully they're closing in on him. If you see, or hear, anything else let me know. But only me. I'll forward the information without getting you involved."

"Actually, there is something else I didn't tell you about when we talked before."

"What is it, Barb? Don't hold anything back this time. Tell me everything you know."

"I would have told you everything before if you weren't so secretive. How am I supposed to know these things are so important if you don't let me know what's going on?"

"I was just trying to protect you, Barb. I wanted to keep you out of it."

"Well, stop being so overprotective. I'm not exactly a shrinking violet, you know."

"Yes, ma'am."

"If you call me ma'am again, next time I see you I'll make your coffee so strong it'll raise blood blisters on your boots. You understand me, cowboy?"

"Yes, ma'am. Just like I like it…uh…Barb?"

"Yeah?"

"You said there's something else you didn't tell me?"

"You don't like it when the shoe's on the other foot, do you?"

"What do you mean?"

"When you're aching to know something and I won't tell you."

"This is important."

"And my feelings aren't?"

"I didn't say that, Barb."

"You could've fooled me, honey. Anyway, Clyde met up with Dr. Doom after he left. I knew Clyde was talking about him when he described that character he met up with. Evidently Dr. Doom was able to catch up with Bonnie and Clyde after the drivers chased them off from your trailer.

"He said he would bail him out in the unlikely event they were arrested because he needed him for something much more important. He dumped Maria off first and then had Clyde turn himself in to the cops after offering him some big bucks. Clyde said he would really be rollin' in the dough when he was finished with the job he was doing.

219

"That man totally disgusts me. He waved money under my nose like I was some kind of two-dollar lot lizard. But I kept playing along, hoping to get as much information out of him as I could. Do you know why I lowered myself to find all this out?"

"I thought you were just curious, and were playing detective."

"Well, you thought wrong, honey. I did it for you. Because I was worried about you. I didn't know what all these characters were up to, but the whole thing stunk to high heaven. I didn't want see you get into more trouble than you're already in. I was worried about you then, just like I'm worrying about you now, because something bad is about to happen in Chicago.

"But, if you don't want to come see me, or talk to me anymore, you can just text me when you get out of Chicago. You can send your address to me then, and I'll mail the bracelet to you." Barb paused for a long moment before speaking once more.

"Good-bye, Bobby Lee."

CHAPTER FORTY-FOUR

HITTING THE PAVEMENT
Monday, 10:15 A.M.

S ugar Dumpling shoved the warehouse door open and trudged down the steps, clipboard in hand. Still seated in his car, the union president watched as he approached Mack. The man avoided the gaze of Mr. President after glancing his way. He slogged over in Mack's direction, pulled paperwork from his clipboard, and snapped it shut.

"You're ready to go, driver."

Mack scanned over the paperwork before offering a hand to the dockworker. Sugar Dumpling looked to Mr. President before he lifted his own limp hand.

"Thank you for unloading my truck so fast." The firmness of Mack's handshake caused the man to nod in cadence with the hand movements. "I'll be able to see the Windy City in my rearview mirror sooner than I thought."

The dockworker slipped his hand away, turned, and walked back up the steps into the warehouse.

Mack watched as the man entered and felt the cool blast of air from inside. He jumped into his truck and pulled forward before hopping down and walking back to close his trailer doors. After catching a glimpse of Mr. President, who still eyed his every move, he turned and walked along the side of his trailer. He smiled, gave the man a backhanded wave, and continued to the back to shut its doors.

Mr. President did not return his smile, or his wave, as he clinched his cigar between his teeth and eased his car away from the warehouse property onto the street.

Scr-e-e-e-ch!

Mack spun back around toward the street. A black Suburban rushed to a stop in front of Mr. President's car, causing him to slam on his brakes and drop his cigar from his mouth. His head snapped forward before banging against his headrest, giving the man a wide-eyed, close-up view of the Suburban now sitting broadside to his car. Another black Suburban rushed to the rear of his car. Its driver slammed on his own brakes, coming to a dead stop just inches from his bumper.

Armed uniformed men poured out from the passenger-side Suburban in front of him. Their uniforms bore insignias of a police or military force, which could only be seen in a flash as the men assumed their positions. A gun barrel appeared over the Suburban's hood followed by a man's head. The man focused his eyes on the weapon's sight, now aimed at Mr. President.

After peeling his hands from his steering wheel, Mr. President showed those open hands to the man. Bolting out from the Suburban to his rear, an officer raced around and aimed his weapon toward the driver's side glass of his car. Mr. President turned to face the new arrival.

"Get out of the car!" The officer jerked the car door open while continuing to bark orders. "Get out of the car now! Hands above your head. Lay flat on the ground!"

Mr. President brought his hands around in sight of the shouting officer before placing them atop his head and locking his fingers together. More officers poured out of the Suburban to the rear. One of the men yanked him facedown onto the pavement as another officer lurched forward and grasped his other arm. The two men dragged him away from the car. An officer trained his gun on Mr. President while another handcuffed him and shouted as he lay on the ground.

"Where is the box?"

"What box?"

As the men were speaking, two of the officers bolted toward Mack, weapons at the ready. One of the men stopped before him and turned his head before aiming his weapon at Mack's heart. The man stared him down as with the eye of a hawk focused on its prey.

"Get on the ground!" Hawkeye commanded. "Get on the ground now and put your hands behind your head!"

Mack knelt to the pavement and spread his hands out before lying face down and then clasping his hands behind his head. The second officer rushed over, yanked a hand down, and slapped a handcuff onto his wrist. He twisted Mack's other arm around and slapped the second cuff on before turning to face the commanding officer.

Hawkeye lowered his weapon and fixed his sight on Mack once more. "Where is the box?"

Mack tilted his head toward Mr. President's car. "It's in his car."

"Where in the car?"

"In the trunk." He wriggled his handcuffed hands behind his back. "It's in the trunk. Can you take these stupid handcuffs off?"

"Anyone else in your truck?"

Mack turned to view his rig. "Who knows?"

After bringing his weapon forward until it was just inches from Mack's face, the officer asked the question in a more persuasive manner. "Is-there-anyone-in-your-truck?"

"There was when I got out. There was a hitchhiker in there. His name is Ricky." Mack twisted his head in the man's direction. "Listen, be careful with him, he's scared enough as it is."

Hawkeye lifted his weapon and turned to Mack's truck, aiming it dead center at the Pete's windshield. "You. In the truck. Get out now!" He motioned his head to the officer who cuffed Mack.

The second officer scurried over to the truck's door, flung it open, and pointed his weapon toward the sleeper. "Get out of the truck now!" He turned to Hawkeye and nodded, before bounding up into the truck. "One last chance, Ricky. Put your hands out first and then I'll tell you what to do next."

Receiving no reply, he threw back the curtain and then brought his weapon from one side of the sleeper to the other. He eased forward, turning his head as he surveyed the contents of the bunk. After spinning back around to face the street, he shouldered his weapon and shouted to his comrades.

"Clear!"

CHAPTER FORTY-FIVE

To-Go Box

Monday, 10:30 A.M.

A large vehicle resembling a fire truck raced up and blocked the road behind Mr. President's car. A green, alien-like figure exited the vehicle. A rounded, dome-like helmet covered his head. His face and neck were wrapped with what appeared to be a covered towel secured with Velcro.

A filtered breathing apparatus was attached to the outfit just below his neck. A hose extended from the top of his head down to his back just past his shoulders. A shell like an umpire's chest protector covered his torso. The rest of his garb looked as if it were borrowed from an Apollo astronaut and dyed green.

Alien Man viewed the situation through oversized goggles affixed to the gear in front of his eyes. He carried a small red box and a container like a fat thermos bottle in his hands as he walked toward Mr. President's car.

Mack lifted his head to view the vehicle and read the inscription on its side: *Bomb Squad.*

Hawkeye returned his attention to Mack. "When did they put the box in the trunk?"

"Just now. Just a few minutes ago. They got it from the back of my trailer."

"Open the trunk." Hawkeye nodded to the officer with Mr. President.

The officer reached into Mr. President's car and popped open the trunk.

A large black truck sped to a stop behind the Suburban in front of Mr. President's car. Huge golden letters spelled out FBI on its side. Below, in smaller letters, were the words *Bomb Technicians*. Another black Suburban raced behind the truck with red and blue lights flashing and came to a screeching halt behind the larger vehicle.

An agent exited the FBI truck barking orders. His face was beet red from the pulsating veins on his thick neck to his military-style haircut. "Secure the area!" Agent Red Face shouted. Armed men wearing FBI jackets spilled from the truck and took up positions surrounding the immediate area.

A shout was heard from the radio in the Suburban behind the FBI truck as the agent in charge exited the vehicle. "Mayday! Mayday! Mayday!"

Mack turned and viewed the agent answering the distress call. His fedora shaded the man's face as his trench coat flapped gently in the wind. The agent turned to survey the scene as he spoke on the radio for a few seconds. Mack's jaw dropped when he caught a glimpse of the man's face. G-Man walked toward Agent Red Face.

Agent Red Face shot his head around toward the agents who poured out from the FBI truck. He raised his hand before pounding it down like a hammer and pointing a finger toward positions surrounding the outer perimeter of the area. "You! There! You! There!" Agents scrambled to take their positions. After scanning the scene, he continued shouting orders. "Evacuate! Evacuate! All civilians out of the area! Now! Go! Go!"

G-Man nudged Agent Red Face around and spoke to him in his low, rugged voice. Mack could not make out what G-Man was saying to the agent.

Agent Red Face spun away from G-Man and resumed barking orders. "No evacuation! Repeat! No civilian evacuation!"

After observing the scene for some time, G-Man nodded. "Great job, guys. Let's get this thing done, so we can be done in time for supper." He looked toward Mack and then motioned Hawkeye his way. The officer shouldered his weapon and marched over to the FBI agent. After the two spoke for a moment, the officer headed back toward Mack, retrieving a key as he walked.

"Okay, driver," he said as he unlocked Mack's cuffs. "Looks like you've got friends in high places." He whacked the cuffs onto his hand before pointing to Mack's truck. "Stay over there by your truck. We'll let you know when we're done."

G-Man returned to the bomb scene and conferred with Agent Red Face. He cast a glance toward Alien Man, who examined the open box in Mr. President's trunk. The agent looked at his watch and shook his head. He turned and walked toward Mack's truck. The agent stopped when he arrived next to his rig. Mack now leaned against his Pete, arms crossed, a boot propped up on the driver's doorstep.

G-Man examined the scene along with Mack. He pushed back the edges of his trench coat before sliding his hands down into his pockets. "Great bunch of guys, Mr. McClain. Best in the business."

"Well, that's good to know. Why aren't you over there helping them?"

"Nothing I can do now. I just turned the whole situation over to the most competent crew out there. I would just get in the way."

"Why did you tell them not to evacuate the area?" Mack turned to face G-Man.

"Seems to me a lot of lives could be saved if that thing explodes."

"Things are not always as they appear, Mr. McClain." G-Man shrugged and stood watching the scene in silence for a moment before he spoke once more. "It would be nice to be forewarned about these things, but that's the way it is in this business. We were expecting something that would take out maybe a couple of city blocks at the most. In that case, a civilian evacuation makes sense."

Mack nodded. "And…this one?"

"We've been preparing for this for some time now, but of course we were hoping it would never happen. These things are getting so sophisticated." G-Man pointed to the trunk of Mr. President's car. "The explosive device in that car? It weighs maybe sixty pounds." He turned to Mack. "That's it. Sixty pounds. A nuclear device weighing sixty pounds. This world is moving way too fast for me."

"A nuclear device?"

"Yes, sir."

"Uh… How did it get into my trailer?"

"We're working on that one, sir."

CHAPTER FORTY-SIX

DOCTORED DEVICE

Monday 11:15 A.M.

"Y ou're working on it?"
"Yes, sir."

"And...?"

"The suspect in your wife's murder? We...um..."

"You know about the demon-possessed doctor who killed my wife? Have you apprehended him, as well?"

"No, sir. He's not actually in our custody, but we know his current location—his approximate location. Whether he is demon-possessed is not our department, but he is certainly a very bad individual who needs to be arrested. He was the leader of a cell, which had planned to set off a powerful bomb in San Antonio, Texas."

"San Antonio? What were they going to do—take out the Alamo? I didn't think San Antonio was on anybody's radar."

"It was to be a symbolic strike. Against Military City, USA."

"You said they *had* planned to hit San Antonio? So their plans have changed?"

G-Man pointed to the device. "Evidently they have, sir. This has been in the works for so long, it was hard for us to believe their plans would change so quickly, but that's what has occurred. Nothing like this has ever happened before.

"Dr. Hashim lived quietly out in Kerrville, Texas, for all this time in preparation for the attack—a town small enough to avoid suspicion, but large enough for a certain degree of anonymity. Also far enough away to avoid prying eyes if anything *was* suspected to happen in San Antonio, but close enough to strike quickly if need be. A good choice, it seems. An off-the-radar location to prepare for an off-the-radar attack.

"When the doctor abruptly changed the location where the bomb was to be detonated, the chatter, both internationally and in this country, became intense. All that chatter caused the ears of the White Hats inside our intelligence community to perk up. Dr. Hashim had evidently decided to go it alone and ignore the cell, intending to get all the glory for himself. This really got the chatter going as the cell covered for themselves to make it look like it was all part of a grand plan to attack Chicago so they could take credit for it when it happened."

"So…you think Dr. Hashim somehow loaded this device onto my trailer?"

G-Man nodded. "All this was so well planned. The doctor worked hard to avoid suspicion for a very long time; he was so close to success with his mission. We don't know what motivated him to make such a radical departure from his plans."

Both men focused on the scene on the street ahead of them once more. Mack shook his head in silence for some time. "Luke 15:7."

"Sir?"

"There will be more joy in heaven over one sinner who repents than over ninety-nine just persons who need no repentance."

"I…um…I don't have my Bible with me. Is there a connection?"

"Dr. Hashim lives in a bizarro kind of world where everything is turned into a mirror image, in the sense of things being the opposite way they were created to be. God has great joy when a sinner is freed from sin or freed from the clutches of the devil. The sinner-turned-saint is then able to do the will of God."

"I'm not following you, sir. I understand the doctor may think he is doing the will of God."

"He *is* doing the will of god—his god. Satan receives his greatest satisfaction when he is able to use God's people to carry out his will. It's been that way throughout history. Of course, the most famous case was when Satan tried to tempt Jesus Himself.

"In his mind, Dr. Hashim thought I was working to pull him away from his mission, but it was actually the Holy Spirit drawing him. When the doctor rejected Him for the last time, Satan was fully able to enter him. He could exact no greater revenge than having a follower of Jesus do his will—to bring such death and destruction to so many people." Mack pointed to the device still being examined in the trunk of Mr. President's car. "So how much damage will that thing do?"

"We just found out from all the chatter we've been hearing that this is a much more powerful device than we had anticipated."

"So...um...so what happens if...if they're unsuccessful out there? If they don't defuse that device?"

"It is calculated that the device, if it explodes, will kill everyone within an area of up to a hundred square miles. Almost half the size of Chicago."

"A hundred square miles? How it was possible for a nuclear device that small to destroy such a huge area?"

"The device alone can't. But it is to be the catalyst for a second device thought to contain enough deadly material to cover an area that large."

"A second device?"

"Yes, sir."

"So where is this second device?"

"Once we locate Dr. Hashim, we think we will find it, as well. Seems he planned on working with you in a more...um...direct manner than we suspected."

Mack shook his head as he surveyed the scene around him. "Half of Chicago... So hundreds of thousands—maybe over a million—people could die?"

"Yes, sir. Seems the Black Hats have bitten off a bit more than they can chew here. The strike they planned was meant to be the biggest attack on this country since 9/11; a huge event, but containable. This will be impossible for them or anyone else to contain. It will be the beginning of a much greater conflagration if we are not able to stop it now."

"A greater conflagration?"

"Yes, sir."

"World War Three?"

"Yes, sir."

CHAPTER FORTY-SEVEN

BONNIE AND CLYDE CLUE
THE CAPTAIN

Monday, 11:45 A.M.

Mack glanced over to see a man exiting the passenger side of G-Man's car. The man placed a cowboy hat atop his head and looked toward the men standing beside Mack's truck. G-Man nodded at the new arrival as he approached. Mack stared in stunned silence.

"Ben?" Mack said as he came near.

"Hello, Mack." Captain Garza grinned. "Looks like you've gotten yourself into a little trouble again."

"What are you doing in Chicago?"

"Came up here to pick up our friend, Dr. Diablo. We got our warrant. I wanted to be first in line to nab that scoundrel and bring him back to Texas before anybody else laid claim to him."

Captain Garza joined the two men in observing the scene as agents exited the FBI truck with a roll of tarp-like material. The agents rushed back to Mr. President's car and rolled it out behind his trunk.

"I flew up here last night as soon as I had the warrant in hand," Captain Garza continued. "Actually, I got here at the crack of dawn this morning. No direct flights out of San Antonio. You know the joke: if you die in San Antonio—"

"It doesn't matter if you go to heaven or hell," Mack finished the joke for him. "You'll have to go through Dallas or Houston to get there. Where is he now—Dr. Hashim?"

"He lawyered up and was released before the warrant was issued. Unfortunately the doctor took off just before we found out about his... um...other plans." Captain Garza shook his head. "We had him, Mack, but he can't be too far. He has to be in Chicago somewhere nearby. He wouldn't miss this for all the world."

Mack looked at G-Man and then returned his focus to Captain Garza. He nodded in silence for some time before responding. "So I understand."

"I was just talking to the agents who interviewed the doctor, and also interrogated Bonnie and Clyde." He cast a quick nod in G-Man's direction. "I was riding with my friend here, and he got me into all of this."

Captain Garza turned to face G-Man. "How's it going? Are they getting it under control?"

"They're working on it, Ben."

The captain slid his hands into his pockets, matching G-Man's pose. The men watched as Alien Man directed two officers to remove the device from Mr. President's trunk. The officers eased it down onto the tarp as Agent Red Face moved his hands down like an orchestra conductor directing the performance of a slow-moving musical score.

Mack joined the men in observing the scene before turning to Captain Garza. "So how did you find Dr. Hashim?"

G-Man looked at Captain Garza and then turned his attention back to Alien Man. He cleared his throat and allowed a slight grin to form on his face before speaking. "We picked him up last night near the truck stop where we met, sir. Seems...um... Seems someone lost track of him before he ever left Texas."

Captain Garza pulled his hands from his pockets and crossed his arms. "Not all of us have the resources of the entire federal government to draw on." He turned his focus back to Mack. "We put together a timeline based on the information we have from the interrogation of Dr. Hashim, and what we've gathered from…" He glanced toward G-Man, "…other sources."

G-Man removed his hands from his pockets and crossed his arms, as well. "Touché."

"The feds were having trouble tracking down Bonnie and Clyde," Captain Garza continued, "so we sent them a little picture book with Bonnie and Clyde and their car in it and told them where they could be found based on the location you provided. As they were on the chase, Bonnie and Clyde all but ran into their open arms."

G-Man looked away and feigned disinterest in the conversation while suppressing another grin.

"The good news is…" Captain Garza glanced toward G-Man before returning his attention to Mack, "…after Dr. Hashim was released and we found out about his…um…other activities, they offered Bonnie and Clyde a pretty sweet deal and the two of them started singing like canaries. It seems Dr. Hashim—"

"Had Bonnie and Clyde put the bomb inside my trailer," Mack said.

Captain Garza exchanged glances with G-Man. "You really should tell us about these things, Mack."

"I found out about it myself shortly before all the excitement started. Haven't really had time to think about it. I just now put two and two together."

"I don't know where you got your information this time, Mack, but as usual, it is dead-on." Captain Garza turned to G-Man. "See why I wanted to keep him in the loop?"

G-Man nodded. "Maybe we should put him on full time."

"I've got claim to him first." Captain Garza motioned to the Suburban he and G-Man were driving. "While I was out there talking to the interrogating officers, I pieced together the last parts of the puzzle, Mack.

"Dr. Hashim was already in Pampa since he had spoken to Ginger and discovered you were heading up there to load. You must have just missed him because he evidently found your truck in the parking lot and waited in his car for you to return. Guess his plan then was to follow you to Chicago and to be here with you when the bomb detonated.

"But once he saw Bonnie and Clyde speeding away when they were caught trying to break into your trailer, he left the truck stop to go after them. After they took off on foot when their car ran off the road, he chased them down and forced them into his car. When he discovered Bonnie and Clyde's plan—"

Mack finished Captain Garza's sentence for him. "He came up with a better plan—to make *me* deliver the means of death for him. Dr. Hashim dumped Maria off and then had Clyde turn himself in to the cops after offering him some big bucks.

"But..." He drifted off into silence for a moment before continuing, "...Clyde didn't say anything before about Dr. Hashim forcing them into his car. Makes sense. Wouldn't make him look like such a big shot. He was scared to death of Scarface *and* Dr. Hashim."

Captain Garza turned to G-Man, shrugged, and lifted open hands before returning his focus to Mack. "Dr. Hashim told Clyde that he would bail them out in the unlikely event they were charged with anything. The doctor kept both packages until those two were released. He paid them a pretty penny to load the device into your trailer and also let them keep the package, which Bonnie and Clyde thought would make them rich. But as you know, the Black Hats had replaced the original package from Scarface with their own bomb."

Mack looked at the bomb scene and nodded. "So Dr. Hashim *has* been following me all this time?"

"That's evidently what he wanted you to think. What he wanted *all* of us to think. All that time you thought you were drawing Dr. Hashim into your trap? You know, how you thought about getting him to attack you so he would be arrested?"

"I thought at the time that would be the only way he would be caught."

"Dr. Hashim had you right where he wanted you—to be fuming about him all the way to Chicago. He knew you would be trying to lure him to you to get justice for Georgia. But he was already on his way here before you ever left Pampa. He went ahead of you to lure *you* to *him*. He wanted you to be looking over your shoulder all the way as you headed to meet your doom in Chicago.

"Dr. Hashim gave notes to Clyde to leave on your truck to make you think he was following you there himself. He had the notes made out already, so he must have originally planned to place them on your truck himself when you stopped along the way. He wanted you to be thinking about their content before he confronted you here and set off the device, which was loaded in his car.

"Clyde was supposed to follow you and load the bomb into your trailer when you stopped again. But he must have gotten a little impatient after you spent such a long time in that truck stop in Pampa. So he made sure you would stop again when he shot out your tire. The bomb was loaded into your trailer when you returned to the truck stop. We assume Dr. Hashim hung around long enough to watch from a distance to make sure his device was loaded into your trailer. Clyde later stuck the note under your wiper to divert your attention back to Dr. Hashim."

"But how did he get the bomb into my trailer? It had the right number on the seal."

"When is the first time you checked the number against your bills?"

Mack stared ahead in silence for a moment before answering. "At the tire shop. After I had my tire replaced. The switch must have been made while I was in the café waiting to bring my truck into the shop. But how did they put a seal on there that matched my bills?"

"The guy at the slaughterhouse where you loaded? He worked for Scarface, too. Trucks were routinely used for illegal shipments, and he would provide seals that would match the numbers on the bills so illicit goods could be placed inside the trailers either en route, or in many cases, right there at the slaughterhouse. Since the numbers matched, the load was unlikely to be searched if the driver was stopped. If the driver noticed the discrepancy after loading, then the guy would just say *oops* and go on to the next truck going to the same destination.

"He gave Clyde a seal and then put that seal number on the bill of lading after you loaded. When you stopped somewhere, the seal you had was to be broken and the new seal would be put on after the package was put in. But the truckers at the truck stop saw Bonnie and him before they were able to break the seal and load the package onto your trailer."

"Why did Bonnie and Clyde try to kill me, knowing that my rig would flip over and whatever they put in there for Dr. Hashim would be recovered?"

"Clyde let it get back to Scarface that Bonnie had stolen the package. He had worked for Scarface for some time, so he knew he would have him kill Bonnie; you would just be collateral damage since Scarface thought Bonnie had sent the money ahead of her and taken off with you. The man does have a flair for drama. When Scarface saw the pictures of your wrecked truck and heard the news about the contraband found in your trailer, he would think Bonnie lied about selling the contents of the package and that his shipment was recovered by the police. Of course, Scarface didn't know about the switch that was made by Dr. Hashim, or that the feds had double-crossed him.

"Clyde assumed the feds would be very interested to know what was inside that box, as well. But he wasn't aware that the feds had double-crossed Scarface, either. In any case, he was sure the feds wouldn't let the truth come out about who the passenger was inside the truck until they knew who had stolen the shipment when they discovered whatever it was that Dr. Hashim had replaced it with. Clyde had watched the feds snoop around the Jordan Unit for some time. He thought the package must have contained something more valuable than the Hope Diamond from the way they were showing so much interest in the goings-on there. That's the main reason he was willing to risk his life once he got his hands on the box.

"It was a valuable shipment all right, but not *that* valuable. The original plan was to break into your trailer when you stopped en route to Chicago, after they were sure none of Scarface's minions were watching. Once Dr. Hashim took it from them, he was willing to do anything the doctor wanted to get his hands on it again. Bonnie and Clyde planned to run off and live happily ever after while Scarface, Dr. Hashim, and the feds were sorting through all this. They really were in love." Captain Garza placed his hand on his chest by his heart and patted it. "Kinda gets you right here, doesn't it?" He turned to face Mack. "But you ruined their plans."

"I did?"

"You did. You ruined their plans when you didn't die and run off the road after Clyde shot at you. At the very least, you ruined the photo shoot they had planned. After Clyde saw you slumped over the steering wheel, he panicked, ran back to your truck, and threw in the card he got from Dr. Hashim to divert attention back to the doctor once more. He assumed you managed to get the truck stopped before you died."

"So if Bonnie and Clyde hadn't been caught back there in Pampa, we wouldn't have known any of this, and I would have just dropped off a bomb that would have taken out a couple of blocks instead of half of Chicago?"

"And we wouldn't have caught up with Dr. Hashim and known of his plans, either, Mack. He would likely have followed you in his car and his device would have detonated after you both arrived here." Captain Garza uncrossed an arm and pointed a finger toward the device Alien Man worked to disarm. "As it turned out, he shipped that thing in your truck and went ahead of you. He was having you deliver the means to your own death. And hundreds of thousands of others."

Captain Garza nodded. "You were hauling a bomb the whole time that is powerful enough to kill you and Dr. Hashim and to take out half of Chicago with you." He pulled a folded piece of paper from his pocket and handed it to Mack. "Before he left with his lawyer, he gave this to the officers and asked that it be given to you when you unloaded in Chicago. I had them run off a copy and said I would hand deliver it to you. Can you make any sense of this?"

Mack unfolded the note before reading it aloud:

"There is one who is before all
Five is the number on which he stands

Alone in the heavens he hears men call
Five times each day in all the lands
But all men great and small
Five times between work with hands
For him who is above each and all
One plus five, three times, he plans
To make all men on him to call."

CHAPTER FORTY-EIGHT

THE CODE

Monday, 12:30 P.M.

A lien Man looked at a handheld gadget and then back to the device on the tarp. He turned to Agent Red Face. Mack could see head movements through Alien Man's goggles. Agent Red Face spoke on the phone and pointed to the device before running his hand through his close-cropped hair. "A code," he said, "some kind of code is needed to disable this thing."

He looked to G-Man and held up open hands. G-Man walked over to Agent Red Face and conferred with him for a moment before returning to stand by the truck with Mack and Captain Garza. He pushed the lapels of his trench coat to either side and slid his hands back into his pockets. The three men watched the scene in silence.

"I learn something new every day," G-man said after some time had passed. "There are one hundred and twenty possible combinations of three-digit numbers." He pointed to the device on the tarp as Alien Man and Agent Red Face stood by. "That device cannot be disabled except by entering the correct three-digit code."

"Why haven't they started going through all the possible numbers?" Mack asked. "If they start now, they may have time to go through them all."

241

G-Man shook his head. "The problem they're having is that if they punch in the wrong code that thing goes off prematurely."

"So they're going to have to guess?"

"We have the best minds in the country working on the puzzle. But, yes, sir, I would say that seems to be the case."

Alien Man scanned the surface area of the device from all angles. Agent Red Face paced about now, waving a hand around as he spoke on the phone. He glanced at his watch once more. "Well, those geniuses down there better come up with something soon. If there was ever a time for them to earn their pay, it's now."

Mack stared at the scene in the street before him. "Dr. Hashim planned to be at the center of the blast when the bomb went off. He was going to be right there in all his glory. And he used me to deliver the means of destruction. I let that serpent pull me right down into the pit with him.

"I don't understand any of this. If Dr. Hashim had not visited our church, he wouldn't have heard me preach the gospel and wouldn't have been so angered about being almost persuaded and pulled away from his mission. He would have just continued with his plan to detonate the device in San Antonio. And the other device would have taken out a couple of blocks in Chicago at about the same time. World War Three would likely have begun anyway after both those devices exploded almost simultaneously."

Captain Garza and G-Man exchanged glances before the captain spoke. "Don't blame yourself, Mack. The guy is brilliant and a lot more devious than you or I could ever be."

G-Man nodded. "The more I learn of this man, the more I think he may have allowed us to arrest him just so he could get a free ride to the area where this thing was going to go off. Yes, sir, he used us all."

"I think he knew he would be released..." Captain Garza continued his old friend's train of thought and then pointed to the note in Mack's hand, "...and he used me as his errand boy to deliver his message."

Mack lifted the note and read it once more before dropping it to his side. "Dr. Hashim must still be in the area. No way would he miss all this."

"Yes, sir," G-Man agreed. He pointed to the device before scanning the surrounding buildings. "That's a curious-looking thing he left for us. Looks like it has eyes or something. The numbers are above its eyes. That's where the code must go. The eyes are slightly elevated above the rest of the device and connected together in a kind of an oval shape—like a large button."

Mack nodded and looked at the device before surveying the area along with G-Man. When he spotted the name above the mission across the street, he stopped and stared at the sign for some time.

He turned to G-Man. "Would you like for me to pray?"

"That might be a good idea, sir." G-Man lifted his arm to view his watch. "The device is set to go off in about fifteen minutes."

CHAPTER FORTY-NINE

IN THE NICK OF TIME
(AND ETERNITY)

Monday, 12:45 P.M.

The scene about him faded away as Mack lowered his head and prayed. He was at peace, but his peace shattered like the window of his truck when he was once again pulled down into the pit by Dr. Hashim. He watched in his mind's eye as a creature tore at his flesh and knocked him to the ground before dragging him into a cave.

When he turned to look at the creature, rock in hand, he saw numbers, coal black and set deep into the flesh above its eyes as if seared with a hot iron. The number was six hundred sixty-six.

Mack's eyes shot open. "One plus five, three times. The number of a man! It's 666! The code is 666!" He turned to G-Man. "Tell him it's 666!"

"Sir, if you are wrong about this…"

"The device will explode."

"Yes, sir."

"And if you don't punch in the code?"

G-Man nodded and walked over to confer with Agent Red Face.

"Hold on! Hold on!" Agent Red Face placed the phone to his chest as G-Man approached.

The men spoke in a low tone before Agent Red Face turned to glance in Mack's direction. He faced G-Man once more and spoke in a loud voice. "666?"

Alien Man looked up from the device and stared at the men through his goggles.

G-Man nodded.

"Sir, with all due respect, we have the best minds in all the agencies in this country and all our allies, working on this as we speak."

"And what have they come up with thus far?"

"Nothing, sir."

"And how much time do we have?"

Agent Red Face glanced at his watch before turning to face Alien Man.

"Do it!" he ordered.

G-Man turned to watch Alien Man. He slid his hands into his pockets as the man prepared to enter the code. Agent Red Face leaned away from the device. Alien Man lifted his bulky, gloved hands and punched in the numbers. *Click. Click. Click.*

The three men gathered around the device. G-man motioned for Mack to come over and join them. Mack hurried over to stand with the men.

G-Man turned to face Mack. "Well, the good news, sir, is the device didn't go off."

"And the bad news?"

Pointing to the timer, G-Man said, "The bad news is—the clock is still ticking."

All eyes turned to watch the timer as it ticked down.

59...58...57...

Alien Man, Agent Red Face, and G-Man raised their heads and turned to Mack.

30...29...28...

Mack returned the stares of the men. "Strike the eye of the beast!"

The men turned to one another and shook their heads.

10...9...8...

"Strike the eye of the beast!" Mack repeated.

3...2...1...

Mack leaped forward and pounded the button on the device with the ball of his fist.

The men leaned away from the device before easing forward once more to see double zeros on the timer. The second timer, to the side of the first, measured time in tenths of seconds. It stood frozen at zero one.

CHAPTER FIFTY

CLEANING UP

Monday, 1:00 P.M.

O nly the heavy breathing of the men could be heard as all stared at the device.

G-Man broke the silence as he raised himself and motioned to the device. "We'll call in a chopper and have this thing taken as far away from civilian population as we can get it." He turned to Agent Red Face. "Maybe we'll send it to the numbers guys and let them deal with it."

Two officers guarding the area came forward to load it into the FBI truck after Agent Red Face motioned for them to do so. Alien Man stood back and watched as the officers picked up the device and marched away step by step in unison with one another before loading it into the truck.

"Clear them a path. Now!" Agent Red Face shouted. "And load it up. Our job here is done."

Mack and G-Man stepped over and stood by Mack's rig.

Captain Garza lifted his phone to answer a call. He walked away and cupped a hand to his ear in order to hear the call in all the commotion around him.

Officers scrambled to clear the road for the FBI truck. The men scurried about picking up materials set up to secure the area and loaded them in their vehicles. The streets in the area began to clear as vehicles drove away.

Alien Man waddled over to the bomb squad truck. Officers gathered about him and helped him remove his gear before they stepped up into the truck with him and pulled away.

Mr. President looked at Mack as an officer grabbed his elbow.

"Okay, sir, we can go now," said the officer as he helped Mr. President up from the pavement.

Mr. President looked at the ground as the officer pulled him up. "Hey, officer," he said as he motioned with his head to a package that lay next to where he had been, "can you get my cigars for me?"

The officer shook his head. The men were close enough to Mack for him to see the officer roll his eyes before he bent down and snatched the cigars from the pavement. He shoved them into Mr. President's pocket before tugging at his arm and pointing to one of the Suburbans still parked at the scene.

"Right this way, sir."

Mr. President turned and talked to the officer as the men walked away. "They're Cohiba Singlo. Fine Cuban cigars. Ever tried one?" Receiving no response from the officer, he continued. "That's too bad. Even an officer of your stature can't afford 'em.

"Listen, I've been watching you. I contribute more money to the police organizations in this town than anyone, so I know a little about police work. I've even awarded some officers individually for their exceptional service. Why are you wasting your considerable talents for such a paltry sum? You can come to work for me. I'll pay you what you're worth."

The man continued to speak but his voice faded as the officer loaded Mr. President into the Suburban before pulling away with him in the back seat. Other officers scoured Mr. President's car and then stepped back as a wrecker driver hooked a line to the car and pulled it onto his rig. The wrecker driver hopped into his truck and drove away with the car in tow.

Mack turned from watching the scene and faced G-Man.

"So what happens now?"

"Well, sir, we'll have supper tonight, go to sleep, and then wake up tomorrow to see what the bad guys have planned for us." G-Man shrugged "Same as yesterday."

He paused, pushed his coat lapels to the side, and slid his hands into his pockets. "I've been thinking about our conversation regarding the Tower of Babel. The Blacks Hats have been working with some very bad individuals to create computer code that would be used by machines, or more accurately, creatures using artificial intelligence.

"It appears the bad guys didn't quit when God confused their language. It just took them a while to come up with plan B. Not a long time in the grand scheme of things—eternity—I suppose. If they are successful in creating these creatures, they won't need many of *us* around anymore. That's the long-term war we face. Plenty of battles along the way, though."

The two men stood in silence for some time, watching as the last vehicles cleared the area, leaving Captain Garza alone in the street as he continued speaking on his phone. Mack nodded, before turning back to face G-Man.

"Actually, I meant Dr. Hashim. What happens with him?"

G-Man nodded toward the street. "Maybe our friend there will be able to nab him for us next time."

Mack turned to see the approaching Captain Garza hanging up his phone as he walked. The captain shook his head at Mack.

"You're full of surprises, aren't you?"

"What do you mean, Ben?"

"Who is this Billy the Kid?"

CHAPTER FIFTY-ONE

GOOD-BYE FOR GOOD

Monday, 2:00 P.M.

"**B**illy the Kid?"

"Our friend Clyde? Seems he got a call from someone calling himself that and telling him he'd better head back to see you because Scarface knew everything they were up to."

G-Man turned to Mack. "Is that the phone call you spoke of when we met, sir?"

"Uh…"

Captain Garza stared at Mack in silence, along with G-Man, for some time before Mack answered.

"It…um…it happened so fast…I…uh…"

"Once again, I don't know how you do it, Mack. We weren't able to do a trace back to his phone since we didn't have anyone who was in communication with him." Captain Garza turned to G-Man. "If he hadn't got someone to make that call, we never would have been able to track down Bonnie and Clyde in time to stop all this."

G-Man nodded. "And the code…"

Captain Garza offered his hand. "Good job, Mack."

"Yes, sir," G-Man said. He offered his hand, as well. "Thank you."

Mack shook Captain Garza's hand and then G-Man's before responding. "Oh, don't thank me. Thank God. He's the one who gave me the code. I just had to go through hell to get it."

Captain Garza and G-Man turned to look at one another before the Captain glanced down to his watch and spoke to the agent. "You were right. You *did* get this thing wrapped up before suppertime." He motioned his head in Mack's direction. "Even if you did have to have a little help from our friend here. But you may have finished a little *too* early. I believe it's your turn to pay?"

G-Man grinned and nodded.

"Gotta head back to Texas, Mack." Captain Garza sighed. "After all this, even if they *are* able to nab Dr. Hashim, I don't think they'll let me get my hands on him to bring him to justice there."

"I understand, Ben, but we're going to keep looking, right?"

"I'll keep dogging him until the day I retire. Then Garza and McClain can take up the hunt?"

Mack shook his head.

Captain Garza chuckled before reaching to slap Mack's arm. "I'll be in touch."

The lawmen walked off in the direction of G-Man's Suburban. Mack listened as the men spoke on the way.

"So how about that steakhouse? You know, the one all the tourists go to? I hope it's as good as advertised. You know Texans know steak better than anyone."

"Steak? The last time I was in Texas you took me to a little place off the beaten path. You said they had the most authentic truck-stop food in the country?"

They arrived at their Suburban and opened their doors.

"Uh-huh?"

"You were right."

The men slid onto their seats and shut the door to laughter.

Mack watched the Suburban speed down a now deserted street and then walked to the rear of his trailer to close its door. Looking inside his empty trailer, he shook his head before swinging the doors around, locking them shut and pounding the door with the ball of his fist. He leaned against his trailer, pulled out his phone, and punched in a number.

"Hello?" Barb answered in an icy tone.

"Two things. Two things I hope will be music to your ears."

"You won the lottery and you're coming to pick me up in your new chariot?"

"You were right, and I am sorry."

"You know me well, don't you, honey? That's even better."

"Listen, Barb. There's something I'm curious about."

"Uh-huh?"

"Does your son ever go by Billy the Kid?"

Barb laughed. "He hated it for a long time. He has such a baby face his buddies teased him without mercy. But they weren't laughing when he made it as a SEAL. Now he wears the name as a badge of honor. Uh… How did you know? Did he get in touch with you, too?"

"No. A little birdie told me."

"Bobby Lee-ee…"

Mack chuckled. "Tell your son thanks. If he hadn't followed his instincts and made that call, things would not have turned out too well for me."

"Uh-huh… And…?"

"And I'll tell you the rest of the story when I make it back to Pampa."

"You're coming to Pampa?"

"I'll come back to Pampa to visit you if you're still there."

"Oh, if you're coming, I'll be here."

"See you soon, Barb."

After walking back around to his truck, Mack opened his door, kicked his boot onto the step, and prepared to climb in as he caught the image of a man crossing the street. The man wore new garments and walked with a confidence he'd never seen before. Mack slipped his boot from his step onto the pavement and pushed his door shut. He stared at the man in silence for some time before speaking.

"Ricky! Where have you been?"

The hitchhiker thrust a thumb over his shoulder.

Mack looked up to read the sign above the mission he pointed to: THE LORD'S BUSINESS.

"You're the one who said it doesn't matter where you've been, but where you're going."

Mack grinned, looked at the pavement, and shook his head. He raised his head once more and viewed the empty road ahead.

The End

CPSIA information can be obtained
at www.ICGtesting.com
Printed in the USA
LVHW030129031120
670552LV00017B/641